I0744121

TELL CITY

TELL CITY

a novel

Kaylin R. Boyd

Boyd's Books LLC

TELL CITY. Copyright © 2018 by Kaylin R. Boyd. All rights reserved. Printed in the United States of America. For more information, address Boyd's Books LLC, 289 W Columbus St. Martinsville, IN 46151.

www.kaylinrboyd.wix.com/stories

Cover artwork and design, illustrations, and interior designed by Lusicovi Creative LLC.

www.lusicovicreative.com

The Library of Congress Cataloging-in-Publication Data is available upon request.

ISBN (hardcover) 978-0-692-15933-0
ISBN (paperback) 978-1-945-182-07-5
ISBN (ebook) 978-1-945-182-08-2

First Edition December 2018.

*This book is dedicated to everyone who supported
me from the start to the finish.*

*This is for my parents, who
never once doubted me.
For my sisters, Devin and Raven,
who always had faith in me.
To my partner-in-crime, Elise Rorick,
for all our jam-packed adventures.
Special thanks to my educators for teaching
me do that which makes my heart sizzle.*

*And finally, I thank the gods for showing me
how to believe in myself.*

To the reader…

This is not a trigger warning.

Starting a new book is like starting a new adventure, and when starting a new adventure, it is unwise to think there will not be dragons. We never know what we will encounter when we set out, but to be brave, we must set out anyway. There will always be dragons, and I wish you luck should they cross your path.

The geography in this book is relatively based in reality, though I have taken liberties. Tell City is a real place, in the real state of Indiana, and it does sit along the banks of the mighty Ohio River, which has flooded. But I highly doubt the city has a magical oracle or has been attacked by gods. I'm fairly certain I made that part up. Santa Claus, IN is also a real place, and I do believe Mr. and Mrs. Claus spend their summers there, but I have no proof.

The places in this book are real places as a reminder that magic can still happen in our world. This is the importance of the contemporary fantasy genre. Mythic tales have always served as the door through which humans and gods interact - safely within a dreamscape.

Books are portals. Even if the people and events inside are all fictitious, the magic of it all is real.

Yours truly,
Kaylin R. Boyd

one
sacrifice
away

A message from the Oracle...

Tell me your secrets.
Tell me your fears.
Tell me your desires.
Tell me what you wish to hear.

I'll tell you answers.
I'll tell you your future.
I'll divine, I'll scry, I'll see
Everything that you might need.

Though hear my warning.
Heed my advice.
This sacred insight
Comes only at a price.

What I do tell
Can change your life.
Knowledge can only come
At a great sacrifice.

So tell me your wishes.
Tell me your thoughts.
Tell me your dreams.
And give me your heart.

Charles could not remember the last time he had seen a road sign. He knew that he was near a place called Calling Panther Lake, forty miles, give or take, outside of Jackson. Walking along the edge of the interstate at night in Mississippi was unsettling enough, let alone treading the edge of Calling Panther Lake.

He had been terrified of cats ever since he'd encountered a black panther on his grandfather's property years ago. It was the way their eyes glowed in the darkness…the way they crept so weightless, so silent upon the ground – the perfect predator. People had called him crazy when he'd told them he had spent what felt like hours clinging to a tree branch just inches above the beast. He had held his breath and his tears, hoping the cat would not hear him, but it had.

It had looked at him with those glowing eyes and had made the conscious decision to spare his life. At the age of ten, it was a miracle he hadn't pissed his pants, but then again it had left him scarred for life. People said black panthers were cryptids…they were only a myth, but he knew the truth: there were black panthers in North America.

Charles had been dreaming about panthers and about apples and raging rivers. His dreams frightened him. They were the reason he was hitchhiking to Tell City.

He tried to distract himself by changing Garth Brooks' song "Calling Baton Rouge" into Calling Panther Lake in his head, but the song lacked melody and rhythm and did not end up making much sense at all, so he wound up just focusing on his feet.

Forty miles was a long way to walk, and having trudged most of the way to Jackson already, he was beyond exhausted. He hadn't had much luck hitchhiking during the day, so he decided it was useless to try to find a ride that late at night. Despite his fantasies of a comfortable seat in an air-conditioned mini-van, he had no choice but to keep going until he reached the nearest exit or rest stop and hopefully find a bench, or even a dumpster, to use as a makeshift bed. In desperation, he prayed for a dumpster. That way he might even find a bite to eat.

Now that he was the one walking along the edge of

the road with no money and just the clothes on his back, he felt guilty for all the hitchhikers he had once passed, saying to his girlfriend in the passenger seat, "Is he serious? He looks like a serial killer. Maybe, if he got a *job*, he could afford a shack instead of a box and maybe a bike or a junker car."

He had grimaced and kept driving, and she had shrugged and said, "Hey, you never know where life will take you. Sometimes people just end up in unfortunate situations."

He missed her, and he realized she'd been right, as usual. Those old men by the side of the road were war vets, whose nightmares and memories would not let them go back to whatever normal existence they'd once had…men who had physically or emotionally lost their families. Kids whose parents were never home and, as a result, had no home to go to. People whose futures and pasts kept them constantly running to or from something or someone, even themselves.

As he walked in the dark along the Mississippi interstate, worried that he may be hit by a car or attacked by a giant cat at any given moment, Charles D. Garrett came to realize that a hitchhiker is a lonely and desperate soul, who is probably more afraid of you than you are of him.

Charles's Texas driver's license said he was only twenty-two years of age. Before he'd had that dream, he had always viewed himself as being more mature than most of his peers, but he had no idea how old he felt anymore.

Walking north up Interstate 55, trying to make his way to Tell City, he felt that his behavior had been more mature when he was younger. Since the night of his dream, he had become more impulsive than he ever had any right to be.

He was thin and with his journey growing thinner. He hoped that maybe the exercise might have increased his muscle mass, but it was unlikely. His brown, wavy hair was short. During his recent hipster phase he had spiked up just the front bangs of his hair, and it had looked classic with his black, wide-framed glasses. When he'd wanted to look like a badass, he'd put in contacts and had gelled his hair all the way up. The James Dean look with his motorcycle boots turned more heads, and that was how he'd caught his girlfriend Jenna. But after he'd had that dream, he stopped caring about everything…even Jenna. He had become a man obsessed, and she'd thought he was crazy. He was still not certain how he felt about that.

Charles staggered up the road in his motorcycle boots, the legs of his ripped jeans half tucked into them. His tight, grey, V-neck shirt seemed even tighter now that the humidity made it cling to him. His shirt was so damp and dirty he couldn't use it to wipe off the road dust and condensation that covered the lenses of his wide-framed glasses. There was no use worrying about his hair. Salty sweat dripped off his bangs.

As he traveled alone with nothing but the sweaty clothes on his back and thoughts of that dream, he decided that it didn't matter anymore if he looked like a hipster or a rebel. Anyone who noticed him walking up the interstate at midnight would think he was crazy. And even that did not matter.

***

Charles was being watched over by a waxing crescent moon. A few hours earlier, when she was still low in the sky, her light shone a brilliant orange. Her craters were intricately detailed in different shades of shadow. Now a pale yellow, the moon hovered just above the tips of the ghostly pines lining the interstate, and she seemed to follow Charles as he walked.

A new light illuminated the Mississippi night as an old truck came over the hill Charles had just climbed. The truck swerved into the left lane behind him and came back into the right lane at the bottom of the hill.

Charles sighed. Another person had passed him on their journey. What took them five minutes in their air-conditioned automobile would be hours for him on foot. At this point he was past being bitter and had moved on to just being wistful.

The truck's brake lights lit up the South Dakota license plate, and the gravel popped beneath its wheels as it pulled off to the side of the road. Charles tilted his head, hesitant to believe that yet another one of his dreams would be entering into reality.

A woman jumped out of the pick-up. Her long black hair bounced around her as she slammed the door and began to march up the hill towards him. Charles slowed his pace. In his daze he saw her as an angel sent from hell. The red taillights of the truck framed her silhouette, which was dramatically curved. Her skin was dark from the sun and her cheekbones were high and defined. She was young, and she wore worn leather boots, cut-off jeans, and a vintage Kansas T-shirt. He watched the glow of the taillights on her ebony hair and the tangles of smoke that lofted from the cigarette pinched between her fingers.

"Are you damned near crazy?" she yelled, wide-eyed.

Charles re-entered reality as she stopped in front of him. "What?" He cleared his throat and tried to speak without a southern accent. Charles hated his southern accent. Too many people thought Southerners were slow and simple. He wanted to sound intelligent.

She popped out her left hip and rested a fist on it. "Do you see how dark it is? And do you know how hard it is to see you in this darkness? Do you?" She pointed the tip of her lit cigarette in his face. "I almost hit you. And I can guarantee, *guarantee,* every asshole drivin' on this road is either drunk, stoned, or sleep deprived, and you're just *strollin'* along.

Are you stupid or something?" She paused to take a long drag from her cigarette, and then forced all the smoke out of her lungs so she could continue. "Did you see your life flash before your eyes?"

"Uh…"

"Did you?"

"No." He cleared his throat again. "No, ma'am." His southern accent slipped through.

"Well, you should have." She scrutinized him in the dim red light. "What the hell are you doin' out here anyway?"

Charles straightened his back and shoved his hands into his pockets. "I'm heading to Tell City."

"Tell City…" She dropped her cigarette and crushed it with the toe of her boot. "Where the hell is that?"

Charles looked off to where Interstate 55 disappeared into the shadows. He sighed and replied, "Indiana."

"And you're just going to walk the whole damn way?"

"No. Yes. If I have to…"

Both of them looked up the hill with squinted eyes as another car came speeding past. The driver swerved into the left lane like she had done before switching over to the right.

"Well, how about this." She looked back over at him, her thumbs in her belt loops. "You tell me my name and I'll take you as far as I can."

Charles narrowed his eyes. "You want *me* to tell you *your* name?"

"Yup."

They stared at each other for a moment, each waiting for the other to make a move. A heavy drop of sweat ran down the corner of his eye, and he blinked to un-blur his vision. The red taillights expanded into luminous rays in the haze.

"My grandfather always says that if you meet a meaningful stranger, you knew him before in a past life. And since I'm not going to drive five hundred miles with a complete stranger you better prove to me you knew me from before."

Feeling confused, Charles watched her as she lit up a new cigarette from a pack she'd pulled from her back pocket. He took off his glasses and rubbed his eyes. "I can't even tell you who *I* am right now," he said. "So I can't tell you who *you* are." He put his glasses back on, believing now that his girlfriend had maybe been right about him being crazy, but there were still people in the world who were crazier than him.

"So, *I'm* not going to get into a car with a complete stranger either. Until you prove that *you* know *me* from this *past life*, I'm fixing to keep walking."

Moving forward again hurt more than he thought it would. His muscles had quite enjoyed standing still for a moment.

"Holy shit. You're Charles Garrett, aren't you?"

He stopped.

"Or at least you used to be." Charles remained frozen as she continued. She looked up at the trees and the sky. "Goddamn it, Grampa!"

"How do you know who I am?"

She looked back at him, her dark hair shadowing her face. "I don't know who you are. I know who you used to be and," she paused, "who you're going to be." She looked back up to the sky and continued to yell at it. "This is real fuckin' funny to you isn't it, Grampa? Bet you're laughin' your old, wrinkly ass off, aren't you? Well, I don't think this is funny." She pointed to her face. "You see me laughing? I'm not doing it. Nope. He can walk for all I care."

She headed back to her truck, mumbling something that sounded like, "You and your damn tricks."

Charles remained motionless, running through the possibility in his head that this was all an illusion. The young woman was imaginary, or even perhaps the angel from hell he had first thought her to be. A feeling of helplessness drained him as he watched her rip open the door to her truck. His exhaustion was nigh unbearable.

The young woman stopped. She sighed and turned around. The tip of her cigarette lit up a vibrant orange as she took another drag.

"You might as well get in," she said, a halo of smoke encircling her face. "'Sides…there are black panthers in these here parts. I bet being mauled to death wouldn't be too much fun."

He stared at her. "You've seen one too, huh?"

She smiled for the first time, her grin crooked and sharp. "Yup."

He headed for the passenger side of her truck. The pain in his muscles was eased just by knowing that in a few short steps he would be able to sit for a change.

"By the way," the woman said, "my name is on the license plate." Her laugh sounded like an animal's cry as she jumped into her truck.

Wile E.

Her custom South Dakota license plate said *Wile E.*

Charles climbed into the pickup. In the darkness it had appeared black, but now up close he could see it was actually a dark blue. The door creaked and clanked as he slammed it shut. The rough metallic sounds made him feel as if he was closing the hatch on a World War One tank.

"Wile E.?"

She put the truck into drive and peeled off the gravel shoulder onto the road. "It's my nickname." She tossed her cigarette butt out the window. "I hate it, but everyone else seems to think it fits, so…"

"So, what's your real name?"

She glanced sideways at him. "Names aren't important."

His frown made her grin.

"Why don't you get some shut-eye and then you can tell me all abouts this Tell City when you come to, m'kay?"

***

He awoke with the heaviness of sleep still lingering in his mind, making it difficult for him to grasp onto reality.

The sky was dark and cloudy, but the eastern horizon was beginning to brighten against the haze. The driver's seat was empty, and the truck was parked in the dark back corner of a truck stop.

The driver's door creaked open, and the tan-skinned Wile E. stared in at him. She had in her hands a drink carrier holding two coffees and two overcooked hot dogs on stale gas station buns, along with a pack of unopened cigarettes.

"You look dead," she said, handing Charles the drink carrier. She pulled herself into the cab. "Smell like it too." She left the door open, letting her left leg dangle out.

Charles wrinkled his nose. "I haven't had a chance to

shower since I left Baton Rouge a few days ago."

"Well, they have a shower room on the inside there, and I can pick you up a couple of shirts and a pair of jeans…maybe a backpack. What size you wear anyhow?"

"Uh…thirty-two, thirty-four."

"Are you kidding? You're skin and bones like a Wendigo." Wile E. reached down the side of her seat and leaned her chair all the way back. "Probably a thirty waist."

"You don't have to do that for me. Really, I'm fine."

She looked him up and down. "I'm not doing it for you."

Charles looked over at her self-consciously.

Wile E. grabbed a hot dog from the drink carrier still in his hands. "Don't be shy. Eat your breakfast, boy, before it gets any older."

Charles's hot dog was hardly enough to squelch his hunger, and afterwards he was not sure whether it was the spoiled meat or the speed with which he'd consumed it that was making his stomach churn. He decided it was both, and leaned forward to rest his head against the dashboard.

"You know," Wile E. said, after swallowing the last bite of her hot dog, "my Grandfather says an army that marches on its stomach is an army that marches on greed."

Charles turned his head to look at her as she opened her new pack of cigarettes and lit one up. "Oh, yeah? And what do you say?"

"I say without food this army will starve to death, and there won't be any marching to Tell City at all." She inhaled a lungful of cigarette smoke. "So tell your little bitch of a stomach there to stop being such a goddamn pansy."

Charles smiled. "It tasted like overcooked road kill."

She stretched her arm out through the open door and flicked the ash off her cigarette.　"It's road food. Soul food. It's what life is meant for." On that note, she grabbed her coffee from the drink carrier.

Charles smiled, lifting his forehead off the dashboard. He removed his glasses and tried to clean them with his shirt. It was still dirty, but at least now it was dry. "Where are we at?" he asked, as he put his glasses back on.

"Arkansas. You slept for five hours there, chief. It's about five in the morning."

"How'd you stay awake?"

"Cheap coffee, cigarettes, and I listened in on your dreams while you had'em. They kept me entertained enough. Let's get you to them showers." She slid out of the truck and slammed the door, heading over to the building. Charles followed her, finding his boots weren't as waterproof as they should have been. Muddy puddles from a summer rain rested on the cracked pavement, and they illuminated the parking lot with the reflection of the rest stop's neon lights.

Charles's confusion had returned, and he found himself rating his new companion's sanity below his own. "You listened to my dreams?"

"Yeah, why not?" Wile E. looked over her shoulder at him. Her long ebony hair again shadowed her face, but the neon lights reflected vibrantly in her eyes. They seemed to glow for a second.

Charles shook his head, trying to understand.

"I didn't want to wake you by turning the radio on," she explained.

"I don't remember any of my dreams."

Under the shelter of the truck stop's extended roof, she stopped and turned to him. "Well, that's because I stole them."

Charles felt like he was on the verge of blacking out. His feet were struggling to find solid ground beneath the haze of the last few days.

Wile E. sighed, and pulled back her hair. Her amber eyes narrowed. "You dreamt about Jenna *a lot*." She began counting on her fingers. "You dreamt you were still walking down the road, and you were confused because you knew you were sleeping. Now that was interesting to watch. You dreamt that your parentals had sent the law off after you, because of the way you got up and left. Didn't call. Didn't text. Left your cell phone and your wallet. You dreamt the cops were tearing through you and Jenna's apartment, as your family and friends hid in the darkness sobbing, hoping the boys in blue wouldn't find a hidden suicide letter written in your delicate, pretty-boy handwriting." She held out all five fingers. "You dreamt just a little bit about Tell City, and then nothing. Blackness. Sleep. Ring any bells?"

Charles began to panic, causing the hot dog to recommence its escape plan. "How do you know all of this?" He put his palm against the damp stone wall of the building to hold himself up.

Wile E. folded her arms across her chest and began tapping her foot. "You're allowed to have weirdo-prophetic dreams but I can't be telepathic?"

Charles took his weight off the wall. "How do you know about my prophetic dream?"

"My grandfather told me."

"Your *grandfather* told you?"

When she nodded in response, Charles ran both hands through his hair, laughing hysterically. "Right. Okay. And who is this grandfather of yours?"

Wile E. tucked her fingers into her belt loops. "Wakan Tanka."

"Who?"

She stared at him for a moment with a gaze that told him he should have known who Wakan Tanka was. "God. Well, it's kinda like God...but not really *God*."

"God…God?" His southern accent slipped through again. "What kind of crack are you smokin'?"

"I'm just kiddin'." She smiled. "Didn't you know you talk in your sleep?" She turned around and walked through the rest stop's front door.

Charles stood there for a moment. So many muddled thoughts ran through his mind, there wasn't any room for anything that made sense.

A minute later he followed Wile E. into the store. The fluorescent lights hummed. The truck stop was crammed with clothing, gifts, and nicknacks. There were ball caps and cowboy hats with embroidered flames, and dream catchers with plastic beads and dyed chicken feathers. There were wooden-framed canvases of wolves and horses, and postcards of half-naked girls, posing provocatively on chromed choppers.

He found himself staring at a picture postcard of a band of big black Harleys parked outside a Coyote Ugly bar. Wile E. came up behind him.

"I prefer old Indian bikes myself," she said. "Either that or a Honda. I mean, at least they don't break down as easy as the first little pig's straw-built playhouse. And not to mention,

Harley riders can be such arrogant, over-compensating little assholes. 'The only good bike is a Harley bike.' 'Harleys are the shit!' 'Harley is *God!*'"

"Apparently, so is your grandfather." Charles turned to look at her. "And Harley's are badass."

She pressed her lips together. "Look, I didn't mean to scare you…"

Charles raised an eyebrow.

"All right, maybe I did, but I'm just trying to help you out. I'm not some Westboro Baptist wacko who's going to preach about fucking Jesus and how everyone's a sinner bound for hell the whole goddamn time. And I'm not some creepy truck driver who's gonna try to rape you with his *little semi* while you're sleeping."

Charles's eyes widened.

"I knew a guy once." She cleared her throat, and led him off to the small clothing racks at the other end of the store. "Anyway, what I'm sayin' is I'm trying to help, and if I don't help, Grandfather God's gonna come down here *personally* and disown my ass. Now I may not be at the tiptop spot on his final will and testament, but twentieth in line ain't so bad. You understand?" Wile E. started browsing through a men's clothing rack filled with tourist T-shirts.

"Can't say that I do."

"Well, if that don't ease your thoughts," she pulled out a shirt and put it up to Charles's chest, "I guess the fact I'm driving all the way to Harrisburg, Illinois won't interest you too much either. It's about a hundred and thirty miles from the *famed* Tell City, but, who's really counting?" She tilted her head while looking at the shirt. "It'll fit." She handed it to him and moved on. He followed. "It's not like I haven't already brought you three hundred miles, and already planned on taking you two hundred more, with a couple extra perks, not to mention, com-plete-ly free of charge, so…" She picked up a bottle of soap from off the rack. "Let's clean you up and hit the road."

***

Charles was trying to decide whether or not Wile E. was holding him prisoner by mandate of God as he sat in her truck outside a roadside motel in Missouri. The sun was beginning to rise and Wile E. had decided it was time to rest. She stepped out of the motel lobby and walked back to the truck.

Charles had his arms wrapped around his chest. He was doing his best not to think about where he had been a month ago and where he was now. It already felt like a lifetime had passed since he'd left Houston, Texas. But he was almost there.

Tell City…a place in Nowhere, Indiana that had been

haunting his dreams for over a month. Now he was only a few days away from finding out why.

"Are you still pouting about the *thank you thing*?" Wile E. climbed into the truck and handed him the motel key card.

"No, I'm not pouting," he said. "I'm thinking."

She put the truck in drive, and began the search around the parking lot for their room number. "Were you thinking about Tell City?"

"Yeah."

She slammed on the brakes, having passed the room.

"Okay. What about it?" She backed up and then pulled into a parking space.

"I don't know." He unbuckled his seatbelt. "I just know I have to go there. The city has something to tell me. It sounds crazy…"

"Yes. Yes, it does." Wile E. got out of the truck and leaned her seat forward. From behind it, she grabbed a worn leather backpack.

Charles got out of the truck and closed the rusted door.

"But I know what you mean." Wile E. pulled her hair out of her face as she walked up to the room. He handed her the key card and she opened the door. Neither of them turned on the light. The darkness was too comforting after driving in it all night. "Prophetic dreams happen all the time," she continued.

"It's just that *sane* people choose to ignore them. That is until after they come true." She threw her bag on the first of the two beds. "Then everyone wants the credit for being the first to know." She plopped down on the mattress.

"Well, my dream wasn't the foreseeing of an event." Charles sat down in a chair by the front window. He pulled off his boots.

"Still counts." She looked up at the ceiling. "It was the foreseeing of your destiny. Like, it's destiny that I just *had* to run into you," she scoffed playfully.

"I don't believe in destiny."

Wile E. looked over at him, puzzled. "So…you abandoned everything for what, then, if not for your destiny?"

Charles leaned back in the chair. "I don't know."

"No, you know." She lay back on the bed and stared at the ceiling. "It's destiny. The old Charles D. Garrett may not have believed in destiny. But *you*, whoever you are now, you wouldn't have done this if you didn't."

"If you say so. You obviously know me better than I do."

"As a matter of fact, I do," she smirked, closing her eyes.

Charles thought about that for a moment, and realized that she was quite possibly right. Every action he had taken since his "prophetic" dream was out-of-character. He thought he would marry Jenna after college, acquire a job in a Houston,

Texas skyscraper, and then live out the rest of his days in a sub-
urban two, maybe three, story house. Never did the thought
cross his mind that he would become a wandering vagrant who
would end up sleeping in a ghetto motel room with a random
woman who was obviously insane. If anyone understood his
newly-found madness, it was this woman, who believed her
grandfather to be God.

Charles sighed, because whoever he was now didn't
seem to care about his current circumstance. He was just grateful
that someone had saved him from the side of the road, and that
this woman did seem to get what was happening. Jenna didn't.
His parents didn't, and part of him, whoever he used to be, sure
as hell did not understand it.

Charles bent over and pulled off the new white socks
they had picked up at the truck stop. As he walked over to
the other side of the room, he again realized just how sore his
muscles were. Every bone in his body cracked as he collapsed
onto the second bed. He never thought a motel mattress could be
so comfortable.

Before he could fall asleep, he looked over at Wile E.
"Why Harrisburg?"

She yawned. "All my brothers are there."

"All your brothers?"

"Most of the good ones, anyway. Bugs will be there, and

Smokey, Tiny, Buzzy, and Jack."

Charles laughed. "Jack? Is he the only one with a normal name?"

Wile E. smiled. "I guess you could say that."

Charles suddenly noticed her smile. It reminded him of The Joker from *Batman*, the Jack Nicholson version.

"How many brothers do you have?"

"A lot," she said. "Now I don't know about you, but I have nocturnal tendencies. We'll shoot the breeze later. Go float, or swim, or sing. Dream. Whatever you do when you're asleep. Just shut up and close your lids, already."

Charles laughed, and put his glasses on the nightstand next to him. He closed his eyes, though he did not float, or swim, or sing. He walked.

He walked into the sunset, past Santa's workshop, and up and down hills with farms and trees on both sides. Road signs told him Tell City was one sacrifice away. He ate an apple grown on the same tree as the apple eaten by Snow White. True love's arrows would not save him. They could, however, destroy him. He was taken to a castle where fear was king, but where it also could not dwell, for if it did the kingdom would fall. It was the most revered of all castles, and the keeper of its gate was blind. He touched his reflection in a well, and all was lost.

Charles jumped awake. Wile E. turned to look at him. She was pouring herself coffee from the room's four-cup coffee-maker. Its digital clock said it was just after two in the afternoon. Charles blinked. The remnants of a dream distorted Wile E.'s face into something dog-like with jowls and teeth. The dog image retreated as the waking world seized control over his mind once again. He forgot all about it instantly.

Charles took his glasses from the nightstand and looked back at her. Wile E.'s black hair was a rat's nest, but she looked rested, satisfied with a good day's sleep.

"Bad dream?" she asked, tearing off the plastic from another coffee cup. She filled it and handed it to him.

"It wasn't bad." He said. "It was terrifying." The coffee cup was almost too hot to hold, so he set it down on the nightstand to cool. "Have you ever watched *Alice in Wonderland* when you were high?"

Wile E. leaned against the chest of drawers, which served as the motel room's TV stand and coffee table. She raised an eyebrow. "No."

"Oh," he paused, "well, it felt like that…watching *Alice in Wonderland*. Or, no, better yet, seeing *The Dark Crystal* while completely stoned."

Wile E. raised her coffee cup to her lips. "Boy, if you find that scary…" She took a sip, averting her eyes.

"It felt like that, but it wasn't…like that. Do you get it?"

"No."

Charles tried to think of a better way to describe his dream, but couldn't.

Setting her cup down on the chest of drawers, Wile E. said, "We missed checkout at noon o'clock, so we gotta git. Wanna grab some grub before we ditch town?"

Charles smiled and got up off the bed. "I'm going to need it," he said, stretching.

They cleaned up and then went to a diner just down the road from the motel.

***

The meal was quiet, much quieter than Charles thought his new acquaintance could be. Wile E. focused intently on her steak as she ate. Charles said nothing. If she wanted to talk she would.

He wanted to thank her again, but he knew she would try to kill him if he did. He had thanked her a thousand times on the ride to Missouri that morning. She had driven him hundreds of miles and bought him food, clothing, and a bed for the night. Charles never expected anyone to be that kind to him. He didn't think he deserved it because he never would have done that for someone else before all of this started. Saying "thank you" was nowhere close to being enough for all she had done for him. But, as she had said right before crossing the Arkansas/Missouri line, "Don't thank me. I am not a saint. Just remember that you owe me."

So, Charles continued to eat, not saying a word.

"Tell me, man-child…" Wile E. set down her fork and knife after finishing her steak. "What do you plan on doing when you get to Tell City?"

He looked up at her. "I don't know really. My dreams haven't told me." He laughed at the way his own words sounded.

"No. I mean…where will you stay? How will you eat?"

Charles looked back down at his plate and scattered

around the remaining bits of food. "I haven't thought about that yet."

"What a genius! I'm tellin' ya…Einstein couldn't compete with your mastery."

Charles grimaced.

"An' what exactly are you gonna do *after* Tell City?"

He avoided eye contact. He had not thought about that either.

Wile E. slurped the remaining drops of her soda through her straw and then set the glass back down. Stretching her arms across the back of the booth she asked, "Houston?"

"Probably not," he replied. "My parents will likely kill me if they ever see me again." He looked up as the waitress slipped the ticket and a pen over to Wile E.

"Probably likely to kill you even if they don't." She picked up the receipt. "Send a hit man after you. That's what I'd do to my hypothetical, illegitimate child if it ever decided to bail like you did."

Charles glared at her. "Thanks…"

Wile E. didn't hear him. A wide smile crept across her face as she looked at the receipt. Her amber eyes beamed over at the waitress, who looked back with the same smile.

"Hold that thought," she said.

Wile E. stood and strolled over to the waitress station,

leaving the receipt facing up on the table. There was a phone number written on it, right above the pink lipstick stain where the server had left a "kiss."

Charles's head tilted to the side as he watched his acquaintance slink up to their waitress. He had not really paid any attention to the girl throughout the meal. He had been busy thinking, but now he noticed that she was reasonably attractive, though she was also what he would have once considered trashy. Her band tee was cut off enough to reveal her lower back tattoo and tight enough to see the sequin detailing on her push-up bra. Her Daisy Dukes were shorter than her work apron, which was tied snugly around her waist. The girl's boots were made of shiny plastic gator skin. It looked like she had stolen Wile E.'s backpack and had shrunk all of her clothes by three or four sizes.

He could not hear their conversation from where he sat, but their body language told him plenty. The waitress stuck out her hip, and giggled as frequently as she twirled her hair, while Wile E. leaned against the wall with a charming smile. There were some hand gestures, some playful eye-rolling followed by more waitress giggles, and then Wile E. quite literally danced back to the table. She spun on her heels and did the Fred Astaire slide back into the booth. She drummed out the final lick to her victory song on the table, and winked at Charles.

He blinked. "What…was that?"

"That?" She threw her elbows on the table and pointed with her thumb back at the waitress. Her smile grew. "Why that was daddy issues at its sunniest, *mi amigo*."

Charles looked at Wile E. wondering whether he should give her a high-five or a good old-fashioned Southern Baptist talk on Adam and Eve.

"And," she said, "a free meal ticket." She smiled at him, grabbing the pen and a napkin. She wrote,

> *Appreciate it, Babe. Will call when back in town.*
> *-Coyote*

"Wile E.," Charles said under his breath. "Like Wile E. Coyote." He pressed his lips together. "I get it now."

She stared at him as they left the booth and exited the restaurant. "You're telling me you didn't get that 'til now?"

He shrugged.

Wile E. patted him on the shoulder. "Like I said… genius!"

***

A few hours later, they were parked out behind a gas station in Harrisburg, Illinois. Charles and Wile E. sat in the bed of her blue pick-up nurturing the beers in their hands. They had said they would only have one, and then go their separate ways, but the both of them were nearly done with their second, and not a word had been spoken until they popped off that third top.

"Meeting up with your brothers, huh?"

She nodded, swirling around her beer. "Most of the good ones anyway." She took a drink.

Charles nodded. His gaze wandered off.

On the rear window of the truck he saw a sticker. It was a circle divided into four sections. One quarter was white, another yellow, one red, and the final quarter was black. Four realistic-looking feathers dangled off the bottom.

"What's that?" Charles took a sip from his beer.

Wile E. looked at the sticker on her truck. "Sioux medicine wheel," she said. "It represents the four winds, four seasons, times of day, life."

"So you're part Sioux Indian?"

Wile E. grinned. "I guess you could say that. I've been a part of many tribes, and I have many brothers in many nations."

Charles raised an eyebrow. "So that Wakan Tanka thing?"

She smiled her sharp smile, and sipped her beer. "Wakan Tanka is…The Great Mystery."

"I thought you said it was your grandfather?"

"It is."

Charles blinked.

"Wakan Tanka is The Great Mystery," she repeated. "That means that it's a *mystery*. You'll never understand it, because it is a *mystery*. So shut up and accept you'll never get it, because it's a *mystery*."

"All right." Charles laughed. "I get it."

"No. You don't. That's the point. It's a mystery."

Charles grinned and took a swallow of beer.

For a moment the conversation died. The roar of the neighboring interstate was beginning to be more than Charles could bear. He still wanted to thank her for all that she had done, but he didn't want to ruin her good mood.

Wile E. busted out laughing. Her laughter sounded strange and sharp, like the previous night when she picked him up by Calling Panther Lake. It sounded like an animal's cry. "You know, you're completely ignorant, right? Everything just *soars* right over your head."

Charles laughed. "Thanks."

"Don't say that word. Do not utter it in my presence. Even if you don't mean it. *Especially* if you don't. Just remember," she paused, grinning. "You owe me one."

Charles let out a sigh. "How can I ever repay you?"

She looked up at him.

"Really," he continued. "How? I'm heading down the road as soon as this beer is gone, and you're fixing to go see your brothers. You don't have a phone. You know I don't have a phone…"

"You know that money I pulled from the ATM?"

Charles remembered back to the hour before when he had helped her navigate the buttons on the gas station's ATM. He nodded.

"Take it," she said, and jumped out of the truck bed.

Charles turned to look at her. "Take it? Just *take* it? I can't."

She pulled out a pack of cigarettes from the pocket of her plaid button down, and lit one up. "You'll be doing me a favor." Wile E. opened up the passenger door to the truck. "If I have it I'll gamble it away. I'm no good at gamblin' when I'm drunk. My brothers know this, and will use it against me." She began rummaging through the glove box to find the money. "And it will put my mind to rest knowing you aren't prostituting yourself out for boxed wine and a Snickers bar."

She looked up at Charles, the cigarette dangling from her lip.

He raised an eyebrow.

"I knew a guy once," she said, and handed him the money. "It ain't much, but it'll do. And don't worry about it. It's a gift."

Ever since Charles was young, having grown up in a

polite southern society, he was led to believe that bad things would happen to you if you did not say *thank you* after someone gave you a gift. Typically, you were beaten. He was even forced for weeks after the Christmas holiday to handwrite thank you letters to every family member near and far who had given him gifts. Consequently, even while biting his tongue and receiving death stares from Wile E., the words wanted to pour out over his lips.

"You want me," Charles said slowly and carefully, "to repay you for all that you've done by taking your money?"

"Yes, Charles. That is exactly what I want." She pulled his bag, filled with all the truck stop goodies, out from behind the seat. "Do I need to use simpler words, or do you think you got the idea?"

"You tricked me…when you kept on saying *I owed you*, I thought you meant like a favor or something."

She smirked. "Like I said, you *are* doing me a favor."

Charles shook his head and jumped out of the truck's bed, leaving his near-empty beer bottle behind. "You know," he said, taking his bag from her, "for being completely crazy you aren't half-bad."

"Says the boy having prophetic dreams," Wile E. quipped, ashing her cigarette. "Listen, in two weeks' time I'm going to Tell City. I got you this far. I need to make sure your stupidity doesn't get you dead in a ditch. All right? Plus, I'm just kind of naturally curious."

"How will you find me?"

Wile E. closed the passenger door. "I have my ways." She nodded to him and pointed towards the east. "Tell City is that way."

Charles smiled, and turned to walk away.

"Hey, brother!" she called after him, and he turned around. "Sun is Wakan. Trust it."

Charles smiled, "See you in two weeks."

Without looking up, Wile E. walked to the driver's side door and got in. Behind him Charles could hear the engine of the old truck clamber back to life.

Thinking over her words, he thumbed through the five hundred dollars she'd given him. *Not a lot,* she had said, *but it will do.* He wondered how far five hundred dollars would take him, and how he could make it last.

Charles put the money in his bag. Tell City was still one hundred thirty miles away. He reached the road and headed east.

***

It was not long after he started walking that clouds

began to roll in and consume the few hours of daylight that were left. He supposed the looming rain was likely to be more bearable than the heat and humidity he had been walking in just a day before. Or had it been longer than that? He could not remember.

Charles wondered if Jenna had left their apartment… if anyone was looking for him. If he could even get in and out of Tell City before he found his picture tacked up on a Wal-Mart entrance sign, or he had a full five-minute segment on the national news with Barbara Walters interviewing his parents and classmates about his disappearance. He thought he should be more disturbed by these thoughts of his loved ones searching for him, missing him, but truly he was more afraid that he might be caught or stopped before he even reached Tell City. He feared they'd catch him and drag him around in chains and a straitjacket, and they'd force him to explain his prophetic dream in front of camera men and news crews. Religious extremists would call him a prophet, and psychologists would diagnose him as having some sort of German-sounding mental problem. Charles was clearly lost, and terribly afraid of being found. It would ruin everything.

***

Robert Wood had a dream about his hometown that morning. Even as he climbed into his patrol car later that evening the damn thought scratched around in his skull, like a maggot gnawing the insides of an apple. He never liked to bring home to work or work to home, and he sure as hell never wanted to think about his *old* home at all. As far as he was concerned, the best memory he had of that place was the day he left it.

It was typical…being the only colored family in a small town, bad things tended to happen. He was a kid after all, and it was the seventies, but it wasn't even that. It was all the holier-than-thou self-righteousness of everyone in town thinking that they *knew* something, and that they were better because of it. He couldn't deal. It was right before he snapped that his miracle came along.

By dream time, Robert had circumnavigated the whole outer limits without so much as a call for domestic violence in the trailer park, or a complaint from Mrs. Craft about someone stealing her lawn gnomes again. His thoughts were itching at him. His coffee was cold. Dark clouds were rolling in, turning the world into a grey canvas for his memories to play on over and over again. He had to avert his mind to something else.

The state roads outside of town were always good for entertainment. There was always someone speeding or driving around with a taillight out. It would put his mind back on track. Help him to forget.

When he'd left that place it had taken him years to forget it all. All the *miracles*. All the bullshit. It took him a while to understand how the real world functioned. The real world does not tell you everything you want to know. You can't sit helplessly by, letting the walls of your life decay and crumble at your feet as you wait for some damned miracle to save you. You have to find it yourself. Find it *in* yourself. It's better that way. Living. Experiencing. The only good thing Tell City ever did for him was letting him escape. That was his miracle.

A cool drink of water read a sign on the gas station window right next to the Uncle Sam poster, and he'd up and joined the Navy at eighteen, never to return.

He rounded a turn on the winding country road. Grey trees guarded him on both sides. Ahead in the gloom, Robert saw a young man walking close to the trees with a backpack on his shoulder. The kid must have seen the headlights for he turned to look back, but he must not have seen the light bar on top, for he stuck out his thumb to grab a ride. Robert flipped on his lights. A hitchhiker on the outskirts of town…the perfect solution to get his mind off things.

He pulled up just behind the kid, who to his surprise did not rush off into the woods. He just squinted into the flashing lights like he was looking off into the sun. Robert stepped out of his patrol car, slamming the door to draw clear attention to the word SHERIFF painted in brown and tan letters across the car. One hand rested on his gun, the other grabbed his flashlight and shined it on the young man.

"What are you doin,' kid?" Robert walked up to him, shoulders back.

The red and blue lights danced around through the trees.

The boy smiled. "Just…walking."

"Just walking, huh? Hitchhikin'? Tryin' to catch a ride?"

The kid looked down, his glasses slipping down his nose. " Listen, I don't want any trouble."

"Oh. Well, hitchhiking is illegal here in Illinois, did you know that?" The kid did not respond. "I just need to see your I.D. and do a check on you real quick. You got your I.D. on you, don'tcha?"

He was just a young college kid. They thought hitch-hiking was some rugged adventure. He just needed a good scare is all, to put the fear of the law in him.

The hitchhiker pressed his lips together, looking back down at the ground. "No."

"No," Robert echoed. He twitched his index finger on his holstered gun. The kid's eyes darted to the firearm. It worked every time, and when it did not work Robert knew he had a long night of paperwork ahead of him. "Please, step up to the car."

The young man's face went white. He walked up to the car and put his hands on the hood.

Robert wrenched the backpack off his shoulder. "What's your name, kid?"

"Charles," the young man said through gritted teeth. "Garrett."

"All right, Mr. Garrett, why don't you have your I.D.?" He began to rummage through the backpack with his flashlight in one hand.

Charles looked over his shoulder at the sheriff. "Isn't this against my rights or something?"

Robert's flashlight landed on a wad of twenty dollar bills in the front pocket. "For a guy living out of a backpack you sure have a lot of cash." He held the wad of twenties in front of Charles' face. "Tell me, stranger, where'd you get this from?"

Now Robert was thinking he might have been on his way to buy drugs. Some dealer was on his way to pick this kid up off the side of the road. That would have been inventive.

Charles looked at him over his glasses. "A friend…"

"And does this friend have a name?"

Charles closed his eyes, and said quietly, "Her name is… Wile E. the Coyote."

Robert tried to contain it, but could not stop the laughter

from bursting out of him. He found himself gripping his knees to keep from toppling over.

The hitchhiker tried to explain, his voice pleading. "That was her nickname or something. She gave me a ride from Jackson."

Rain began to sprinkle from the sky. After the fifth raindrop fell on the deputy's uniform his laughter vanished. Robert stuffed the money back into the bag and pulled his handcuffs from his belt. He ripped the kid's hands off the hood of the Ford. The metal clashed as Charles's body fell against the car. "And then this *Coyote* just gave you hundreds of dollars?" He slammed the handcuffs around the kid's wrists and pulled him back up.

"Actually, yes!"

"Yeah. Right." Robert walked him to the rear passenger door. "You know your rights?"

"Like they've mattered so far?"

He ducked the kid's head as he put him in the car.

"Good." He slammed the door and walked back to the other side. "Wile E. the Coyote," he said, chuckling to himself.

At least the punk made his night interesting, and possibly even the rest of his month. With five hundred dollars he had to be either buying or selling drugs. He tossed the backpack into the shotgun seat as he got in.

"You'll stay in the town jail for tonight 'til I figure out what to do with you tomorrow." He buckled his seatbelt and turned off the light bar.

"I was just walking. I'm no harm to anyone. And the money, it…" The kid looked at Robert's reflection in the rearview mirror.

"No harm? Hitchhikin' is against the law 'round here, kid." Robert looked back at him via the mirror, making sure his gaze was stern and cold. Dominance was how you gained their cooperation.

"You got no I.D. You've got a roll of cash you can't reasonably justify. You're a stranger. As far as I'm concerned you intend harm. To *my* town. Ain't happenin', kid. You got that? Not 'til I clear you…if I clear you, and in that case you'll get the hell out of my town as fast as you can, you got that?"

The kid rolled his eyes and sunk into the backseat. Robert turned the car around and headed back towards town.

"So, let's get to know each other then, all right?" The kid didn't respond. "Where you traveling from, Garrett?"

Robert met Charles's fearful gaze in the mirror once again. "Houston," he said.

"Texas, huh?" Robert picked up the coffee he had bought on his break a few hours ago. The red to-go cup felt like ice to the touch, but he took a sip anyway. He regretted it immediately.

Charles's eyes followed the cup as he set it back down in the holder.

"So, kid." Robert glanced at him. "Where were you hitching to? Chicago to make some connections?"

Charles raised an eyebrow, still gazing at the coffee cup sitting in front of him. Robert looked back at the cup. It was just a red paper cup with the Folgers logo: the sun rising over a mountain.

"Look," Robert focused on the road as he made the turn to head back towards town, "if you work with me, I'll get you a cup of joe at the station. Hell, I'll get you a sandwich, too. So, where were you headed?"

Charles looked at the back of the deputy's head, and said, "Tell City."

The patrol car came to a screeching halt, fishtailing on the slick pavement. Charles's body tumbled forward, having no balance with his hands behind him. He hit his nose against the barrier that separated him from the deputy.

Robert whirled around to face the backseat "What the hell did you just say?"

"Tell City," Charles repeated, squirming back into the seat. With his wide-framed glasses slipping off his nose, he smirked. "You've heard of it?"

The cop clenched his teeth. "I grew up there."

"Seriously?" Charles laughed to himself, and whispered to Robert's coffee cup, "Sun is Wakan."

Robert stared back at him. The blue lights glowing from the radio equipment painted his worn face, and reflected off the grey in his hair.

"Listen," Charles began, "I know about the small-towns-don't-like-strangers-thing, but I've been traveling for over a week trying to get there. This can't happen to me now. Please. I swear I never planned on causing *any* trouble. I've never done anything illegal in my life. Well," he paused, "okay, but my record is clean. I was a good student, had a 3.0 G.P.A. I've never even had so much as a traffic ticket and I—"

Robert waved his hand. "Stop. Stop. I get it. Okay? Shut up." He saw the kid take a deep breath. "What you so hell bent on Tell City for? Ain't nothin' there 'sides a floodwall and antique furniture."

"Please don't call the insane asylum, but..." He glanced again at the Folgers cup for reassurance. "I had a dream about it."

"A dream?" Robert was skeptical for a moment, but not a long moment as moments were concerned. He recalled the dream he'd just had that very morning. It wouldn't leave him alone, that dream. It had wormed its way into his core.

Robert jumped out of the car. He tore open the backseat

door. "Get out."

Charles inched out. Robert spun him around, and rummaged through the lint and gum wrappers in his pocket to find the cuff keys, then remembered they were on his utility belt. "Can I allow you in the front or do I really need to call the asylum?"

Charles smiled. "I promise I won't push any buttons."

"Good." He unlocked the handcuffs from the kid's wrists. "Get in."

***

Robert could not think clearly. Numbness took over, and there was no escape. Not even the humming of the road or the patter of the rain could bring him back. He had witnessed too many evils in his hometown, and somehow he had done well forgetting them. But all it had taken was one damned dream to make it all rush back.

That dream…the hitchhiker. This was the work of Tell City. It was trying to tell him something.

He and his companion traveled in silence until they pulled into the rest stop off the interstate.

The kid cleared his throat. "So," he began, "what is Tell City? Why is it so…" He made a mess of hand gestures trying to explain what he was thinking.

"Listen, kid. Tell City is a place of *miracles*. Messages from *God*." His tone was heavy with disdain. "It's a place that tells you what you need. It gives answers, kid. But it...it's not right. It's not natural. The things it tells people. The things it hides. It can kill a person more often than it can save'em. You're better off hitching back to where you came from."

"Miracles and answers and messages from God don't really sound like a bad thing."

"Some things people are better off not knowin'."

They got quiet for a minute. Rain drummed on the roof, only emphasizing the silence.

"What happened to you there?"

Robert's dark eyes, previously hollow and lifeless, were now rimmed with tears and memories. The last time he'd cried was in 1987 on a burning ship in the Persian Gulf. He tried to force the tears back down this throat.

"My mama at a real young age just wanted to know that the Lord was watching her. She wasted her whole life, every single hour of it, waiting for a sign. She died waiting. But I saw it plain as day. She never got a sign that He was watching, because He wasn't. He don't watch any of us." Robert fought back the tears. "My baby cousin wanted to know her future...wanted to know who she'd grow up to be. Apparently, Tell City told her.

She killed herself the very next day. This one man I knew…his miracle, it…it made him blind."

The kid looked at him with sympathy – or maybe pity – in his eyes. "What about you?"

"I was one of the lucky ones," Robert said, and took a breath. "Look, if miracles exist, if God *exists*, it's not supposed to be like that, kid. Not like in Tell City. So go home. Whatever you're tryin' to do, it's not worth it."

He saw an expression on the young man's face that was a mixture of fear and confusion. He should not have said anything. He should have known this would be too much for the kid to handle. Something like that was too much for anyone.

"Sheriff," Charles said, "I appreciate your advice, and you giving me a ride in this weather." He let out a humorless laugh. "But I've gotta know what all this shit means." Charles looked off into the rain. "I am so terrified…of all of this. Of everything that has happened to me over the last month, let alone what is going to happen once I get to Tell City, but…" He paused, sighing. "If I let the fear take over, I'll call up my mommy and daddy, they'll fly me back to Texas, and then it was all for nothing. So thanks, but I've gotta go." Charles opened the car door and stepped out into the pouring rain.

He bent over slightly to make eye contact with Robert, his glasses already as foggy and as wet as the Ford's windshield.

"Thanks for not arresting me." He grabbed his bag, closed the door, and splashed off through the puddles to the rest stop shelter.

A long breath escaped Robert's lungs. He looked around at his patrol car and down at his uniform. The numbness in his soul subsided, but it left a strange aftertaste of something he had not felt in ages. But he could not remember what the feeling was or if there was even a good word to describe it. The only word that came to mind was *spring*.

***

The next morning was clear and bright. The rays of sunlight evaporated whatever puddles were left over from the rain the night before. Robert sat down at his desk with a warm cup of coffee, and he thought about Tell City. This time he allowed the memories passage into his consciousness. He did not fear them.

There was little paperwork to be done and only a few emails to read. After completing those tasks, he typed the name Charles Garrett into his databases. After glancing through about one hundred males in Texas with that name, including the various different spellings, he found the right kid from Houston.

Charles was twenty-two. Brown hair and brown eyes.

He was five-eleven and about one hundred forty-five pounds.

He was missing, and the entire state of Texas was looking for

him.

Charles had a nightmare as he slept on the dirt floor of an abandoned barn.

The king was approaching.

Crouched between himself and the well was the black panther. It just sat there, watching him, its tail moving back and forth. He stared into the cat's golden eyes, feeling like he might hyperventilate. He was sinking, choking, but he could not move. The king was nearby. The well was so close, but still unobtainable. He heard the ticking of a clock. The panther remained motionless except for its swishing tail. The king had to be defeated, the apple eaten, the toll paid, the sacrifice made. The sign said WELCOME TO TELL CITY.

It should not have been a nightmare but it was, probably because of the panther, though it had not been the most harrowing dream he had experienced thus far. His first dream had been the worst. He had awoken in a cold sweat that night. Jenna had been trying to shake him awake for several minutes, or so she had said.

He woke up from this nightmare in what he hoped was an abandoned barn. The darkness was unsettling. His chest tightened in panic, but he told himself it was just the dream making him feel that way and nothing more. After all, he had been walking in the darkness all night until he'd found the barn. So it was not the darkness causing his fear, it was just the dream.

And then he remembered that he didn't believe dreams were *just dreams* anymore. His chest tightened again. He couldn't breathe. Panthers...

From his book bag he pulled out a tattered spiral notebook and a pen, courtesy of his last ride, a seventy-year-old hippie named Rufus. The old man had picked him up in his custom-painted 1975 microbus just east of Eldorado, Illinois, and had dropped him off at a sketchy gas station off of Interstate 64. It had been a two-hour ride filled with smoke, philosophy, stories and The Beatles. Charles did not remember most of it. He did remember Rufus having a Wile E. Coyote bobblehead on the dash, though, and recalled that the old dude had given him the journal for the purpose of recording his dreams.

Charles shuffled across the dirt until he found a spot where he could see the lightening sky through a hole in the roof.

In the darkness, he tried to write down a few words about the dream so that he might recall it in full later.

He closed the journal and stood, stretching his arms and legs. Grabbing his backpack, he left the barn. The soft glow of the sky was a welcome sight after the darkness of the shadowy farm. The coming of dawn mirrored the optimism he felt inside his soul. Right now he was in Santa Claus, Indiana. Later on that day, he would be in Tell City.

Everything about that morning felt fresh and cleansing. The dampness of the dew cooled the air and glistened on the overgrown grass he had to wade through to get back to the road beyond the trees. The birds sang as they fluttered about, and the crickets chirped loudly to welcome the rising sun – until a gunshot rang out.

Silence fell across the land, and for a moment Charles thought he was dying.

It might have been his heart pounding in his ears, or maybe the shot had blown out his eardrums, but his whole head felt numb.

He stood frozen for a minute, and the effect on his hearing wore off…just in time for him to hear the sound of a gun being cocked behind him.

Without breathing, he pivoted around to face the barrel of a little old lady's pump-action twenty-gauge shotgun.

"What are you doing on my property? You're tres-passing." The lean, elderly woman had a Minnesota accent that was as thick and as sweet as syrup. Her hair was almost completely white. She wore it in a braid off to one side. With her aim fixed on him, she walked up closer. The fraying hem of her mid-calf length dress was dirty from tramping through the mire, which was caked in a thick layer on her boots.

"Ma'am?" Charles's softened southern accent came out as thick as Mississippi mud. "I was asleep in the barn over there. I thought…I thought it was abandoned. I'm just passin' through."

Her hands were steady on the gun. "We've had a lot of *passersby* coming through here lately, and I'm not about to trust any of them."

"Oh…okay. Um…" He tried to find words or his breath or whatever came first. Growing up in Texas, hunting and going to the shooting range were typical pastimes, though he did not really like hunting. Most everyone had at least one shotgun hanging on the wall. However, he had never had a loaded one aimed at his heart before.

Charles noticed the dark red stains on her hands and his vision blurred.

He stumbled a bit. "I'm sorry. I'll leave."

The old woman's eyes narrowed as she looked at him.

"Fine. Go. And remember, I checked you once." She paused. "I won't be checking twice."

Charles nodded.

"Dash along now."

He ran. Like a deer he jumped through the grass and over fallen logs. He did not stop to look back or even catch his breath until he could see the road through the trees, and when he did, he collapsed to his knees on the dirt. He thanked whatever god might exist out there – Wakan Tanka maybe – for sparing his life.

***

The old woman stepped onto her porch with her muddy hessian boots. A bloody burlap sack had flung on her back. Her quaint little farmhouse still had icicle holiday lights twinkling along the roof, and the smell of cinnamon and peppermint wafted through the screen door.

She dropped her burlap bag, filled with her rabbit kills to be skinned and flayed later, on the porch. Two ravens swooped down from a nearby tree and landed by the steps. Their beaks clicked and heads bobbed at the sight of the rabbit blood.

"You get your rabbits at dinner like the rest of us. Now

shoo." The woman waved her hand, and the ravens flew back up into their ash tree. They waited and they watched.

She set her shotgun down against the porch's wooden rocker and leaned over to reach the outlet behind it to unplug the holiday lights. Then she entered the house through the creaking screen door.

"Skadi!" A deep, jolly voice called out to her from a big green chair by the fireplace.

She took off her boots in the doorway. "Yes, dear?" She passed the living room and entered the kitchen, where she washed the rabbit blood and dirt off her hands in the sink.

"You won't believe what Rudolf tweeted!" Her white-haired husband turned in his chair to look at her with his one good eye. His accent was different than hers. It had been roughened by tobacco, and sounded almost Scandinavian.

Mrs. Claus shook her head. Despite his age, he was delighted by the new world's wonders, and often played with Apple's newest devices before they hit the market. He often told her that if he was going to grant wishes, he was going to make sure they worked first. To grant a broken wish would be a nasty trick, the kind he'd often let his blood-brother play on those who made the naughty list.

"He said—"

"Nicholas!" Mrs. Claus interrupted her husband. "I

cannot believe you're *already* playing on the interweb. It's only six." She pulled down her off-white apron, which hung from a knob on one of the kitchen cabinet doors, and cinched it around her plump waist.

"I know, I know." The old man appeared in the kitchen doorway. "But I have to keep in touch with the boys." He pouted as he readjusted his suspenders. "Plus, it's not like they're on the same time as us anyway."

The old woman did not respond as she walked over to the kitchen table, where there sat a long-stemmed pipe and a vintage Christmas tree ashtray. From the ashtray she picked up a half-smoked stale cigarette and lit it up.

"Did you catch any rabbits?" Stroking his white beard, Nick strolled across the room to the coffee pot. The cups were hung on hooks by the coffeemaker with care. Mr. Claus took down a Holiday World novelty mug.

"They're on the porch," she said grumpily, flicking the ash off her cigarette.

Nick set the coffee cup down with a bang. "Woman, you said it yourself, it's only six, so what could have *possibly* ticked you off already? It's too damn early."

She sighed, and left the butt of the cigarette to burn out in the tray. "Sorry, dear. You know how we've had so many… *visitors* recently."

He nodded, slipping his thumbs behind his suspender straps.

"Well, we had another one this morning. Sleeping in the reindeer's barn, so he said."

He furrowed his heavy brows as he turned to pour himself a cup of coffee. "Who was it this time? Pan? Cernunnos?" He let out a deep, jolly laugh.

"No. No one like that." She sat down in a kitchen chair. "Do you remember…oh, what did they name him…Charles Garrett? The little boy in Houston who always wished for a horse and a bow and arrow to play cowboys and Indians? And we persuaded his guardians to buy him the Nerf bow and arrow instead, but we never could make them get him a horse. They did live in such a small apartment, after all."

"Yes. Yes, I do remember. That was not long before he stopped believing." Saint Nick sat down at the table and picked up his tobacco pipe. "He was a good boy. Became selfish after his father received that promotion he had wished for, though. That's the way it goes, I suppose." He waved his hand around the pipe and it began to smoke. After a few puffs it was perfectly lit. "What about him?"

Mrs. Claus hit his arm with the back of her hand. "He was the one sleeping in the barn, you ol' fool." She leaned back in the chair. "I believe he's going to Tell City, just like the others."

Nick took a sip of his coffee. "I wonder what he has to do with all of that rubbish."

"I don't know," Mrs. Claus said, standing up. "But I do believe we better find out."

Nick nodded. "I do agree you ought to."

Mrs. Claus rolled her eyes. "I'm going to go skin those rabbits. Now, why don't you tell me what Rudolf said on the Twitter?"

"Ho!" Old Saint Nick slapped his knee, his laughter making his big belly shake like a bowl full of jelly. "He said, 'Right now I have the worst cold I've ever had…if you thought my nose was red before!'"

Mrs. Claus laughed along with her husband, and then she walked back out onto the porch to skin the rabbits for dinner.

***

It all seemed too familiar, like déjà vu. The road sign said TELL CITY 9 MILES. Charles had seen that road before. He had seen the sign before. It must have been in one of his dreams.

The Indiana summer sun beat down on the countryside. Mossy twisted trees and shrubs lined the fence rows between properties. Yellow and white farmhouses popped up atop rolling green hills above fields of corn and soybeans. Weaving through the hills and trees, gravel lanes branched off of the paved main roads, disappearing into the landscape. Bugs buzzed all around him with an all-consuming surreal hum that saturated the air. The buzz seemed to creep along the surface of Charles's skin. It was the mock applause and cruel laughter of the earth as it waited for him to cross the threshold. There was no turning back, even if he wanted to. There was only going forward into unknown danger. The bugs knew this as they watched and chattered and placed bets on his life.

Gravel crunched beneath his feet as he walked on past the green road sign. Nine miles would take him about four hours if he kept a good pace, but the road was winding up and down hills a majority of the way, so he was not sure how long it was realistically going to take, especially on tired legs and an empty stomach.

When he'd crossed through downtown Santa Claus earlier in the morning, he had dipped further into Wile E.'s generous donation to buy himself a few nutrition bars from a gas station. After his traumatic experience with the farmer lady's shotgun, he'd decided to treat himself to some food to calm his nerves.

Santa Claus, Indiana was a strange and slightly creepy place. Even in the height of summer, the town was decorated with weathered reindeer and timeworn Santa Claus statues from the city square all the way out to the campgrounds in

the country. The oldest Santa statues in the world guarded the

town's winding back roads, perpetually judging the residents

and passersby. The statues' concrete eyes and fixed smiles

forever watched, always knowing who had been naughty or

nice. It was in this place that the Christmas holiday never ended.

Even the town's biggest attraction, a theme park, was called

Holiday World.

Though Texas had a few strange towns itself, Charles

had never seen anything like Santa Claus, Indiana before, and he

decided that if Saint Nick really did have a home outside of the

North Pole, that would be the place. His white beard and jolly

cheeks would blend right into the scenery.

***

Charles had eaten the last of his nutrition bars, and his

stomach was still growling. He looked up and saw an old white

pickup with a *Born to Kill* bumper sticker parked along the side

of the road. He slowed his pace as he came closer to it. The truck

was empty aside from crushed Coca-Cola and Monster cans and

a camouflage ball cap sitting on the dash. He walked on past, but

froze at the sound of tramping feet and breaking twigs on the

other side of the road.

Two young men, about the same age as Charles, emerged from the woods carrying fishing poles, tackle boxes, and a cooler. When they saw him standing by the truck, they stopped.

A moment went by without anyone making a sound. Then the big man with a beard and a ball cap nodded. "Sup, son?"

Charles nodded back. "Not a lot."

The two men walked across the road to their truck.

"Sorry," Charles continued, "I was just walking and saw the truck. I was just making sure everything was okay."

"S'cool. We was just down by the river throwing our rods." The bearded one started to dance out the motions of throwing out a fishing line and reeling it back in.

Charles raised an eyebrow as he watched. "Right." Behind him, the other man, who was much thinner and taller than Charles, laughed as he lowered the tailgate and put his fishing pole and the cooler in the bed.

Charles felt awkward. Both of the young men had their eyes on him, sizing him up for a reason he could not discern. He just knew every word he said would be a crucial factor in their judgment. "C-Catch anything?"

"Yeah," the bearded man answered. He licked his lower lip, and looked at his companion by the tailgate. "Go ahead,

Steve. Show him *the loot*."

The skinnier man grinned. With his boney hands, he dragged the cooler across the bed, close to his chest. He looked at Charles and winked before he ripped open the lid.

Charles expected to see organs and blood from a sacrificial deer, but instead he saw ice, beer, and fish. There were several bluegill and bass, all gasping through their gills and begging him with their glassy eyes to be put back in their aquatic home.

Charles laughed. "Looks like y'all had a good morning." He added, "You had me going for a second there."

Steve closed the cooler as his bearded friend snickered and put his own fishing gear in the truck bed.

"Yeah, well, we've had a lot of creeper visitors around here lately. And with you creepin' around our truck…"

"I didn't mean to *creep*." He paused. "I've just been walking for a while and I thought there might be someone who could give me a ride."

"Where you going?" Steve asked, closing the tailgate.

"Tell City."

"I don't know, Brandon." Steve looked Charles up and down. "Think he passed the *'aight* test?

Brandon nodded. "Yeah, he's 'aight." He looked at Charles. "Hop in the bed, jack."

Charles took his backpack off, and though it wasn't that heavy, it was a relief to free his shoulder of the burden. "I really do appreciate it."

"Tha's how we do." Brandon opened the passenger door and slid into the truck.

With Steve at the wheel, the truck roared to life and peeled off the gravel shoulder.

Brandon opened the rear window and introduced himself over the sound of the wind. They shook hands through the open window.

"So, you live in Tell City?" Charles asked.

"Yup. Both of us do." Steve leaned sideways and pulled out a container of chew from his back pocket.

"What's it like?"

Brandon and Steve glanced at each other. To Charles it seemed to be a look that reminded them both to keep the town's secret.

"It's 'aight," Brandon said. "Kind of boring. Why are you and all these other people coming to town all the sudden?"

Charles's eyes narrowed. "Well, I don't know about the other people, but I'm just passing through." He wasn't a good liar, but the two young men in the truck didn't seem to notice. "So, who are all these *visitors* I keep hearing about?"

"Dunno," Steve said, spitting out his window. Charles

watched the chunk of tobacco spit catch in the wind and fly behind them. "Hand me that can, will you?" Brandon handed Steve an empty soda can. "That spit didn't hit you did it?" He glanced back towards Charles.

Charles tried to smile, but it was more of a grimace. "Thankfully, no."

"Good." He spit into the can. "All these people are coming to town with their suits and weirdo accents. My dad thinks they're looking for real estate, or something."

"Maybe they want the old factory?" Brandon added.

"I dunno," Steve said. "They're just weird. Strange. Not like me or Brandon here." He hacked again into the soda can.

Charles laughed, looking up as they sped through a crossroads. He hadn't realized they were going so fast. Then he saw the sign, TELL CITY 1 MILE. It disappeared behind the trees as they curved down the road.

***

When Tell City appears, it just kind of hits you. One moment there are farmhouses and barns and the next thing you know you're in town. Your brain finally realizes where you are when you see the giant sign showing an apple with an arrow piercing through it. It's a beautiful sign that says WELCOME TO

TELL CITY, painted in elegant white script. When Charles saw it, he thought his heart would stop beating. He had seen that sign in one of his dreams.

The sign was quickly left behind and Tell City lay before him. Compared to the skyscrapers of Houston, though, it was hardly a city. It had a small-town ambience that Charles had rarely seen before, aside from family reunions and television shows from the sixties. Everything looked so quaint and so quiet compared to the hectic uniformity of the big city townhomes and suburbs he had grown up around.

Charles remembered the sheriff, who had abducted him in Illinois. He found it hard to imagine that this terrible secret he'd been warned about was being kept locked away. Hidden behind the walls of the little shops, and buried underneath the mulched and weeded garden beds of the little houses. On the surface, it all appeared to be too fragile for something so ominous.

Charles looked back into the truck cab. "Seems kind of peaceful."

Steve scoffed and spit into his can, and took a sharp right turn into a gas station. Charles's fingers gripped the edge of the truck bed to keep from rolling out.

Brandon looked at Charles as they came to an abrupt stop at a gas pump. "Yeah, well…"

Steve jumped out of the truck.

Brandon continued, "Small-town U.S.A. really isn't like what they say."

"Hey," Steve said, peering in through the window, "Brandon, you want a Monster?"

"Yeah."

"And what about you, er…?"

"Charles," he said, laughing. "That'd be great, if you're offering. I could use an energy boost."

Steve wandered off inside the gas station.

"Well, nowadays," Charles said, looking back at Brandon, "TV shows and movies say small towns are filled with vampires, witches, and…supernatural mysteries. That's obviously bullshit." Charles grinned, and watched the expression on Brandon's face change. "What else do they say about small towns that's not true?"

"W-well," Brandon said, avoiding eye contact, "you know, they say everybody knows *er'body*, but that ain't true. You see, you know who you know, and they know who they know. That's it. Maybe in *really* small towns…"

"What's the population here?"

Brandon turned his head to meet Charles's gaze. "Hell, maybe seven thou? Might be small to some. Where you from?"

"Houston. Population about two mill."

"Damn, son." Brandon stroked the stubble on his cheeks. "I don't think there is one goddamned white picket fence in this hole, not that I know of. And it's not Andy Griffith's Mayberry, that's for sure."

Steve stepped out of the gas station and walked up to the truck. He tossed a can to Charles and reached through the window to hand one to Brandon. "Where we taking you, Charles? Know anyone in town?" Steve opened his Monster and started chugging.

"Nope." Charles opened the tab and took a swig. "Is there a motel somewhere close?"

"There's a motel at the other end of town. Want us to take you there?"

"If it's not too far I'll walk." Charles jumped out of the bed. "Y'all have helped me enough as it is. I appreciate it." He reached out his hand.

Steve shook it, and gave him directions to the motel. Charles grabbed his bag from the back and hung it on his shoulder. With his free hand he waved to them both.

"See you 'round, jack," Brandon yelled, as the white truck sped from the gas station's parking lot.

***

Amanda Wood was out in her mother's old flower garden, ripping away the lives of invading dandelions and clover. She was thinking about her own life – all the people who had been ripped away like weeds. It was strange to think about death that way.

Life is what it is, she thought, made of comings and goings. Amanda was not sure how she *felt* about that, though. It might have been acceptance, but she wondered if it was more like numbness, not wanting anything, not feeling anything.

She could not imagine one thing she wanted back, or wanted to change, or wanted to know. She did not want anything.

Everyone her age had already gone to the Oracle, some lucky ones had even gone twice, but she had not. She could not think of a thing to ask for or a reason to go. Her remaining family thought it was strange at her age, that with everything that had happened over the last year, she had not gone. It was like a Tell City coming-of-age ritual that she had failed to complete.

Sweat dripped down her brow. Amanda wiped it away with the back of her gloved hand.

"E-Excuse me?"

Amanda looked up to see a man about her age standing on the other side of the wrought iron fence. She thought right away that he had a boyish charm. He was tall, thin, unshaven, and he wore those old grandpa glasses that college kids thought were all the rage.

Amanda took off her mother's gardening gloves. "Yes?"

"I was looking for the motel in town, and I think I got myself lost."

"Not quite. Go straight until you reach the traffic light. Take a right and that will put you back on the main drag."

"Thanks," he said with a southern twang, and waved.

Amanda continued weeding after slipping her gloves back on. She wondered if she should have been more hospitable. She wondered if she should have offered him a place to stay or a ride at least. The drive would have only taken a minute. And maybe she should have offered him something to drink. It would have been the so-called Christian thing to do, but he was a stranger.

Her aunt and everyone at mass were gossiping about the strange visitors coming around, and how they could not be trusted, but the young man did not seem odd. He just looked like a college drop-out, one of the romantic ones that dreams of traveling the world as a stowaway on a ship, and ends up hitchhiking to tribal villages in the Amazon. But those people are not *strange*, Amanda decided, just adventurous, and perhaps even naïve. She wondered if everyone in town was just being paranoid. They told her to do one thing, and then they did another.

At the end of it all, no matter what they said or did, Amanda did not care.

***

The man at the front desk of the Days Inn motel looked as if he had been working the graveyard shift for too long. He was pale and boney. His long gray hair was oily and stringy. There seemed to be no soul residing inside, so his body only moved due to obligation. The man's sunken eyes told Charles he was nothing but an inconvenience.

The old clerk dropped the key onto the desk and hissed, "Sixty-three eighty-eight."

Charles pulled four twenties out of his bag and handed them over.

"One of the last rooms," the man grunted, and the cash register opened with a ding. He handed Charles his change.

"Really?" Charles asked. "A big event going on or something?"

The man slammed the register closed. "Not a goddamn thing," he deadpanned.

He walked off towards the back room. "Checkout's at

noon," he growled over his shoulder, and shut the office door.

***

Charles found his room. He showered and cleaned himself up the best he could. In the mirror, he saw how thick his facial hair had grown. Since puberty, he had always been clean shaven. He had no idea his stubble could grow so thick or so evenly. He looked much older than he felt.

While he was still used to moving, he decided to put off resting until after he found food. Wile E.'s money wasn't going to last for long at seventy bucks a night, so he had to stick to the essentials.

He walked back the way he had come and found a gas station. He piled his arms full of all the canned beans and cheap microwavable meals he could carry.

"Bunking down for the apocalypse?" the lady cashier asked, while bagging the cans.

Charles just smiled politely.

"I know I am…I see the signs," she said with a straight face. "Have a good day now."

Charles continued to smile as he inched out the door.

During the entire walk back to the motel, he thought about the apocalypse and prayed it would happen many years after his death, or at least after he figured out all this Tell City dream stuff.

By the time he arrived back at the motel, the sun was beginning to set and all the other visitors had returned for the night. The parking lot was full of cars, and Charles couldn't help but notice they did not fit into the scenery: Cadillacs, Audis, Mustangs, Bentleys, Mercedes, B.M.W.s, Jags. They were either brand new or classic and chromed. Though Charles was never much of a gearhead, he still found himself lusting after them.

Charles watched as a rusty old truck pulled from the parking lot, and then there was nothing left but a shining sea of polished classic and luxury cars.

Once inside his motel room, he made himself the dinner of champions: cold beans in a can and microwaved macaroni.

He turned off the bedside light and laid his glasses on the nightstand. There was a stand up card next to his glasses. It thanked him for choosing Days Inn, and it had the motel's logo on it: a rising sun or a setting sun, Charles could not tell, but he thought of the Folgers coffee cup and of Wile E.'s words. *Trust it.* He stared into the sun on the standup card until his eyes closed.

Before he fell asleep, he wondered if he should give his parents a call to let them know he was all right, perhaps even persuade them to send money. For the first time in his life, the thought of taking money from his parents made his stomach churn. This time, unlike the other times, he might actually *need* it once Wile E.'s cash was spent.

Jenna did not cross his mind that night. The girl he'd met weeding the garden, though, her eyes looked familiar. Charles could not remember where he'd seen them. It wasn't déjà vu. It was not from a dream. He just knew he had seen them before. Hollow and dead.

***

Steve and Brandon had the truck backed up to the banks of Windy Creek after nightfall. Both men sat on the tailgate with one hand holding a fishing pole, the other gripping a bottle of beer. The case of beer was nearly gone. Country music played from a Smartphone sitting on top of the blue cooler.

"Here's what I'm thinkin,'" Brandon said.

Steve looked over at him while finishing off his beer.

"If this magic shit can make Desiree psychic and her old man a *priest* of the Oracle…why can't it share the love, huh? When I go I'm asking for money."

Steve chuckled in response. "Yeah." He tossed away the empty bottle.

"I could get myself a truck and a huntin' lodge up near Bloomington or something. I'd get out of this podunk town. Live the good life."

"Hell…" Steve opened up the lid to the cooler and then handed Brandon the phone. "Change the song, dude. I'm tired of that whiney-ass shit." He pulled out two beers, setting one on the tailgate for Brandon. "If that were all possible I wouldn't just ask for money. I'd become a rapper. They make bank, get women, free weed. Doobies the size of your thumb, man."

Brandon scrolled through the phone to find a song, and an upbeat tune began to play.

Steve opened his beer. "Women and herb all the damn time, 'round the clock, twenty-four-seven."

Brandon smiled and licked his lower lip. "You got a problem with that, son. *You* can't rap."

"Yeah, well. That's what the Oracle's for…if it could."

"But it can't. What the hell is magic good for if it can't *do* anything?"

"Now, boys…" A male voice spoke up from behind them, the accent deeply southern.

Steve and Brandon turned around to find a man standing there in jeans and a dress shirt. His hair was a shade of dirty blonde, his eyes were the murky brown of a river.

"What if…what *if*," he said, walking up to them, "magic *could* do something?" He sat on the tailgate in the narrow space between them and took ownership of Brandon's beer. "Like what you were just asking for?" He paused, taking a swig. "Actually, it can do all of that and *more.*"

Steve looked the man up and down and said, "You…are sittin'…way too close."

The blonde man stood up, looking offended.

"Yeah," Brandon mumbled, "an' what in the hell you doing at *our* fishin' spot?"

"I'm trying to make you a deal." The stranger handed the beer back to Brandon and pushed up his shirt sleeves.

Brandon looked at Steve. "Now he's startin' to speak our language, son."

Steve laughed. "Yeah, buddy!"

Brandon stood on his drunken feet and raised the beer. "But here's the thing, *jack*. We don't make deals with people."

"Nope," Steve chimed in.

"People make deals with us."

"Yup."

The blonde man's mud-colored eyes darted back and forth between the two of them.

"Cause we got something *you* want." Brandon poked the blonde stranger in the chest with the beer bottle.

"Yup. So what's it gonna be?" Steve smirked.

The man's expression went cold and rigid. The creek behind him began to rise. It crept up the bank.

Brandon felt the water seeping into his boots, and Steve jumped to his feet, standing on the tailgate, looking down at the sudden flood. Their drunken mumbled cries tangled together as the rising water swept across the bank

The blonde man sighed, running his fingers through his hair. "Sorry, boys, I must have lost my temper." The water subsided quickly. The only sign of the flood was the water dripping off Brandon's clothes.

Brandon stood motionless on the bank, soaking wet from the knees down. The beer bottle dropped from his hand, and he stared up into the blonde man's face.

"Now…where were we?" The man put a fingertip to his lips. "Ah, yes…making a deal." He smirked. "Either of you interested?"

There are some things people are better off not knowing, and Desiree Hart wished she'd never known what had happened to her father that night.

***

It was dark and cold when Jon Hart found the shack in the woods. He had been the first and only person to find it alone. The tradition was, and still is to this day, that only a person who has gone before can show you where it is. Others had tried to find it on their own and failed.

He had found it though, on that chilly November night, but later in life he and others close to him wondered if he really had been truly alone.

Jon had been drinking at McGrath's Pub, trying to swallow more than just the whiskey. But it was hard to drown the memories when everyone that talked to him felt the sympathetic urge to mention her name…Marie.

She had given him the world, and then she was gone and he was alone. A black hole had begun to grow in his chest; every part of him was slipping away. He knew that soon there would be nothing left of him.

Jon kept waking up in the middle of the night, and he would roll over in bed to hold her, to feel her warmth against his flesh, but she would not be there. He felt the urge to run to her for comfort, but there was no one to run to. Without her, his soul and his entire being were lost.

Jon was barely holding on.

He had to see his wife again. If he could just see Marie, she could save him. She always did.

He stumbled from the bar and ran into the woods.

His cries rang out through the night as he crashed drunkenly through the trees. The whole forest bowed to the sound, for it was the echo of a dark and tragic death.

A heavy frost covered the trees and the ground. The world was fragile and still.

Jon rested for a moment against the rough bark of an oak to wipe the icy tears from his face. His vision was blurred with both the *tears and the liquor, so when he walked out into the barren meadow, he almost did not see the tiny crooked shack.*

The shack was decrepit and leaning. Vines crept up along the wooden panels. They were thick with thorns, and they guarded the shack and all its magic.

As Jon opened the door, the bones of the structure moaned. The hinges creaked.

Candles lit up the walls, and the dripping wax had hardened in puddles on the dirt floor.

Jon stepped across the threshold. "Hello?"

"Greetings," said a man's voice. In what a second ago had been an empty corner, a pale man now stood. He had a white beard and was dressed in black.

"M-my name is Jon Hart." He walked in further.

The old man nodded. "I know who you are. The Oracle foretold your arrival." His voice was as deep as the night sky, and he spoke with an authority as wise as the stars.

"I…I…" Jon looked off into the flickering light of the candles. "I lost my wife. She died."

"This I also know. The Oracle told me so."

Jon looked back up into the old man's shadowed face. "I have to see her again. I have to. I need her!"

"The Oracle cannot undo what is already done, my son. It cannot bring her back."

"That's not…" Jon's breathing was ragged, his voice wavered. "That's not what I mean. I just…I need to see her. Hear her voice just one more time. I need that."

The man walked carefully up to Jon. His feet were bare, and each step he took had a timeless grace and a ritual purpose. He moved as if he were walking across water or floating in a dream. "There is something the Oracle told me of many eons ago," said the priest, "but it requires a great sacrifice from you, Jon."

Jon gazed into his eyes. They were white. He was blind.

The old priest's bones creaked as he raised his wrinkled hand. He was older than the shack itself. "Our secrets are buried in our hearts." He touched his hand to Jon's chest. "Revealing them is nothing less than the sacrifice of human art."

"Name it," Jon pleaded. "I'll do anything."

He released a deep breath. "You are ready, my son."

The priest glided his fingertips up Jon's neck and face until they rested on his brow. The palm of his hand covered Jon's eyes. And all went white.

***

Daniel and Robert Wood were young men at the time. They found Jon Hart kneeling by the side of the road that night. He was drunk, and blood dripped from his eyes. They offered to take him to the *nearest hospital, but he demanded they just take him home.*

They dropped him off at his mother's house, which was where he had been staying so she could help him take care of his three-month-old baby girl.

With blood still dripping down his face, he stumbled through the front door. He could hear the late-night rerun of Bewitched *playing on the television, but all he saw was static. Though he could not see her, his mother was asleep on the couch. Jon searched with his hands until he found the stair rail and climbed the steps. He felt his way down the hall to his baby's nursery and reached her crib where she was sleeping.*

He searched around through the blankets until he found her tiny body. He picked her up and held her close to his chest. Her sleep disturbed, she began to whine.

"I'm so sorry, Desiree." Jon began to cry. The salt stung his eyes. "I am so sorry, my little girl."

He fell to his knees, and holding her tight in his arms, he rocked her back and forth. His body shook with violent tears. "I am so sorry..."

The baby girl began to wail.

***

The night her father became priest to the Oracle was forever burned in her mind. It was the first thing she saw when she was given her mother's gifts.

Desiree pulled her eyes away from the crystal ball in the center of the table. It was actually glass, not crystal, but her clients didn't need to know that. She glanced over to the spirit altar on her right. The wax from the lit candles had begun to puddle on the table and drip onto the floor.

"Shit."

Desiree flew from her seat and blew out the candles. The wax had already done its damage to the carpet. She would have to try to clean it later once it dried, but it would not be the first time or the last. The damage deposit on the building was not too outrageous, but Mr. Spencer, the landlord, was nitpicky with her because of her line of *work*. Being the town psychic, her reputation preceded her.

Desiree looked down at the offerings on the altar she had left to honor the dead. There were clippings from obituaries, along with candies, pennies, and shells. She picked up the picture of her mother, Marie. The photo had been taken at McGrath's Pub. Desiree never used to think she looked much like her mom. Marie had straight black hair, smooth tan skin, a lean feline face. Desiree looked more like her father – curly brown hair, pale skin, and a squared jaw. But as she grew older, she began to see the resemblance. It was in her eyes. The box of black hair dye she used to hide the grey every few weeks helped

a little, too.

Desiree was sixteen when she went to the Oracle. She

just wanted to know what her mother was like. As its priest her

father could not refuse the request. Jon Hart never spoke about

his wife after the night he became priest, and because of his

silence, she never knew who her mother was, or how powerful

she was, until the Oracle showed her. It gave Desiree her

mother's power.

Desiree touched her lips to the picture of her mother,

and set it back in its place on the altar.

The bells on the front door jingled. Even before she

peeked through the curtains, Desiree knew who it was.

Amanda's aura had a dull, hollow taste. It had been like that

since her parents passed away the year before.

Desiree parted the doorway's red curtains and saw

Amanda reaching out to touch a doll on the voodoo altar.

Desiree had set it up in the front room, and it was just for show,

really. She kept the real thing upstairs in her apartment, but her

clients didn't need to know that either.

"Don't touch that." Desiree smiled.

Amanda ripped her hand away and turned to look at the

psychic.

Desiree was old enough to be her mother, but she never

looked like she could be anyone's mom. She dressed like a rock star in dark, low-rise jeans and fitted shirts.

Desiree walked up to the altar. "You don't want to upset the Loa now do you?"

"The Loa?"

Straightening the voodoo doll on the table, she said, "Vodoun spirits."

"Like…" Amanda raised an eyebrow. "Like voodoo?"

Desiree touched the statue of St. Peter on the altar. "My mother was a voodoo priestess back in New Orleans. That was before she met my father." She looked over at the young woman. "What can I do you for, Miss Wood? Your aunt would kill you if she found out you were here on a Sunday instead of at Mass."

"I already told her I'm not going anymore," Amanda said. "They wouldn't stop staring at me with that look, you know? After a year you'd think they'd stop pretending like they care." She paused, glancing around the room as she readjusted the purse hanging from her shoulder. "I understand the polite sympathy, which is customary when someone is mourning, but after a while it's like *they died,* I'm over it, now leave me alone." Amanda added, "Mom and Dad always hated her side of the family, anyway. They never approved of their marriage…until after the funeral. Then they made it into some sort of Romeo and Juliet tragedy."

Desiree interjected, "So, what is it that ails you, hmm?" She smiled. "You want me to curse all them over there at the cathedral?" She sat down in one of the armchairs she had bought for the front room. They appeared to be antiques from the Victorian era, but really they were cheap reproductions that Desiree had distressed and recovered with fabric she had gotten at a yard sale. Again, it was for aesthetics, and her clients did not need to know.

Amanda looked at Desiree with dark, hollow eyes. "No, nothing like that." With a dismissive wave she continued, "I don't know…I *think* there might be something wrong with me."

"And what's that, honey?"

Amanda glanced around the room at all the draping fabric, the animal bones, the bottled potions, the herbs. She looked back at Desiree with a shrug, and said, "I don't feel anything."

The bells on the door jingled, and a young man walked in. He was skinny, and wore wide-framed glasses. The young man had a backpack on his shoulder. He was a little ragged around the edges, but still had some innocence about him. His aura was strange but vaguely familiar, and it lit up at the sight of Amanda. They knew each other.

"Can I help you?" Desiree was suspicious of strangers walking into her shop. She had grown up with all of her clients or her clients' children. It was unsettling to have someone step into her shop that she did not know.

Charles leaned back out the door and looked at the glowing neon light that said OPEN PSYCHIC. As he leaned back in through the door frame he smiled. "I hope so."

Desiree stood as Charles approached her. She took his money, and told him she'd help him soon.

Amanda followed her to the back room. Drawing back the curtain she asked, "Do I owe you anything?"

"Hell, no, baby." Desiree sat down in her chair at the reading table. "This is on the house."

***

Charles sat in the waiting room, his backpack by his feet. His old self screamed in the back of his head, calling him an idiot for spending precious money on a whack job, a scamming psychic. His new self did not respond. It was not worth the fight, and that one girl was there, the one he saw weeding the garden. She looked normal enough, and she was seeing a psychic. Not to mention he was in no position to be calling anyone else a whack job.

The curtain parted and the girl walked out. The psychic stood behind her, and Charles could see she was almost his height. She was well into her forties, but still had a body that would make any woman jealous – slender, fit, and perky. Charles never expected to meet a psychic who looked and dressed like she did. They were supposed to wear long billowy skirts and dangling jewelry, but she wore tight faded jeans with a black studded belt and a Harley Davidson tank that hugged every curve.

"Come on in." Her voice was deep and smooth, and Charles had trouble ignoring all the things his old self was saying as he watched her tramp stamp swaying with her hips as he followed her into the back.

The room was much like the front of the shop, only darker. There were no windows. The room was lit only by the flickering flames of black candles. There was a table in the center and it was draped with a long burgundy cloth. Charms and symbols decorated the walls. There were altar tables covered with candles and trinkets and wax. Along the walls were shelves that were cluttered with jars filled with herbs and colored oils.

A tingle went up Charles's spine, and he knew that behind the decorations of her psychic stage, she was no whack job scamming con. Behind the trumped-up act, behind the curtain, was something real. He could not see it, but he felt it.

"Have a seat," she purred, sinking into her chair at the table.

Charles pulled out the Victorian chair on the other side and sat.

"Why have you come to me?" she asked in a voice that was flirtatious, rehearsed, and used on all new clients.

Charles held in his laughter, knowing that some things have to be done to fulfill clients' fantasies and stereotypes. He cleared his head and tried to remember the reason he had come.

"Do you do dream interpretations?"

"I do." She smirked with a glint in her eye.

"Great!" Charles dug into his backpack and pulled out his spiral-ringed dream journal. "Because I have a few of them."

The look on her face changed from the phony façade to something much more real. "You have dreams often?" Her ring-covered hand reached out over the crystal ball in the center of the table and took the journal.

"It was a dream that brought me here. I live…lived…in Houston. I had a dream about this place."

Desiree began thumbing through the pages that described the dreams he had had the last few nights.

"And that's when it started, and that's why I'm here," Charles explained.

Desiree chuckled. "You had a dream about this shit-hole?"

Charles's gaze narrowed. "I know the town's secret," he

said in a hushed tone.

"Oh, yeah?" She leaned back in her chair, still skimming through his journal "And what secret's that?"

Charles leaned back as well. "I don't know really. I just know that the town…it *tells* you things, like an Oracle, I guess."

Desiree looked up. Their brown eyes met, and she dove into his aura. It was humming. It was electric. It felt like a storm.

She closed the journal and set it on the table. "Yeah, well," she said, lacing her fingers together and setting her elbows on the arms of the chair. "It's still a shithole."

Charles cracked a smile, and she continued, "Tell me about your dream then, the first one."

Charles's gaze drifted off as he remembered.

"There was a flood. People were screaming. There was a war going on and…there was magic. Not like Houdini magic, but something…subtler. I didn't see it, but I knew it was there. And there was this castle that everyone was running to. And the flood was alive and it…it was trying to get there, too. But when I was running I found this apple tree, and it was the castle. I tried to tell the other people but they wouldn't listen. Then I was sitting on this stone well in the castle, but it wasn't in a castle it was in a forest, and I had an apple in my hand from that one tree." He looked up at Desiree. "There was a road sign in front of me that said TELL CITY. I remember looking at it and knowing

I had to go there, but this," Charles paused, laughing, "this *king* was coming, and there was a black panther, and I *hate* cats. I mean, I'm terrified of them because of a black panther I saw as a child. And I had to eat the apple, but…I woke up."

***

Desiree and Charles walked out into the lobby of the psychic's shop. Amanda was there waiting, and she stood as soon as she saw them.

"Amanda, this is Charles Garrett," Desiree said. "Charles, this is Amanda Wood."

"Hello." Amanda nodded.

Charles smiled and shook her hand.

Desiree was slightly unsure of herself. Taking these two to the Oracle had two separate but equally horrible consequences if anyone were to find out, and she could sense it. This would not turn out well, but their issues were things her father, the priest of the Oracle, needed to handle. Her spells and charms had little power on this terrain.

"Why don't you two follow me?" She walked over to the front window and turned off the OPEN PSYCHIC sign. "There is something I need to discuss with both of you."

She led them down the hallway where the restrooms

were located. They had not been used since Mr. Bright's dental office had closed down after his death. He had gone to the Oracle when her father had first become its priest. He had wanted to know how to be successful in such a small town. The Oracle told him to become something the town did not have. At the time, the town did not have a lot of things, including a dentist. He had renovated the building into Bright Dental, and it was the only dentist office in town for many years. After his death, Mr. Spencer bought the building, thinking someone would rent it out for a similar, practical, useful business. Instead, it became a psychic shop.

Desiree opened the door to the stairs that led to the apartment above.

"You live up there?" Charles asked.

"Well, business isn't what you would call *booming*."

Charles and Amanda followed her up the stairs to a small landing.

"Don't look at the mess." Desire opened the apartment door.

"I'm sure it's fine," replied Amanda, following her into the living room.

***

Charles stood on the threshold and glanced around the apartment. The décor was much like downstairs, but the walls were painted a simple white and it was much brighter.

"See," Amanda said in rehearsed pleasantness, "it's not that bad. Not as messy as my place. I just haven't had any reason to clean, I guess."

One of Desiree's three black cats hopped off the couch and strolled to the door. Charles felt something warm brush up against his leg, and he froze.

Over the pounding of his heart, he heard someone ask him if he would like anything to drink, but Charles couldn't breathe. Then the voice said, "Aw, it looks like Luna likes you."

Trembling, throat clenching, he peered down. A pair of yellow-green feline eyes stared back at him. The black cat's razor-sharp teeth flashed as it let out a shrill ungodly noise. A low rumble echoed within the depths of the beast, as it leaned forward to attack Charles's leg once again with cuddles.

Still panicking, Charles kept backing away from the tiny black cat, and his heel caught on the edge of the landing. He fell backwards down the stairway, hitting step after step until he crashed into the wall at the bottom of the staircase, and everything went black.

***

He woke up on the couch. A wet rag was on his forehead, and Desiree was sitting on the coffee table in front of him.

"You okay?" she asked, with a hint of panic in her voice. "You scared us to death."

"I...*hate*...cats." Charles looked around the apartment, the events rushing back to him. He covered his face with his hands, mumbling into them. "This is so embarrassing..."

He heard Amanda's voice ask, "You have a cat phobia?"

He lowered his hands and saw Amanda sit down next to Desiree on the coffee table.

"Ailurophobia," Amanda said, handing him a glass of water. "I was a psych major."

Charles took the rag off his head and sat up. He sipped the water.

"It's normal for a phobia to be embarrassing," Amanda continued. "First, to be afraid of something to the point of severe anxiety is stressful enough, and then the phobia itself is often socially humiliating and debilitating, which can lead to a number of other psychological issues in conjunction with the phobia."

"Uh...thanks?"

Desiree smiled. "The cats are locked up in my bedroom. Are you feeling okay? You hit those stairs pretty hard."

"I think I'm okay. At least...I don't think I should go to

the hospital." He thought about that for a moment. Insurance and parents and family doctors would mean inquiries and notifications. "Yeah, please, don't take me to the hospital."

"What?" Desiree said, smirking, "you afraid of doctors, too?"

"Nosocomephobia," Amanda stated.

Charles turned to look at her in bewilderment.

She stared back at him. "Desiree wants to take us to the Oracle tomorrow."

Charles blinked. He'd hit his head, but he knew he had understood her correctly. Looking back and forth between them both he asked, "I'm not crazy?" He set the glass of water down on the table and put his feet on the floor. He discovered his ankle was sore, and grimaced. "It's all true? There actually is a secret here? There's…magic?"

Desiree's eyes were hazy and unsure.

Amanda's were dark and empty. Where had he seen them before?

"Tell City has an Oracle," Desiree said. "My father is its priest." She reached behind her and picked up Charles's journal. Apparently, she had been reading it while he was incapacitated. "You've been having dreams about this place. I don't know why. But we've had a lot of out-of-towners visiting recently, including you. Things don't just happen. There's a reason." She handed him the journal. "I want to take you to my father tomorrow. Maybe the Oracle will," she paused, "tell us something."

"How does it work?" Charles asked.

"That," Desiree said, standing up, "would be an excellent question for my father when we see him. You in?"

Charles smiled. "I'm in." Maybe he'd suffered a minor concussion from falling down the stairs, or maybe it was pure excitement, but whatever the reason, his head was spinning.

He was not crazy. He had made it to Tell City. He had found out the secret, and, in a few more hours, he would be face to face with the answers he'd sought. He had succeeded.

"You're staying at the motel?" Amanda asked, and Charles nodded. "You can stay at my place. If you stay here with Desiree, you face further injury, and I have three spare rooms. I thought about it yesterday when you stopped for directions. So, you're welcome to take the guest bedroom if you like. I don't mind. I don't use it. Someone should."

He thought about the quickly dwindling supply of funds that Wile E. had given him. He wanted to make it last for as long as possible, so he smiled. "I'd appreciate that."

***

Jon Hart stood in front of the lost well. He was in the

void before the Oracle. He saw nothing, but the Oracle could see everything, because it *was* everything. It whispered to the priest in the voice that only Oracles have, but there was no voice, for it existed in a void. The Oracle echoed through Jon's mind, and Jon came back from the void with only one thought: *Sacrifice.*

It was night. Marie Deveraux felt the cool Mississippi mud between her toes. She could hear the faint sound of a saxophone playing with a street band a short distance away up by St. Louis Cathedral. There was no moon, but the glistening of the city before her lit up the darkness.

She smiled. The Mississippi River lapped around her ankles and misted her legs. She took in a breath and closed her eyes. The soul of the city enveloped her. It was her city after all, and it was her life.

Her veins began to pulse with the rhythm of a snare drum, and her hips and shoulders began to sway with the notes of a clarinet. Then the music slowed to the beat of a leather-skinned drum in her mind; she could hear feet stomping in the dirt. In her vision, ancient words were whispered underneath the breath of the song, and an intricate sigil was made upon the ground with a handful of white powder.

"Hello, Marie," a voice whispered from behind her.

Marie fell away from her trance, and again was standing in the shallows of the Mississippi with the city of New Orleans behind her. She turned to see the man who had interrupted her. The bangs of his blonde hair shadowed his face.

"I'm sorry." She smiled, and stepped out of the water. She placed her bare feet on rock after rock until she reached the level dirt of the levee. "Do I know you?"

"Why darlin', I'm slightly offended. You don't recognize me? You were just talkin' to me, after all."

She tucked a long, black strand of hair behind her ear. "That's impossible." She had been in a trance searching for the guidance of the Loa, and no one else was around.

"Not quite, darlin'. Nothin' is impossible."

"You're a Loa?"

The blonde-haired man smiled and bowed to the young voodoo priestess. "In the flesh."

Marie's breath caught in her throat, her heart pounding. The smile on her face was unstoppable. "How?" She reached out a hand and put it on his bare chest, where his shirt fell open. "I've heard stories, but..."

"The ancient ways can do many things, Miss Marie."

His deep voice slipped across the night into her mind, and she was entranced. He laid his hand upon hers. The energy of his soul was like a torrent of water. Rushing. Crashing. Spilling out onto the land. Clermeil, the Loa of flooding waters.

"But the old ways are dying, and not just ours, Marie, but all ways of magic and ways of the Earth." He paused. "There is an Oracle. One that can regain what we've lost…lower the veils between the worlds. It can restore this faithless, hopeless wasteland so that the blood of eternity can flow through its veins once again. Without it…this reality is lost to the mundane prison cell you are forced to call home."

Marie's dark eyes stared into his. She pushed his bangs out of his mud-colored eyes. "You're afraid," she said. "You're sad…and you're desperate."

She turned to walk away, but he grabbed her wrist.

"And how do you feel? When you can feel the power, the energy of the universe right there, but it is nowhere to be seen? How do you feel on those nights when the moon is high and you know there are voices calling you, and you want so badly to understand what they are saying?" He stepped closer. "You feel alone…and desperate. We can change all that, Marie. Think of how you feel right now." He released her wrist. "I am a Loa standing before you, physical in this reality. Magic…physical in this reality. It can all be tangible. It can all be real, Marie…if you help me."

She was silent, listening to the sounds of the city and the gentle murmur of the Mississippi. Shivers crept across her flesh. "What do I need to do?"

The Loa smiled. "I need you to go to Tell City."

***

Charles awoke from a strange dream, and all he could remember was the sound of a saxophone.

He sat up on the bed. The morning light was muffled by the grey curtains covering the windows. The room looked like a page from a magazine, but everything was covered with dust. From the mod vases on the dresser to the square shade on the chandelier, nothing had been touched in that room for a long time.

There was a picture frame on the nightstand, next to where he had set his glasses. It was a family portrait. The wife was pale with dark, teased-up hair, and her lipstick was a vibrant shade of pink. Her husband was a handsome black man with a smile that stretched from ear to ear. He wore a red sweater that reminded Charles of *The Cosby Show*. Between them sat Amanda. She was about five, and her hair was wild in all directions. They all seemed truly happy, unlike most family portraits Charles was used to seeing…the ones with fake smiles.

He got out of bed and jumped into the jeans he had left on the floor. Grabbing his shirt from off a retro armchair in the corner, he walked out into the hall.

Amanda stepped from her room at the exact same time. Charles smiled, surprised to see her. He opened his mouth to say something, but nothing came out; he was distracted by how long her brown legs looked in her purple cotton shorts.

"I was just about to wake you up."

Charles smirked, and leaned against the wall. "I have a habit of waking up before noon nowadays." He realized his shirt was still rolled up in his fist, and fumbled to put it on, leaning back against the wall as soon as his head reemerged from the cotton.

He remembered wishing that all that walking would give him some muscle tone, but with the fatigue and lack of nutrition, he knew he looked haggard instead.

"How long did it take you to hitchhike here?" Amanda asked, folding her arms.

Charles tore his gaze away from her long limbs.

"Uh…" He jerked his attention upward, all the way to the ceiling, as if contemplating the answer to her question. "I don't remember really. What is today?"

"The thirteenth of June."

Charles looked into her ebony eyes, and noticed they were not as beautiful as they should be. Her eyes were glazed over and lifeless, and their familiarity nagged at him.

"Then it's been about two weeks." Charles shook his

head. "It feels longer than that, though. I rode a bus to Louisiana. A lot of people there gave me quick rides to the next major town or wherever they were heading, and I stayed longer than I should have with some fellas at L.S.U. I got lucky in Mississippi, and in Illinois I almost got arrested." Charles laughed.

"Hmm, well, I made some coffee, and if you want a shower there are towels for you on the sink." She disappeared down the stairs.

Charles stood in the hall for a moment before walking to the bathroom. Something was wrong with Amanda Wood. He knew she was antisocial and quiet. But, perhaps it was a Yankee thing. He knew Yankees didn't hug as much. He also knew that his aunt, who lived up in New York, was an ice queen, but Amanda did not seem normal even in a cold-hearted Yankee sort of way. There was something off about her, and that something made Charles uncomfortable.

After finishing the morning hygiene ritual he had taken for granted for so many years, he bounced down the stairs. He felt fresh and almost normal again with his stubble-free face.

Amanda had changed into leggings, a T-shirt and sneakers. She sat on the couch tying her shoestrings.

"Is it your first time going to this…Oracle?" he asked.

She looked up at him. "Yes."

"Excited?" Charles smiled, barely restraining his own

enthusiasm.

Her brows narrowed, and she pushed her lips out, contemplating. "No." She grabbed her bag and her keys, and headed toward the garage.

He followed. "No way. Not even a little bit?" Charles desperately needed to see something human in her eyes. "Come on! You don't even feel the slightest hint of excitement or anticipation or—"

"No." She pushed the button on her key fob. The locks in her Nissan clicked open.

His enthusiasm vanished. Charles climbed into the passenger seat.

***

A few hours later, Desiree's rusted Oldsmobile pulled off a country road onto a hidden dirt drive. Charles got out and closed the passenger door, looking up at the trees. The morning was quiet and still, except for the occasional call of a blue jay or a crow. Desiree began to lead the way to the Oracle.

In the future, if asked, Charles would not be able to tell someone how to get there, but he would be able to show them. That is just how these sorts of things work.

He would remember following Desiree through the

trees, Amanda by his side. They had not talked. They had just listened to the sound of the leaves and twigs beneath their feet, and they had watched the squirrels scamper up the trees. He would remember hearing the sound of a deer traipsing through the brush in the distance. But that would be all.

The shack was huddled in the field, and Mother Nature's breath made the tall grass around it sway. The vines that embraced the sides of the little shack were the only thing keeping the walls standing. Lying against the frame of the door was a piece of plywood that had once been bright white, but now was dingy from weather and age. Upon it was spray-painted the word OFFICE, the letters overlapping and askew, as if it had been inscribed by a blind man.

Charles wiped the sweat from his forehead, and noticed Desiree and Amanda were already at the door. He tucked his hands deep into his pockets and walked up to the crooked little shack that sat in the middle of nowhere.

***

Desiree pushed open the little door.

"Hey, Dad."

Against the opposite wall was a rickety card table with two chairs. Jon Hart stood up from his chair, a smile crinkling his kind weathered face.

"Desiree…Amanda," he greeted them as they entered. "And who's the boy?"

Charles stood in the doorway, his hands still buried in his pockets. The priest was blind, but knew each of them. Charles examined the man. In the heat of the summer he wore a brown tweed blazer that was frayed and tattered from age, and dark slacks. He had on round, wire-rimmed sunglasses, and he acted as if he were staring right back at Charles.

"This is Charles Garrett, Dad," Desiree replied, looking around the shack.

The old man seemed confused. "Charles?"

"Dad, it's sweltering in here. We need to get a generator and some fans. It's too hot for you to be staying out here like this each year." Desiree slipped back out the door and looked for something to prop it open with.

Jon Hart said nothing in reply to his daughter's fuss. He just smiled.

"Amanda," he said, grabbing his wooden cane, which was propped up against the card table. "I've been worried about you for a while. I wondered if you'd ever come to see me." Jon's voice was mellow and calm and as soothing as honey.

Amanda's gaze narrowed as Jon stepped up to her.

"Your father and I, well, we didn't know each other,

not in the way most people know each other, but we secretly understood one another, I suppose. He grew up to be a good man, a good husband, and certainly a good father."

Charles looked over at Amanda. Despite Jon's sympathetic tone, her face was rigid and her expression seemed a little bored, as if she was listening politely to someone chit-chatting about the weather.

It dawned on Charles that her four-bedroom house and newer model Nissan had been inherited because she had lost both her parents. And yet she shed not a tear at the mention of her late father. Finally understanding, Charles excused her quiet and emotionless behavior.

Desiree finally found a large stone, and shoved it under the door to keep it open. "There. That'll help."

"Amanda," Jon said, placing his hand upon her cheek, as Desiree re-entered the shack, "you've gone numb…closed off your heart. You died along with your parents to protect yourself. The Oracle cannot undo what is already done."

Amanda shrugged. "Okay. I understand."

"But you can live again." Jon's hand slipped down to her shoulder. "It cannot undo what's been done, but it can still heal." Jon raised his head as though he were looking into her eyes. *"The past is written by the story told. The truth is kept by the only one who knows."*

Amanda shook her head. "I don't see how that applies."

"Neither do I," he said, chuckling, "but there are a lot of things we don't *see*. That is what the Oracle is for."

Desiree stepped around them and sat at the card table.

"Now, my boy, the Oracle didn't mention a *Charles Garrett*."

Charles stared back at the Oracle's priest. Amanda took a seat at the table with Desiree.

"My daughter must have seen something in you."

"He's had dreams of this place, Dad. Prophetic dreams."

Charles pulled his hands from his pockets. "They aren't *really* prophetic. They don't *prophesize* anything."

"Yes they do," said Desiree, "and we need to know what. With all the strangers coming into town for no reason and—"

Jon raised his hand. It was a weak gesture, but it silenced Desiree. "Sonny, what do you think?" He stepped up to the boy, as if to study his face.

"Me?" Charles grimaced. "I don't know. I just…well, I just wanted to know what was going on in Tell City, because of my dreams."

"And now that you know that there is an Oracle here, now that you've found what you came for, what will you do?"

Charles didn't know how to respond.

"*Why?*" Charles finally asked, more to himself than the priest. "I wanted to find out what the dreams were about, but...I don't know why I'm having them."

Jon smiled. "Good. Now you are beginning to think!"

There were a few moments of silence.

"Well, Dad?" Desiree asked, leaning forward in her seat. "Why?"

"He is beginning to ask the right questions, Desiree, but that does not mean he has asked *the question* yet." Jon lifted his hand to Charles's face, and searched it with his fingertips. "You are not ready...my son." Jon lowered his hand. He still held his cane, but did not use it as he walked over to the table.

"There is something happening in the town that has happened before. *Unrest has brewed along the other shore, and an unquenchable thirst will thirst no more. An army has sailed across the tides, in the Ferryman's boat they all did ride. Where the sun does set upon the west, is where the gods will see their rest. A bribe for an eye at the well's gate, and if the bribe is taken, so sealed is our fate.*" He paused, smiling. "And don't you worry about those fans, Desiree. I'll be fine."

***

The three of them stepped out of the shack, and Desiree

shook her head.

"I hate it when he does that." She looked over at Charles. "I'm sorry about that, Charles."

"Are you kidding?" Charles's smile stretched from ear to ear. "That was *awesome!*"

Her dark eyes squinted, and she tilted her head. A roar crashed its way through the trees, the sound of revving engines and snapping limbs.

They looked towards the noise. Through the brush, three four-wheelers tore their way into the field. The camo figures riding atop the A.T.V.s hooted and cheered their arrival.

Desiree's teeth clenched. "Are you fucking serious?" In a fury she began to storm towards the men. "Hey!"

Charles caught up to her quickly. "Hey, Desiree, calm down a sec."

She ignored him.

Amanda waited behind in the shade of the woods, avoiding whatever confrontation was about to be had.

The roar of the engines ceased. "Well, how you doin', girl?" The older man took off his helmet, revealing his baldness. His gaze wandered up and down her body. "Lookin' good." He spat off to the side of his A.T.V.

"Shut the hell up, Rick." Desiree folded her arms across her chest, one boot tapping in the grass. "You know, I'm a little lax on the sanctity of this place, because he's my *dad*. I grew up in that damn shack, but this?" She threw up her arms. "God, Rick, you might as well take a shit on it!"

"Aw, hell, Desiree, it ain't that big of a deal. I'm takin' the boys. It's their first time." The bald-headed man got off the four-wheeler, and the other two followed suit, taking off their helmets. The two of them looked over at Charles.

"Aw, shit, Brandon, look who it is." The tall one gestured with a gloved hand to Charles.

The bearded one turned to look. "Didn't recognize you without the facial hair, jack."

Charles smiled, and stuck out his hand. "Hey, y'all."

Steve shook his hand. "What the hell you doin' out here?"

Rick walked up to them. "Who's this?" He shook Charles's hand.

"This is that hitchhiker we tol' you 'bout," Steve said.

Charles let loose his southern twang. "Nice to meet you, Rick."

Rick guffawed. "Desiree. Baby. Bringing a stranger here? You know," he said, wiping his nose on his plaid sleeve, "I'm a little *lax* on the sanctity of this place, but bringing a stranger here…might as well wipe your ass with it."

Desiree glared at him and he glared back. Jaws locked.

"Don't tell anybody?" Her eyes softened. "I have my reasons, just…don't tell anybody."

Rick pushed up his lower lip, and after a moment nodded. "'Aight. But you gotta do one thang for me."

Desiree smiled. "What?"

Biting the corner of his lip, he walked up to her. "Tell me my ride's sexy." He glanced at his four-wheeler.

She shoved his shoulder. "Fine…your ride's sexy." She turned and headed back towards where Amanda was still waiting.

Charles nodded to Brandon and Steve. "Catch y'all later."

Desiree yelled over her shoulder. "You're a no-good influence, Rick O'Conner. Take care of them boys."

"Yes, ma'am," Rick yelled back.

"Don't mind him, Charles," Desiree said. "He won't tell anyone."

Charles grinned. "Got him wrapped around your finger, do you?"

She arched a brow. "Something like that."

"Okay. I didn't need that image. You're forty."

"So?" She paused. "Do I look like I'm forty?"

Instead of responding, he just cleared his throat.

They joined Amanda, who forced a smile. "I used to

babysit those two. I hated it."

Charles laughed, and then asked, "Is Rick their dad?"

"No," Desiree said. "They aren't brothers, and Rick is just the local pest, but he's looked out for those two for a while now. Their real dads were friends in high school, and are still pieces of shit." She led them back into the woods.

"Hey, Desiree," Charles whispered. "So, for bringing me here, are you going to get in trouble?"

She smiled and wrapped her arm around his shoulders. "Nah. Just as long as the council doesn't find out, and Rick doesn't like a single one of them. We'll be fine."

***

Just as the sun was beginning to set, Steve's truck pulled into the parking lot of the Days Inn. It parked in between a sleek black Jag and a 1940s Bentley.

Steve and Brandon straightened their ball caps before they knocked on the door of Room 126. The door swung open as if by magic, and sitting across the room in a chair was Clermeil. He was fiddling with a glass of water.

"Come on in, boys. Have a seat."

They walked in and sat on opposite ends of the motel bed.

"How did it go?"

They looked at one another, not sure who should start.

Brandon cleared his throat. "Well, nothing happened."

"He said we weren't ready," Steve added.

The Loa's muddy eyes narrowed. "Who said you weren't ready? Ready for what, exactly?"

Brandon leaned forward. "The priest of the Oracle."

"He said we weren't ready for, you know…" Steve looked at Brandon for help, and received none. "The Oracle."

Clermeil sighed. "Well, where is it?"

"The shack?" Brandon asked. "It's in the woods."

The Loa smiled. "In the woods. Well, that does a great deal to narrow it down, now don't it, boys? Because we're only in the marvelous state of *Indiana,* which is *nothing but woods*!" The water in his hand exploded like a geyser from the glass. "Give me somethin' useful, boys, or you'll find yourselves clawing your way out of the rocks at the bottom of the Ohio!"

"Charles!" Steve shouted. "He's an outsider. We found him hitchhiking outside of town. He was there at the Oracle. Desiree the psychic, she took'im."

"And how is that useful?" The water in his glass began to spin like a whirlpool.

Brandon continued. "There's a rule, jack. You don't tell out-a-towners about the Oracle or the council will…"

"Who's the head of this council?"

"I don't know. The mayor, I guess. Or the sheriff, maybe?"

Steve added, "It's the mayor, man."

"You sure?"

The Loa smiled, and the water in his glass grew still. "Now, that, gentlemen, is the kind of information I need. I need to know everyone that might stand between me and this Oracle. Find out more about this council, and come back tomorrow."

Steve and Brandon started for the door.

"And boys…"

They turned to face the Loa of flooding waters.

"Don't let me down."

***

Charles had had some awkward family dinners, but sitting in the back corner of the local greasy spoon with Amanda took first prize for awkward. She hardly said a word. Even as he tried to stir up conversation, Amanda only smiled and nodded.

Charles had paid for the dinner, and they took some drinks to go. It had been an unspoken decision that she would show him around town. So Charles kept up with her as she strolled along the streets.

"Those fries were great." Charles smiled.

Amanda nodded.

"So is that like the town hangout spot?"

"No."

"So, er, what is the local hangout spot?"

"There across the street."

Charles looked up to see tall concrete walls stretching along Tell City's border. In the quiet small town setting, the obtrusive walls of solid concrete were just wrong. It was as if the city had once seen a great ancient war. It looked like the Berlin Wall or the Great Wall of China had been dropped into a tiny river city in Indiana. It was neither of those, though. It was the Tell City Flood Wall, and those giant concrete borders had become art. Murals stretched across the wall, telling elaborate stories of the town's history. The wall told of floods and furniture factories and life along the river.

Through a gap in the wall large enough for vehicles to drive through, Charles could see the river and a park. Children ran to and fro along the riverbank as their parents sat on benches facing the water, gossiping and keeping watch over the playground.

"You know, back in Texas there was this park I used to go to with my parents and we used to… " Charles bit his tongue.

"Used to what?" Amanda did not look up as they

walked past the gate to the park.

Charles took a deep breath. "Amanda what…how did they…your parents…" He paused. "How did they pass?"

Amanda shrugged. "It was a year ago. It was raining. They were driving too fast."

"Oh…I'm sorry." Charles lowered his eyes to the sidewalk.

"It was their own fault, really. No sympathy needed. I get enough of it as it is."

Charles racked his brain to understand. He could never blame his parents for something like that. He loved them. He would forgive them. Accidents happen, and sometimes it is the road, not the driver.

"Were they drunk?" That might explain any bitter feelings or grudges.

"No," Amanda answered. "They were just driving too fast, and they should have known better. They knew their fate."

He furrowed his brow, puzzled. "What do you mean *their fate?*"

Amanda sighed. "I've never talked about this with anyone, but they both went to the Oracle before they knew each other. They both told the Oracle that they wanted to find true love. A love to die for."

When she saw that Charles still seemed confused, she

continued. "Miracles aren't free. There's always a cost…a price to pay, and when you ask for *a love to die for*, well…" Amanda lifted her dark eyes to look at Charles. "What else can you expect?"

Cupid and Psyche divorced eons ago, back when the real Roman Empire lay down to die and took its gods with it. The divorce was a long, drawn-out spectacle, where, of course, she took him for everything he owned. His mother rubbed it in every chance she got. *I told you so.* It was an embarrassment; he had become a laughingstock among the gods. The god of love himself had failed at keeping a woman happy.

As the gods began to fade from this world, Cupid's heart grew bitter. His love had left him. The world and the people had abandoned him. No one believed in love, true love, anymore. Not like in the older days when the lovers would die for love: Odysseus and Penelope, Achilles and Patroclus, Thisbe and Pyramus, Apollo and Hyacinth. No one, not people, not gods, not even Cupid himself, loved that hard anymore, and if they did, they might thank his mother, Venus, or Aphrodite, but usually they thanked Jesus. Cupid himself never got any thanks. He was now viewed as a chubby little cherub with a diaper rash – which, in all honesty, was more of an embarrassment than the divorce.

Thus, when Clermeil let him in on his plan for the last remaining Oracle, Cupid gladly readied his arrows.

***

The wind was blowing strong at the top of the Tell City water tower as the mayor pleaded for his life. Clermeil's knee pinned the mayor down to the metal grate of the catwalk, and kept him from tumbling off the edge, while Cupid, bored and disinterested, tucked his hands into the pockets of his blazer as he fought back a yawn.

"I swear! I'm not on the Oracle council! I sit in my office and read emails and sign paperwork all day. I know as much about it as anyone else. Please!"

Clermeil laughed. It was a polite, deep laugh that made Cupid's flesh crawl. "I find that very hard to believe, Mayor."

The gentleman's robe rustled in the wind, flowing like a flag from the tower. "I'm just an elected official."

"You're the mayor." The young and beautiful god,

Cupid, rolled his eyes. "Certainly, if you don't know, you must know someone who does."

Clermeil's hands gripped the mayor's bedclothes and threw the man to his feet. The water tower made a metallic moan as the mayor crashed into the guardrail.

"Answer him," the Loa snarled.

His eyes tried to find an escape, but the only way out was down, and in the darkness the one-hundred and thirty foot drop looked like eternity.

From his quiver Cupid drew an arrow. His gentle fingers glided to the golden tip.

"The priest, Jon Hart! He has a daughter. Her name is Desiree."

Clermeil's eyes became dark dangerous pools as he pulled the mayor's body up closer. "Jon Hart is your Oracle's priest?"

The mayor only nodded.

Clermeil and Cupid met each other's gaze, and Clermeil gave a solemn nod. Releasing the man from his grip, the Loa turned into the wind and stormed away. The young god approached the man, and with each step of his polished Oxfords his boyish smile grew. This was the part he had been waiting for.

"Who do you love?" he asked.

The mayor looked confused. "My…my wife and kids."

Cupid grimaced. "No, you don't. You cheated on her last month, and you always assumed the boy wasn't yours. So, you don't love anybody. Not even yourself, do you?"

Cupid touched the golden arrow head to the man's neck.

"Please don't kill me. I'll…I'll treat them better, I will. I'm a good man."

"I don't really care what kind of man you are…but everybody needs somebody to love." Cupid spun the man around to gaze at the dark silhouette of his little town and the arrow pricked the soft flesh of the mayor's neck. The small red beads trickled, and at the bottom of the water tower stood the Loa, looking up at the mayor and the young god.

Cupid could hear the mayor's heart pounding, his short, raspy breaths.

"He's beautiful, isn't he?" His boyish smile returned as he stroked the politician's thinning hair.

"Yes," he whispered.

"You love him, don't you?"

"Yes."

Cupid stepped back away from the mayor. "And love can make all things possible, so fly to him. Fly to him on the wings love hath given you."

The mayor took off his slippers and placed both bare feet upon the guardrail. His robe tangled in the wind as he tried to fly.

***

Clermeil stood still, looking over the misshapen corpse. He lit up a cigarette as Cupid approached. The Loa offered one to his accomplice, but the god refused, so he put the pack back into the pocket of his jeans.

"Why did we not make him love you then leave him alive?" Cupid pulled his quiver off over his head. "He would have done anything you said. You know that."

Clermeil smiled. "How many arrows do you have, lover-boy?"

"As many as we want." He loosened his tie. "Why?"

"We can make the world fall in love with us later." He exhaled a cloud of smoke and continued. "Cupid, I'm a gamblin' man, and I'm feelin' lucky. I just want to see what happens."

Though Cupid disagreed with Clermeil's gambling problem, he did not dare to challenge him. The Loa could be unforgiving and ruthless if crossed, so for now he would fold. He nodded his head.

The Loa turned and headed back towards town. Cupid took one last look at the mayor, his blood seeping into the soil, and then up at the water tower, upon which was written in red,

TELL CITY.

The first tribute to the Ferryman had been paid. Sacrifice was such a messy thing.

***

5:03 A.M. Charles and Desiree could not stop the ground from coming. The moment their bones cracked against the earth, they were torn from their dreams. Their bodies convulsed. Their hearts spun inside their chests. Tears flooded down in torrents. Neither of them could stop their muscles from trembling underneath their goose-pimpled flesh. They were halfway across town from each other, and they were both alone in darkened bedrooms.

***

Amanda awoke to a scream coming from down the hall. She shot out of bed and ran to Charles's room. She sat down on the edge of the bed and shook him. His body trembled beneath her touch. He was awake now, but Amanda was sure he did not know that.

She did what she was supposed to do, what her mother had done for her. She held him and rocked him, and attempted to coax him back to reality.

***

Charles did not realize where he was, for he had just leapt from a water tower to his death. He did not know who Amanda was or that she was even there, but when he came back to his senses, he did not care that he barely knew her. Charles fell into her, and stayed there for five more minutes. She was warm and she was gentle, much unlike the place from whence he fell.

Birds began to chirp, and a muffled, grey light crept underneath the curtains.

Amanda was humming. She had such a sweet voice.

"I died," he managed to mutter. "I was dead. I fell."

"You really do have some intense dreams," Amanda said. "They say you never die in your dreams, and if you're falling you always wake up before you hit the ground. And if you don't... But, see, you're still alive. It was just a bad dream."

Charles smiled. It really was just a dream. Just a *dream.* His gaze found his journal on the nightstand.

"*Oh, shit!*" Charles, within seconds, was dressed and flying out the bedroom door.

"What's going on?" Amanda was still sitting on his bed in her cotton shorts and a tank top.

Charles ran back to the doorway. "My dreams. They're prophetic. Either your mayor is dead or he is going to be. We have to go to the water tower."

"You honestly believe that?" Amanda raised an eyebrow. "Charles, I get the whole power-of-dreams thing, but to take it literally? I mean, it's all metaphorical. It's in your head."

"Amanda! We've got to go."

***

A storm was coming. The water tower was taped off. Red and blue flashing lights danced off of the morning fog. The local police department and investigators were scurrying around attempting to collect whatever evidence they could before the storm washed it away. The mayor's wife and children were curled in each other's embraces as they watched the stretcher being laid next to the corpse of their beloved.

Charles stood frozen – but not in disbelief. His dreams, until now, had been much more intangible, surreal. This dream had turned into reality. A bitter taste was on his tongue, and his body began to tremble as it had when he first awoke. The edges of his world began to blur.

Amanda touched his arm. Her lips moved, and at first he heard no sound.

"Charles." She sounded so far away. "Are you okay?"

Desiree was standing with the sheriff. She held her raincoat closed against the wind.

They were whispering.

Everything Charles heard, everything he saw, was muffled in fog and in white noise. He had died with the mayor only hours ago, now in the blurry corner of his eye, he saw the medics fumble to get the remains of his distorted frame into a body bag. He tore his gaze away from the image, and found Desiree.

The sheriff was walking away from her, his phone to his ear. She looked up across the clearing, and their brown eyes met.

There was something in her gaze. She knew he had been there on the water tower, and suddenly Charles understood that she had been there, too. They'd had the same dream.

Charles's chest tightened as he remembered placing his bare feet – *the mayor placing his bare feet – on the rail of the water tower. Sitting in a boat on a river inside the earth was an old man, who sang a funeral dirge as the mayor fell in love. He was so sure as he fell. He had always wanted to fall, and he fell and fell straight through the earth, where the man in the boat was floating, signing, waiting, to ferry him to the other shore.*

The world came back sudden and harsh and crystal clear. Charles felt his insides jolt, and he could hear the shuffling of pant legs and boots weighed down by the morning dew as EMTs and coroners and police officers rushed around. He heard the zipper of the body bag so crisp and final. He saw the clouds rolling and tumbling, looking like National Geographic had filmed them and then put them in the sky. The blur and the numbness had vanished like magic. Charles stood in the damp grass, very near where the Loa had so recently been standing.

"Charles," Amanda said again. Her voice was flat. "Seriously, are you okay?" But she already knew the answer, and her eyes lacked any sympathy.

When he looked back up at Desiree, she simply nodded to him. His motor functions sitting on his bed returned, and within seconds he had passed Amanda and was at Desiree's side.

"What was that? I was all…and then it was all—"

"So I helped then?" Desiree craned her neck to look into his wondering eyes. "Looks like you were having a vision there."

He was confused, and it must have been written all over his face for she laughed a little.

"I know the look, and I could taste it in your aura. When you have visions the world just kind of melts and you're somewhere else, sometimes literally." Desiree glanced around. "I grounded you, ripped you out of your vision. Now's not a good time for your eyes to roll back into your skull and for you to start speaking in tongues. People are already spooked."

Charles gulped. "The eyes bit, would that have happened if you hadn't…?"

"No," Desiree said, and then added, "but it could have."

"Who is this?" The sheriff marched back up to Desiree through the grass and leaves, while looking Charles up and down, uncomfortable with a stranger at the mayor's murder scene.

"Pat, this is Charles." Desiree put her hand on Charles's shoulder.

"He's a friend of mine," Amanda added, as she approached. "From school."

Desiree nodded. "He's psychic. I've been teaching him."

Sheriff Pat tipped his hat. He was younger, but still had a gruff, old-fashioned air about him that made him seem as if he belonged in an old western.

"You, uh…" The sheriff scratched the side of his nose. "You saw it, too?"

Charles gave him a nod. "Yessir."

"You guys know who the two men were that—"

"One was a boy," Desiree interrupted. "Couldn't have been more than seventeen."

"He was in a suit," Charles added, "and the other one was in his thirties or forties and was wearing blue jeans and a dress shirt. He had a Louisiana accent."

The sheriff's eyes squinted. "Louisiana?"

"Right." Charles paused. "Deep-southern, but not thick back-water, not Cajun."

He gave Charles a belittling look. "So, a southern accent?"

Charles pressed his lips into a fine line. "Yeah, just southern."

The sheriff laughed. "I don't believe any of this shit. You called me at five A.M. and now…"

"Believe it." Desiree was stern.

The man just shook his head and took off his hat. "What the hell am I going to tell Joanne and their kids?"

"Just let the investigators figure it out."

"Aw, hell, Desiree, you know I can't do that!" The sheriff was losing his nerve. "Everyone is all up in arms about all these strangers anyhow. This is going to be a nightmare." He paused. "No pun intended. You said they were asking questions about the Oracle? We got to get the rest of the council together. And what are we going to tell your ol' man?"

"Chances are, he already knows," Desiree said. "I'll talk to him, but there is no telling if that will actually be useful or not."

"Yeah. All right."

The sheriff looked up at the rolling sky. "Get on out of here for now. I'll, uh, let you know if I find anything. Go home. Stay safe." He put his hat back on and made long careful strides toward the grieving widow and her children.

Amanda stood quietly by Charles's side.

"Desiree," Charles said in a concerned and hushed tone, "the mayor told them your name. They know who you are. What—"

"Shut up. Not here." She closed her raincoat around her. "Come on."

***

Amanda followed Desiree's car into town towards the shop. Charles was nervous. He rubbed the stubble on his face, his gaze lost out the passenger window, which was streaked with the first sprinkling of raindrops.

"Charles?"

He looked over at Amanda. Her dark eyes were blank.

"Should I be afraid? I don't feel afraid. I mean, I know something is wrong, but…"

"Amanda," he said. "Thank you."

She glanced at him. "For what?"

"I…I'm freaking out. I have no idea what's going on. I

watched someone get murdered this morning *in my dreams*. I was almost arrested. I had a gun pointed at my face. I'm a thousand miles away from home." Charles paused, and closed his eyes. "It's just nice that you're not freaking out. It's keeping me sane."

"Oh," was all she said, and then they arrived at Desiree's shop.

***

Desiree hurried them in, and locked the door as they entered. She rushed up the stairs to the apartment above, and made Charles and Amanda wait on the landing until she had herded all the cats into her bedroom for Charles's sake.

"Desiree, are you all right?" Amanda asked as she entered the apartment.

"Frankly, no. No, I am not. None of us are." She was in the kitchen now, spilling a whole container of red pepper into a mixing bowl.

Charles tried to grab her hand. "Desiree, what are you doing?"

"Making makeshift brick dust."

Charles looked at Amanda, but she just shrugged.

"*Brick dust?*" he asked.

Next, Desiree ripped off the top of her salt shaker, and

dumped all the salt into the bowl with the red pepper. "It's a protection charm."

"Protection from what, Desiree?"

Her fists slammed on the countertop, and her gaze snapped over to him. "I will tell you when I'm done."

She hurried to every window, every door, and every mirror in her tiny apartment, and sprinkled before each a thick line of the red powder. Any altar she had on her end tables and on dressers she encircled with the powder. Anything that could have served as a portal between the worlds, she encircled or lined with the brick dust. Above her front door, hung like mistletoe, were a handful of little twigs tied with black ribbon. She removed them from their hook and whispered to them, and then put them back. Standing still in the middle of the living room, she faced her palms outward and closed her eyes.

Charles felt something go through him – a wave of electricity. The hair on his arms stood on end. His heart skipped a beat. Shivers crept across his flesh, and the pit of his stomach began to turn and twist.

"What was that?"

"A protection spell," she said. "Charles, what do you remember about the dream?"

Amanda sat down on the couch to listen.

Charles shifted his weight. "The mayor gave them your

name. They're after you, and your father, and the Oracle. We have to do something before they…"

"Who's they?" Amanda asked in her monotone voice.

"The Loa. One of them is a Loa, and you don't *fuck* with the Loa. So *we* aren't doing anything. *We* are laying low." Desiree sank into an armchair.

"Loa? You mean like on the altar downstairs in your shop?"

"Yes, exactly, and he was physical. They were both *real*. Not figments. Not concepts or spirits. Real."

"Desiree," Charles said, "we can't just hide in your apartment. This isn't something that will just blow over. If they're looking for you, if they are really here, will the red pepper really stop them?"

Desiree frowned.

"And the kid that was with him… "

"Was a god," Desiree finished.

They were silent for a minute.

"Gods and spirits aren't physical," Desiree continued. "They can't be. And until we know what's going on, *yeah*…we're laying low."

Thunder began to rumble through the clouds, shaking the earth. The storm began.

***

Charles could not sleep. The three beasts locked away in Desiree's room howled and wailed throughout the dark hours. Their claws scratched and ripped through the crack at the bottom of the door, clawing to pry it open. He was afraid of them, and afraid to dream. The King had come. Fear…he could not fight it.

Charles tossed and turned in his makeshift bed on the floor of Desiree's apartment. He longed for the comfort of the bed in Amanda's house, or the bed at a motel, or his bed back in Houston. At least he was not on the floor of that barn in Santa Claus. That he could be thankful for.

He turned over onto his side again and saw Amanda sleeping on the couch. She looked so calm, like she could not hear the pouring rain, the crashing thunder, and the evil cats. Maybe it was a blessing, not feeling anything. She shrugged off the impending danger, and could not care less about, well, anything. But Charles knew that was not true. There was something stirring in her. Something was trying to come back to life. Her calculating thoughts had to be triggered by something.

Charles rolled onto his back. He thought of the Loa and gods, and wondered what his grandmother would say. She probably would drag him back home with a lasso made out of Bible pages, singing along to contemporary Christian radio the entire way back to the good Lord's belt, and she would be wearing that huge pink, floppy church hat. She always wore that ugly hat.

Charles sighed, and closed his eyes.

There was a knock on the door.

He sat up in the darkness. The rain had stopped. Amanda was still asleep.

He heard another knock.

Slipping out from the sheets, Charles approached the door. Everything was grey. Everything seemed to move in slow motion. His hand inched towards the knob. He opened the door.

The man on the other side seemed confused.

"I apologize," he said in a charming deep-south accent. "I thought you were…" He paused, correcting himself. "Is Miss Hart here?"

Charles saw him clearly in the dark like he had seen him clearly on the water tower. The Loa's eyes were muddy.

Charles's Texas accent came out thick, and deeper than he thought possible. "She ain't available."

The Loa smiled. "Well, well, well, a southern gentleman, not much unlike myself. I suppose you'll be kind enough to let me come in out of the rain." It began to pour on the landing to Desiree's apartment. "I'd like to wait for her." He tried to step through the door, but something blocked him.

Both the Loa and Charles looked down at their feet. A thick line of brick dust drew a wall between them. He could not enter.

Charles lifted his gaze and looked into the Loa's murky eyes. "Like I said…Desiree ain't available."

Clermeil smiled a gentleman's smile. "Why this sure does put a damper on things, but y'all can't stay in there foreva'. You know that don't you, boy?"

"Don't plan on it, sir, but maybe like the gentlemen we are, we can leave the woman out of this?"

"Well, that certainly can be arranged. I have a sudden inkling I should get to know you anyway."

"Three hours. The restaurant on the corner in town."

"How about something a little more private?"

"No."

The Loa of flooding waters smiled. "Fine."

"Oh, and jus' so you know…I ain't walkin' there in the rain." Charles slammed the door, and woke up tangled in his sheets on the floor.

He sprang to his feet. It was morning. The cloud cover was dense, but the rain had ceased.

Amanda was still asleep, and the nocturnal beasts in Desiree's room had been quieted by the dawn light.

Charles paced around the living room. He was uncertain

whether or not it had been a dream, or if it was still real even though it had been a dream. He wanted to wake Desiree, to let her know, so she could explain to him what was happening inside his brain, but he himself said to leave *the woman* out of it.

"Why did I say that?"

He continued to pace, running his fingers through his hair.

"Why was I that stupid? Stupid…I can't believe I said all that."

Charles stopped pacing and hurried into the kitchen. The microwave said it was 7:03 A.M.

"Three hours…" Charles had no idea what time he had had that dream. He did not know if the three hours had passed or not. He had no idea what he was doing.

Without considering other alternatives, he got dressed and left Desiree and Amanda sound asleep as he tiptoed out the door.

***

"Late." The Loa smirked as Charles entered the restaurant. He still wore a white button down and jeans, just like in his dreams. "Late to a meeting you yourself arranged. You are fallin' short of my expectations."

Wide-eyed with disbelief, Charles stood motionless in front of the table.

"Uh…er…"

Clermeil raised an eyebrow. "Very, very short."

Charles sat down. "So that was a dream? You can do that?"

"I can do a great number of things." A curvy woman with fiery red hair stopped at the table and set down two plates. She poured Charles a cup of coffee.

"I took the liberty of ordering for you. I assume you like home-style grits?"

"Yessir. Much appreciated. Uh…who are you exactly?"

The blonde man smiled, cutting off a piece of country fried steak. "You don't know?"

Charles looked around. No one else seemed to be paying either of them any notice. "I know you're a Loa," he whispered, "a voodoo-spirit-thing, and I know you killed the mayor."

"I did, and I am. The Loa of flooding waters to be precise…Clermeil."

Charles picked up the coffee cup. "Why are you here? What do you want with Desiree?"

The Loa dabbed his lips with the cloth napkin. "She's the daughter of a woman I used to know and the daughter of the *priest*, and I'm here for the Oracle, of course."

"Why?"

"*That's* the big question on your mind?" He laughed. "Charles, you're starin' at a god."

Charles fell silent.

The room clanked with silverware and dishes. Grease sizzled on the grill behind the counter. The cash register opened with a pleasant ding.

"You ain't my god."

Deep laughter echoed in Clermeil's throat. "Son, you got a lot to learn about gods." He set down his fork and knife. "Do you see this world? Godless. People have faith, but it's not unwavering. And your god, their god, where is he exactly? You have no actual *reason* to be faithful. No miracles. No divine mysteries. No real reason to drag yourselves to church each week. What is faith without reason?" Clermeil pushed up the sleeves of his dress shirt. "I'm goin' to give your world, I'm going to give humanity, a reason. I'm going to *bring* the gods back and deliver magic, miracles from the other side, straight to your doorstep."

"You're a good salesman."

Clermeil snapped his fingers and pointed at Charles.

"There he is. There's the man I met this mornin', but here's the thing: y'all, humanity, wouldn't have to wonder anymore. You won't have to cry and beg for life to be different, for magic and angels and wishes to be real. It all will be." He picked up his coffee, and leaned back in his chair. "I know how it is. I know your struggles. I hear all those prayers on the other side. I can taste humanity's longing. I feel all those hearts pounding that just *know* there is more out there. That passion. That sadness. Just think, all your prayers will be answered. You need not wonder anymore."

Charles had wondered if he was insane, being drawn to a place all because of a dream. Jenna had thought he was acting crazy for having fixated over some small town in Indiana for weeks. Even he believed he had indeed gone off the deep end the day he got up and left. Jenna had already left for school before he had woken up that day.

What it must have been for her to come home after class. His car would have still been parked in the same spot. The door wouldn't have been locked. His wallet would have still been sitting on the kitchen table next to his phone still on the charger, and he would have been nowhere. Gone.

And what a relief it was to discover he was not crazy. He was right. He wasn't insane. Magic, miracles, his dreams, they were real, but at what cost?

"The catch is you need the Oracle, and the mayor and others may have to die for you to get this?"

The Loa grimaced. "Every venture, even the holiest, has

necessary casualties."

"Necessary?" Charles's teeth clenched as he held back all the guilt rising in his chest for all the collateral damage he'd left behind in Houston.

"Unfortunately."

Charles took a steadying breath, and set down his coffee. "And what's in it for you?"

He leaned forward. "Ain't it obvious?" Charles didn't respond. "I, we, the gods, can rejoin with the Mortal World. Our world and yours have been separated by walls for far too long, and you'll find many other gods and humans alike agree. We're tired of whispering and kissing through the cracks. When we get the Oracle, we will knock down those walls. Neither man nor god will need to long for one another anymore."

"How can the Oracle do that?"

"The Oracle can tell me how to do it."

"It only gives riddles."

"The riddles would need to be deciphered, which is why I must possess it. It will take time."

"How are you going to decipher it?"

"I have a million gods that can help with that."

"If you have a million powerful gods, why do you need an Oracle? Can't you do it yourselves?"

"There are limitations."

"Like what? As you said…I'm staring at a god. So, what, you can't stay? You can only be here so long?"

"Something to that effect."

"Do you have any other weaknesses in your master plan I should know about?"

The Loa's eyes narrowed. His patience was wearing thin, and the coffee in his hands began to boil. "Boy, I'm doing you sad, miserable human folk a favor. You spend your lives tryin' to reach the divine. I'm taking away the divide. I'm letting you in on our little plan, because you may be of some use, and I pay my friends very well." He set his cup down. "Well, boy, what say you?"

The Loa's words hung thick in the air. *Our little plan.* Charles looked around the restaurant. No one there was from Tell City. The suits were too clean-cut. The purses were too vogue. Each one of the grease joint's customers were perfect archetypes of themselves. He was surrounded by gods.

"We've done just fine mucking up the world by ourselves, thanks. We don't need you crazy, power-hungry god folk making things worse, and I don't need your money." Charles stood, taking out his wad of cash. He paid for the food he did not eat by laying a hundred dollars down on the table. "If magic exists, if gods exist, it ain't supposed to be like that. You're better off goin' back to wherever the hell you came from."

"You're making a mistake, boy. Ain't a lot of people on your side of the fence. I suggest gettin' an umbrella," he said, his reserve coming back to him, "or an ark. There's a good chance of rain."

Charles stormed out of the restaurant.

***

In the back corner reading a newspaper was a boy in a clean-cut, all-black suit. His cufflinks were little hearts, with the aorta and all the proper ventricles and atriums, set in silver.

"Cupid."

The boy looked up from his newspaper with an indifferent smile as Clermeil approached.

"Do you think," asked the young god, "he's the one the Fates warned about?"

Clermeil's eyes narrowed. "Distract him."

***

That was when the rain began. It started as a drizzle, and then with a crack of lightning, it began to surge from the dismal heavens. The gutters overflowed. Puddles became ponds. Creeks became rivers and their banks became swamps.

***

The old stone well, lost in the woods, lost in time, stood like a sentinel. Its water's surface, once as smooth and black as a mirror, began to ripple and dance with each captured raindrop.

Jon sat alone at his card table in the shack, but he was not entirely alone in the depths of his mind. He knew each raindrop that fell into the well, and the Oracle sang, in a way that only Oracles can. The music soothed its priest's hidden fears, and told him the flood was back and that destiny had come.

Charles returned to the psychic shop saturated from the sudden downpour and quaking due to his nerves. He stood there in the darkness of the waiting room. The only sounds were the rain, and a clock ticking.

"Hello?" Charles cried, and soon the building racketed as Desiree's feet flew down the stairs.

"Where have you been? You're shivering!" She began to mother him, sitting him down in one of her distressed chairs. She ran her hands up and down his arms trying to warm him up.

"Amanda, bring some towels!" she yelled up the stairs.

Amanda appeared a short time later in the waiting room.

"We went looking for you." She handed a towel to Desiree, who started drying him off like one would a wet dog.

"But then it started raining, again."

"Where the hell were you?" Desiree's voice was stern. Her nostrils even flared.

"I…I couldn't sleep." Charles's southern accent had disappeared. "I went and got breakfast at the corner diner."

Desiree did not believe him. "Why? I have food. Didn't I say to help yourself to it?"

Indeed she had.

His eyes darted back and forth between her and Amanda. "Because…I…well…I asked the Loa to meet me there."

Amanda just tilted her head in confusion, but Desiree snapped.

"*You did what?*"

"He came to me in a dream," Charles explained. "Actually, he came for you, but the brick dust wouldn't let him in."

"So you decided it would be a good idea to invite him out for a cup of *coffee*?"

"Kind of. Yeah. But I was dreaming, Desiree. I wasn't myself."

"Well, who were you then?"

"I don't know, but I wasn't Charles D. Garrett that's for damn sure!" He paused. Briefly, he remembered Wile E. cursing at the sky, at God, at her grandfather.

"That's great," Desiree continued. "Pat, the sheriff, called and he got the council together. We're late for the meeting. But, you can tell them all what you two chit-chatted about when we get there."

"You're on the town council?" Amanda asked.

"No. The council for the Oracle."

***

They met in the gym of the high school. It was dimly lit, and the floor was scuffed and scratched. The basketball nets hung limp and torn from the goals, and the wooden risers were folded flat against the wall. It had that echoing, haunting feeling that only a school after hours has. Sheriff Pat was there, pacing in front of the crowd sitting on metal folding chairs. Charles guessed a few of them were teachers or coaches. Others were business owners. It was a small group, and each of them had an aura of authority he could almost taste.

Pat rushed over to the doorway as he, Desiree and Amanda walked in.

"What are they doing here?" He stared at Charles and Amanda.

"Whether people like it or not, they're in this. I was looking after them, and they got dragged into it, too." Desiree stood her ground.

"Amanda is…still in a delicate place right now," he whispered, "and the boy may see the same fucked up shit that you do, but that doesn't mean he belongs here. They have to leave."

"No." Desiree was firm. "Ladies and gentlemen," she addressed the council and they all turned in their chairs to look back at her. "What is going on in our quiet little town is huge, bigger than we can imagine right now. Our mayor is dead because someone is after the Oracle, which is why Pat called you here."

"Then why did you bring a stranger here?" A petite woman in a boxy grey suit stood. "This is *our* business. Who is he? We need to be taking every precaution we can. What if he is one of them?"

"I promise you he's not."

Charles had never felt that nervous, even when he had been surrounded by gods in a tiny little diner with only one exit.

"He's like me. He has visions, dreams. That is why he traveled all the way from Houston to come here." Desiree looked at him. "Tell them, Charles."

"Uh…" He grimaced. "It's true?"

"Really? That's the best you got?"

He shrugged.

"Who is after our Oracle, Desiree?" asked a man in sandals and socks.

She took a breath. "A Loa, a voodoo spirit."

"Clermeil," Charles interrupted her. "The voodoo spirit of flooding waters…and he brought gods with him. Uh…" He looked at the group now. "He…he said he wants to use the Oracle to break down a wall to come into our world. And he has a group of gods with him, but they only have so long. I don't know how long," Charles admitted, "but they have a time limit, I guess."

"And how do you know all this?" asked a middle-aged man in a stained Saints vs. Colts Super Bowl T-shirt. "One of your visions?" he scoffed.

"He told me."

Pat scratched the side of his nose. "You talked to him?"

"Yessir. He came to Desiree's last night, but couldn't get in because of…a protection spell."

"We can't trust outsiders, and dammit, Desiree, you should have known that." The woman in the boxy suit glared at Charles.

"I am *so* glad you teach Tell City's kids to judge people because they are different, Principal Dawson," a gentleman in a sweater vest said with a smirk.

"I also teach them not to take candy from *strangers*, Mr.

Burton." She folded her arms over her chest. "You're welcome."

"All right, people." The sheriff put his hands in the air. "Can we focus on the issue at hand?"

There was a loud boom and the walls of the empty building shook. It sounded like thunder, but the chill on everyone's flesh told them it was not. Silence fell amongst the group. Everyone looked at the ceiling of the gymnasium as if it might bring some sort of revelation, or another roll of thunder to quell their unease.

The sheriff's cell phone rang. With the speed of a Texas Ranger drawing his pistol, he pulled it out and answered. "Sheriff." Seconds later the faint sound of sirens brought everyone to their feet.

Pat ran out the door, one hand pulling his keys from his belt, the other still holding the phone to his ear. The people in the gymnasium clustered into small whispering groups. Their expressions ranged from anger to complete panic.

"I think I have a bad feeling about this." Amanda grabbed Charles's arm.

He turned to her. "Okay. What do you feel?"

"Something in my stomach, like I'm going to throw up. Is that normal?"

Charles smiled. "It means you're scared. Don't you remember what being scared feels like?"

She shook her head. "It's been too long, and it's more about what I'm thinking. We shouldn't be here. They're right. Why does Desiree think you and I can help? This is the council's problem. That is what the council is for… keeping the Oracle safe. I know you might help with your dreams, I guess, but… what are dreams going to do against gods? They aren't even real, right?"

"Come on," Desiree interrupted, pulling her car keys from her jacket pocket. "We're following Pat. That wasn't thunder. That was an explosion." Desiree turned, and left the gym with hurried strides.

Amanda looked back at Charles with a furrowed brow. He only shrugged in response, and they rushed to follow Desiree out through the halls of the school.

Principal Dawson followed behind, and soon the whole of the Oracle council was filing out to their vehicles in the school's front parking lot. They followed the sound of the sirens and the straggling patrol cars out to the trailer park in the northern hills of the town.

****

Steve and Brandon sat on the lowered tailgate. They were parked up on a high country road overlooking their trailer park down below. They were covered by trees, but they could see the burning trailer below just fine. The flames and the smoke that came from Brandon's trailer spiraled into the sky. The rain sprinkled down on them, but they cracked open their beers anyway, and settled down to watch the show.

Inside the trailer were both their fathers. It was the place the two men always chose to smoke and drink.

Fire trucks and ambulances ripped across the gravel road. The firefighters reeled out their hoses. Residents of the trailer park gathered around the flames, and stood in their driveways and on their porches. When the deputies and police sped in they began putting up tape and barricading off the spectators. Minutes later, Pat's vehicle came to a screeching halt on the gravel road, followed by each of the council members' cars that had been parked in front of the high school.

"I tol' you the sheriff was the council leader." Brandon took a sip of his beer. "Not the mayor. That fuckin' Democrat didn't know shit about nothin', let alone the Oracle."

"All right. But we still don't know if he was the leader." Steve leaned back on the truck bed, using his elbows to prop himself up, so he could still see the flames. "And I'm the one who saw'em meetin' at the school, you fat fuck. What else would all those people be meetin' the sheriff at the school for?"

"Well, why the hell would I have believed that? That's a

retarded place to meet. All out in the open and obvious."

"Yeah. It was fuckin' retarded. That's how I knew." Steve took a drink, and suddenly he pointed down the hill. "Hey, look, it's the bitch principal at the middle school that was always givin' us shit. You remember her?"

"Yeah, I remember that cunt face." Brandon spit off to the side of the truck. He turned his camo ball cap forward to keep the rain off of his face. "You gonna miss him?"

"Pops?" Steve sat up. "No." He spat, imagining he were spitting on his father's grave. "He always gave me shit. He's a fucking prick. *Was...*" He stood on the truck bed and climbed onto the cab.

"What the hell you doin'?"

Standing on top of the cab of his rusted white truck, Steve howled into the trees, and he raised his beer to the towering flame. "Burn, bitch! Burn!" He took another swig.

"Git the fuck down, Steve!" Brandon looked down at the trailer park below. No one could hear Steve over the roaring of the flames, and the little explosions that kept the fire going, despite the rain and the firefighters.

"How's the celebration goin' boys?" Clermeil said, appearing from nowhere. "Did I not tell you? You come through for me, and I'd come through for you. I make good on my promises. I sent Ishtar, and she did an amazing job, didn't she?

Two-for-one, or should I say three-for-one, 'cause we got the council out from hiding?"

Steve jumped off the cab of the truck, beer splashing out of the bottle. He stumbled to keep his balance, and shook Clermeil's hand.

The Loa clasped his shoulder. "Ishtar will keep the fire fueled for a while, and we made sure there was no chance they made it out alive."

Brandon slipped off the tailgate. "It worked. That's all of them down there. Steve was right, that was the council meeting at the school. Has to be them."

By this time Steve was again standing on top of the cab. "See, that's Desiree there with that hitchhiker we picked up, and…I think that is Amanda Wood."

Clermeil nodded. "You might have mentioned a hitchhiker once. Charles, you said?"

"Yeah."

"Hmm…remember, boys, I could get for you what that Oracle said you weren't ready for. I want a list of names of everyone down there. Names and professions. Keep up the good work, and I can give y'all that new start you were askin' for. Enjoy your fathers' funerals, boys."

Clermeil walked away and disappeared into the woods.

"Yo, Steve." Brandon looked up at him.

"Yeah."

"Look, I know our daddies were assholes and fuckin' meth-heads, right? I get it, but do you think they…I mean nobody's gonna believe it, Steve. That's bigger than a meth explosion, man. That was like a fucking bomb."

Steve shrugged. "Whatever, man, they're not going to look that deep. They ain't that smart and ain't even gonna give two shits even if they were. They're gonna walk in, see two white-trash burnt guys along with the crystal. Case closed."

"That explosion was huge. They couldn't have afforded all that chemical and shit for anything that big. They weren't running a ring or nothing, they were just—"

"You pussying out?" Steve turned on Brandon with narrowed eyes.

"No. It's just—"

"You feeling bad or somethin'?"

"No."

"Your daddy beat your ass senseless, man."

"I know, but this ain't right."

"You're pussying out."

"Dammit, I ain't flakin'!" Brandon rubbed his face to get the rain out of his beard. "Look here, jack. I'm jus' sayin' we got to be careful. This is deep fuckin' shit, dude."

Steve jumped off the cab into the bed of the truck. "I

know, but, boy, we got this. If we do what this fucker asks, we'll be rollin' in the green. Man up, and drink your beer. Those pieces of shit are dead."

"Yeah." Brandon raised his beer. "Here's to the good life."

***

Amanda, Charles, and Desiree sat in the corner booth at McGrath's Pub. Amanda sat quietly, sipping her lemon water. Charles kept glancing up at her, trying to decipher the expression on her face. It was either intense contemplation or a vacant look that revealed the lack of all thought. The fact that he could not tell which it was disturbed him somehow, and no matter what he did to distract himself, ripping the label off his Bud or even counting the number of floor tiles, he could not stop himself from wondering.

Desiree finished off her whiskey. The ice in her glass rattled as she set it down with a disgruntled sigh.

"That was *not* a meth explosion," she said.

"Yeah, but they are going to have to say that it was." Amanda's tone was flat.

So she had been thinking about the night's events, Charles thought. Though she said she could not *feel* anything, that did not mean she could not think about the situation; it just meant she was not afraid of it or worried by it or upset about the deaths. Though, she had seemed to be concerned with the fact she could not feel. Could it have been pure logic that drove her to believe she needed to go to the Oracle to get her emotions back? If it was all pure logic, then the other morning when she had ran to his room and soothed away his nightmare, or his vision, was she just doing that because it was a polite or logical thing to do? No. There was more to it than that, or so he hoped.

"Charles?"

"Huh?" He looked up from tearing his beer bottle label into even smaller pieces.

"You okay?" Desiree raised an eyebrow at him.

"Yeah," he said. "Just thinking."

"About what?"

Charles looked at Amanda. He could not say he was thinking about her, contemplating the way the world looked through her dark brown eyes.

"You know." Charles scooped all the bits of paper into a pile. "All this crazy Tell City voodoo-gods-Oracle stuff."

Desiree eyed him suspiciously for a moment, then returned to her rant. "They *cannot* write that off as a meth explosion! It was the Loa!"

"Why would a Loa want to kill *them*, though?" Amanda

asked. "They had no connection with the Oracle or the council."

"Maybe the gods were trying to break up the council meeting?" Charles took a sip of his beer. It took every fiber of his being to focus on the conversation and not just Amanda.

Desiree fiddled mindlessly with her empty glass. "Well, if that was the plan it sure as hell worked, and now the council is going to be *very* busy cleaning up this media nightmare...yay." She rolled her eyes. "We aren't going to have time to get to the issue, which is the Loa. This is going to be chaos. All the media wanting to show up for interviews with their cameras and their microphones asking about the mayor, asking about the river levels, asking about the," Desiree made dramatic air quotations, "meth ring."

"But their job is to protect the Oracle," insisted Amanda. "That should be the priority."

"It is. To keep the Oracle secret from other *people* – not gods from parallel dimensions. The mayor is dead. Otherwise, he would have handled the media bullshit. Now Pat is going to be tied up with this explosion, along with the rest of the council, and two of them work for the damn newspaper. Tim, Mike, and Karen were voted into office for something or other," Desiree waved a hand, "and everyone else is still a teacher, principal, police officer. And who am I? The town psychic. I can't help them. They will have to answer to journalists every five minutes, and pissed off Tell City residents more often than that. I'm not sure how hard it will be to hide from the rest of the world that a voodoo Loa caused the biggest meth explosion ever, and killed our mayor."

Desiree threw her hands up in frustration, and then waved down the bartender for another round.

Amanda shrugged. "Just say everything is still under investigation until the media gets bored and moves on to the next story."

No one said another word until the bartender had set down the next round of drinks, and had moved on to the opposite side of the room to chit-chat with one of the regulars.

Having finally averted his mind from the lace on Amanda's white tank top, Charles asked, "If the explosion was to break up the council's meeting, was the mayor killed just to get the council together?"

Desiree and Amanda looked up at him. There was a definite look of realization on both of their faces, though each expression was drastically different than the other.

"He needs the people that look after the Oracle disoriented and scattered so he can get to it, maybe." Charles grabbed a new beer.

Desiree took a gulp of whiskey, and smirked. "So he can break down a wall into our world and vacation in Maui?"

Charles laughed. "He tried to make it seem like he was tired of hearing humanity's cries and prayers for, you know, something more, but I think he wants the glory of it all, being a savior, like Jesus."

Sheriff Pat busted through the tavern's front door, his hand resting on his holstered firearm, his gaze scanning the crowd until it landed on Charles Garrett. He headed straight for the booth with long powerful strides.

When he reached their table, Desiree tried to speak, but he cut her off before she had the chance.

"You mind telling me why I had an Illinois sheriff's deputy in my office looking for you?" he asked Charles.

"An Illinois sheriff?" Charles had to think for a second, but then the answer was obvious. "Oh, what's he doing here?"

Pat leaned on the table. "You know him then?"

"Yessir, I do. He…uh…is a friend."

"A friend." Pat squinted.

"Sort of," Charles answered. "Not really." He was trying to reason out why the sheriff would be there anyway. He had tried to convince Charles not to go to Tell City. He had made the town sound cursed.

"Then what is he doing here?"

"I don't know!" Charles raised his chin and his voice. "Is he still at the station?"

"No." Pat hesitated, and then said, "He's at the Catholic church."

Charles gave him a sardonic smirk. "Then I guess I'm not under arrest, am I?"

Sheriff Pat glared at him. "Not yet anyway."

"Amanda," Desiree interrupted, "why don't you take Charles to the church. I want to have a word with our sheriff."

Amanda shrugged, and took one last sip of her lemon water. Again, she was indifferent to everything going on around her. She and Charles got up from the booth.

Charles heard Desiree ask in an angry whisper as he and Amanda walked to the door, "What the hell are you trying to prove?"

"I am doing my job, which frankly, is hectic enough right now without having to deal with the new stray you adopted, but go ahead, enjoy your drink."

Charles did not hear the rest of their conversation, because in a booth against the front window was a beautiful boy in a tailored black suit. Their gazes locked. The god's eyes had an expression as sweet as ambrosia and his smile could charm the devil. He propped his elbows on the table, showing off his heart-shaped cufflinks while his hands fiddled with something green. He laid the green object down, and winked.

"Charles?"

He looked up at Amanda. She held the door open for him, the stormy wind tossing her hair like black silk ribbons. The neon lights behind the bar reflected in her dark eyes. Staring into them was like staring into the black and peaceful void of eternity. Her eyes were like an endless night with hidden secrets and mysteries begging to be explored, begging Charles to find them. Rain droplets trickled down her delicate chocolate hand, and her lips…

Charles shook his head, and looked back at the booth by the window. The god had vanished. All that was left on the table was a one-hundred dollar bill folded into an origami heart.

Charles rubbed his eyes, and followed Amanda out the door.

"You okay?" she asked as soon as they were inside the car.

Yes, Amanda was gorgeous. Yes, she was an enigma to him, but he was no longer enchanted by her lace top or her smooth skin or her lips.

"Yeah…fine." Charles cleared his throat and stared out the window at the falling rain.

Charles thought about Jenna, and the sound of her laughter, and how her eyes got all squinty when she was deep in thought, and then he forced himself to stop.

***

The Catholic church was in the center of town. It was an ornate stone building, with a cross atop the tallest spire. Amanda parked as close to the door as she could. The windshield wipers batted back and forth.

"This is the cop that arrested you in Illinois?"

"No, he didn't arrest me." Charles unbuckled his seatbelt. "He just handcuffed me and pushed me into the backseat of his car for hitchhiking." He smiled, and shrugged. "But he let me go."

"Why?"

"We had a bro-moment."

Charles got out of the car. Amanda did the same, and they ran up to the doors of the church.

The church was dark, aside from the track lights shining on the altar and on the giant cross upon which Jesus' tortured body hung limp, his crowned head low. The savior's eyes were wide open though. No matter where you stood in the church, no matter where you sat in the pews, those eyes looked right at you, right through you. The pews were all empty except the third pew from the front. There sat the sheriff in his civvies, looking up at the ghost staring down at him.

Amanda nodded to Charles, telling him to go ahead,

that she would wait for him.

He took a deep breath and walked up the aisle. Maybe it was in comparison to the gods he'd had the pleasure of meeting in Tell City that made this one, with whom he was so familiar, seem so far away. The altar seemed surreal. His Bible Belt Christian relatives would have looked at him in shock if he had told them he had entered the house of idols. However, the thought of saints and the Virgin Mary hardly seemed comprehensible as a threat to his Christian upbringing in the shadow of the false gods and demons he had been dancing with recently.

He stopped next to the third pew from the front.

"Sheriff?" There was no response. "What are you doing here?"

The church echoed with the sound of his deep and bitter laughter. "Because life doesn't make any sense, kid." He turned his eyes away from the Lord and looked at Charles. "If it did, none of us would be here."

Charles did not know what to say, so he sat in the pew behind the sheriff. In front of him in a cubby on the back of the sheriff's pew was a worn red copy of the Holy Bible. Charles stared at it, but could not bring himself to pull it out and thumb through the thin wax-paper pages.

"You know you're a missing person?" Robert said,

glancing over his shoulder and stretching his arms across the back of the pew.

"I assumed," Charles said.

"You know that legally I've got to do something 'bout that?"

Charles leaned forward, putting his elbows on his knees. "Makes sense." He laughed. "The local sheriff will be happy you're arresting me. I don't think he likes me that much."

"Arresting you? If I was gonna do that, I wouldn't have let you out of my car that night unless I was throwin' you in a cell."

Charles nodded.

"No. I just have a couple of questions for you, kid. This isn't exactly the correct way to do it, but we're in the house of God. I guess that counts for something." He paused, expecting a reply from Charles, but Charles just looked at him perplexed. "Did you leave your home in Houston, Texas on the first of June of your own free will?"

"Yes."

"Have you been physically injured?"

"No."

"Are you in good health? Not ill?"

"No. I'm fine."

"Do you want to go home?"

Charles had to think, but only for a second. "Not at the moment."

He nodded. "And do you want your folks to know where you're at?"

This one took Charles a minute. He removed his glasses and wiped them on his baggy T-shirt. Charles wanted his family to know he was okay. He wanted them to know he was not dead in a ditch or passed out in an alleyway, but did he want them to know where he was? Charles would not put it past his uncle to drag him back by the short hairs, and force him to grovel at his mama's feet for her forgiveness. Or his grandmother might guilt him into coming back. She would then make him read the Holy Book aloud cover to cover, while she sat in her floppy church hat sipping iced tea.

"No," Charles said, and he saw the sheriff's head nod. "Wait..."

The sheriff turned to look at him.

"You don't have to take me back?"

"You're a grown man. This was your choice."

Charles exhaled slowly.

"All the authorities legally have to tell your family is that you're safe, seeing that you were not abducted and at risk."

"Good to know. I'll remember that next time."

"Next time?"

Charles shrugged.

The sheriff turned away to face the front. "I ran away from home once, too. Ran away from here."

"Why?"

"Tell City told me to. I told you, kid… I couldn't handle this shit. People having their questions *answered*. The meaning to their lives spelled out for them in some damn riddle, like they were special, like they had the secret to life. Well, I went out there, into the real world, and you know what I found?" Charles said nothing. "The same damn thing. Life is a riddle. Everyone has their own riddle that is unique and special to them that they have to work out. Some special purpose to their life, some holy quest or special gift or a fucked up past. You don't need an Oracle or divine intervention to receive the answers or for life to mean something. You know what makes life mean something?"

He did not wait for Charles to answer. "Death. That's it, kid. That's all it takes. Knowledge that someday you gonna die. And it's what you do with that knowledge that counts. That is how you figure out who you were, who you are, and who you gonna be. You figure out how you want to live by figuring out how you want to die."

Robert paused and his voice softened, "My mama wanted to die knowing her babies would be safe, me and my little brother, Danny; that the Lord would protect us and watch over us. She sat here and prayed and prayed, looking for the sign the Oracle told her would come. Hmm…" He chuckled. "Maybe we were wrong all that time. Maybe it wasn't that she didn't get her sign. Maybe she just didn't see it." He gestured to the cross.

Charles's gaze followed Robert's to the crucified personification of sacrifice, to those eerie eyes that followed you around the room. No matter where you stood or sat in the mass, his fixed eyes burrowed into your soul. He was watching you, always.

Charles and the greying deputy exchanged a look and both laughed uneasily before being interrupted.

"Uncle Robert?"

Charles and Robert Wood looked up at Amanda Wood. Robert's and Amanda's hollow empty eyes met.

"Are you really my Uncle Robert?"

"Amanda?" Robert stood, using the back of the pew for aid.

Charles looked back and forth between them. He now remembered where he had seen Amanda's eyes before. They had the same hollowness as the eyes of the sheriff.

He hugged her, but she did not hug him back. Robert laughed boisterously. He almost glowed.

"Let me look at you." He held onto her shoulders. "I last saw a picture of you when you were in diapers. How's your mama and daddy?"

"You mean your brother and sister-in-law?"

"Yeah, girl!"

"Dead."

His hands slipped from her shoulders.

"No one knew how to contact you. I'm sure this comes as a shock. I'm sorry for your loss."

Charles stood, placing his glasses back on his face.

"How?" Robert's voice trembled.

"I thought you knew what they both asked the Oracle for. They asked for a love to die for. Let's be honest. It was naïve, unintentional suicide."

"How can you say that about your mama and daddy?"

Amanda did not respond.

"I thought they would have raised you better. You're mad 'cause you lost people. I get it. We all lose people, but that is no reason to disrespect the people that brought you into this world, and cradled you with all the love in their hearts."

"I mean no disrespect, but fact is fact."

"Well, you got your facts wrong, little girl!" He pointed a finger in her face. "In that picture they sent me of you, all those many years ago, when I was still in the Navy, you know what your mama and daddy wrote?"

Amanda remained motionless.

"They said they made a mistake."

An abashed look appeared on her face.

"They said their love to die for wasn't each other. It was you."

Amanda's eyes filled with tears. "What?"

"That's right. You were the love of their life. Despite the racist bullshit of the mixed marriage. Despite how your Aunt Nancy disowned your mama. Through all that hate and all the slander and the pain, they had you. You were the most beautiful thing in their lives, and they said that they'd die for that baby girl in that photograph. Where'd she go?"

Tears were streaming from Amanda's eyes now. "It's all my fault," she said, looking up at Robert. "Uncle Robert, they died in a car crash. It was raining and Daddy was driving too fast, because…because…" She put her face in her hands. "I called them, because I was going to hurt myself." She fell to her knees, her tears spilling upon the floor of the church. "It was all my fault! I was so selfish. So fucking stupid."

Robert knelt down, and held his trembling niece, there on the floor of the church, in the house of repentance and forgiveness, the image of sacrifice personified watching over them.

Charles stepped out of the pew, and around the remnants of the broken family.

The past is written by the story told. The truth is kept by the only one who knows. Miracles do happen, thought Charles, as the words of the Oracle echoed in his memory. Maybe they weren't supposed to happen the way they did in Tell City, he wasn't sure, but he knew he didn't belong in this miracle. He walked from the church into the pouring rain.

The sky was rolling with different shades of grey. The ground was saturated. The streets were turning into rivers.

He went around the side of the building where there was a small cemetery. It felt ancient. The grave markers were old and weathered. The Latin inscriptions above the deceased's yellowed images were barely legible in spots. He spotted white poster board staked next to a grave. In bleeding Sharpie it read HE IS RISEN.

Charles wondered if it was a sign for the second coming of the savior. Or if it was someone's sign from the Oracle. Or if the sign was meant for him. He stared at it in the pouring rain. The words continued to bleed.

Risen.

Rising.

The river.

He ran. Splashing through the pounding rain, Charles headed eastward towards the town's floodwall. It stood resolute, a large solid concrete wall lining the edge of the Ohio's banks.

Its painted murals spoke to him of past floods. Disasters caused when the Ohio flowed over the roofs of houses, and destroyed old buildings and the lives of Tell City residents.

Charles ran past the concrete wall into the park. The swings rocked back and forth in the wind. The merry-go-round creaked as it circled on its own. The trees bowed down to the rushing stampede of the Ohio. The river had already passed its banks and was rising ever higher onto the land. The dark water thrashed like a large and angry snake against the shore.

It could not be contained for long. It was alive. The river was alive, and it was trying to get to the Oracle. Charles looked over his shoulder at the floodwall. The gates would have to be closed, or the town would flood.

His eyes landed on the sole mural painted on that side of the wall in the park. It said in large bold letters TELL CITY, and between the words was painted an apple, pierced by an arrow.

Charles had to get to a stone well – he knew that much. And there was an apple he had to eat before the king arrived, and somehow there was a panther involved. He was not sure what it all meant. Charles had never been good with riddles.

Snow White was beautiful. She slept so soundly in that tiny crooked shack. It was such a shame she would not wake. He loved her, and knew her even though they had only met once before a long, long time ago. Charles was hers. Love was so many things, and this felt so natural.

He looked down at the apple in his hand. It came from the same tree in the garden as the apple that had put her to sleep. It was poison, but he knew he must eat of it.

You are ready, my son. The Oracle's voice rang like bells.

Charles wanted to be afraid, but fear would make the dream sky crumble and crash to the earth like the rain in the waking world.

Light slanted into the shack from the slats in the wood roof. The black panther was outside the door, his raspy purr shook the wooden boards, and the gleaming sunlight trembled.

Charles could not be afraid, that was the toll that must be paid. He must fight the king by ignoring the king's reign on this place. Fear could not dwell here.

My son. *She sang like a siren.*

He raised the apple to his lips and took a bite.

***

There was a siren, not the mythical kind. It rang shrilly, and then faded, and then rang again.

Charles sat up. He felt the remnants of a dream weighing on him like a hangover, but he couldn't remember it.

Rain pounded on the roof, overflowing from the gutters. He tossed the purple comforter aside and got out of bed. As he pulled on his jeans and fastened his belt, he looked at the pictures of Amanda and her family on the nightstand. Something ached in his chest.

The siren rang out again.

He grabbed a shirt from his backpack, which lay on the floor by his feet, and pulled it on. Charles smiled, thinking of Wile E. Would she come find him in Tell City? Had it already been two weeks? He could not remember. Too much had happened and the days had blended together.

Amanda and Robert sat on the couch downstairs. They

were facing one another, and speaking in whispers.

"What are the sirens?" Charles interrupted.

"Emergency weather warning. They are closing the floodgates." Amanda's emotions affected her tone of voice. She was worried, and Charles couldn't help but smile. She could feel. Her curse was broken.

But acting excited about someone being terrified and finally coping with a terrible tragedy did not seem to be an appropriate thing to do, so Charles blinked it away, still smiling.

"Is it true?" Robert asked, distracting Charles.

"About the floodgates?" Charles asked.

"No, nimrod. The Oracle? The gods? The mayor? Your crazy ass dreams?"

"Yes."

"Shit."

Amanda grimaced. "I told him everything."

Charles shrugged, his stupid smile coming back. "You had a right to." He cleared his throat. "Is there coffee?"

"Yeah, help yourself." She smiled back, and Charles staggered into the kitchen.

No, he told himself. This was that god's doing. That boy with the arrows and the…

"Cupid?" He pondered aloud, as he took a coffee cup from a drying rack by the sink.

He poured himself some coffee.

No, he could not believe in Cupid. But he could believe in prophetic dreams and voodoo Loa? He thought of the look Wile E. would be giving him if she knew he was thinking this, but then again she would believe anything. She thought her grandfather was a god or Wakan Tanka or whatever. What if her grandfather was whatever she said he was? The great mystery? What would that make her? Wile E. the Coyote the goddess? Charles did not think Native Americans had goddesses, but maybe they did. And what did that make all her brothers? Smokey the Bear and Tiny the Spider and Buzzy the Crow and…

"Holy shit." Charles laughed aloud. Either her brothers were all cartoon characters or they were all Native American animal spirits. She was right. Everything did go right over his head.

Dazed, Charles stumbled back into the living room. The TV was on, but the sound was muted. Images flashed showing a pretty news reporter and images of the raging Ohio.

Robert pointed at the TV. "It's a good cover…for a god. With this town's history no one would be surprised it was underwater."

"How does that help them?" Amanda looked at up Charles as if he had the answer.

"Immobilizes everybody?" He blew the lingering steam

off the surface of his coffee.

"It would immobilize them, too."

Robert busted out with laughter. "Gods? You think a little water's gonna hurt them?"

"How do *you* believe this so easily?" Charles asked, squinting at Robert.

Robert thought for a moment. "Remember when I dropped you off at the truck stop?"

Charles glared at him. "That was after you threw me against your car and handcuffed me, right?"

"Right." Robert just smiled. "You told me you had a dream, and that dream made you hitchhike all the way here from Texas."

"Yeah." Charles raised the coffee to his lips. A flicker of recognition sparked to life in the back of his mind as the smooth glaze of the mug touched his lips. The black coffee was bitter. It tasted like poison. Something was familiar, like déjà vu, like the memory of a dream.

"How'd you believe your dreams so easily?"

It was an eternity before the cup hit the floor. The steaming black liquid seemed to levitate in the air as it fell. The mug bounced and spun, before rocking to a stop. The coffee followed, bleeding into the carpet.

Before Charles's mind could react, his mouth said,

"Desiree."

"You okay?" Amanda bent down and picked the mug up off the floor.

"Desiree!"

Amanda looked at him. "What about Desiree? Charles, did you have another dream?"

"Yes."

***

The neon OPEN PSYCHIC sign was off as Robert, Amanda, and Charles pulled up to the shop. The windshield wipers were at full speed, and still the rain flooded the glass. All three of them stepped from the car. Desiree's Buick was parked in front of the shop, but she never came to the door as Charles pounded on it, trying to wrench it open.

"Hey," Robert yelled over the pounding rain, "the back door." He led both of them around to the alley. The rear door to the shop was smaller and weaker than the front entrance. Robert motioned for them to stand back, and with a sturdy kick caused the pine frame to give way.

The three of them walked into the reading room of Desiree's psychic shop, but Charles did not stop to call out for Desiree like Amanda did. He did not evaluate the scene like Robert. Charles headed for the stairs, hurrying up to her apartment. He did not knock on her door, which was still guarded by a solid line of brick dust on the floor. Nor did he stop for the cats, as they ran to hide under the furniture. No thought of southern-gentleman law crossed his mind as he entered her bedroom.

She was sleeping soundly despite the storm.

"Desiree?" He sank down next to her bed. She did not hear him. "Desiree." He shook her shoulders, and still she slept. Her lips were pale and cracked. Her tangled black hair lay across the pillow.

"Wake up!" Charles demanded.

A strong, dark hand rested on his shoulder, and Charles moved away.

Robert pressed his fingers against Desiree's neck, and then held them beneath her nose for a few long agonizing seconds. She was alive – the look he gave Charles said so.

"What's going on?" Amanda's voice quaked.

Charles recalled his dream. "She's asleep, and she's not going to wake up."

Robert turned to him, giving him a hard look. As easy as it was to believe in it all that morning, he was evidently struggling to believe it now.

"What do we do?" Amanda asked, as the two men

stared at each other. "Charles!"

He looked up at her. She was expecting him to know what to do because of his dreams, because he foresaw it, but he had no idea what they meant. Desiree would have known.

"I was in the shack," he recalled. "There was a woman, like Snow White, that had fallen asleep and wouldn't wake up."

"Okay. Find someone to kiss her." Amanda sounded angry.

Robert's eyes met Charles's gaze. "And?"

"There was an apple I had to eat. It's been in a lot of my other dreams, but I never ate it. We were in the shack…" He paused.

"Yes?" Amanda urged.

"And the Oracle said…"

He looked over at Desiree. She was as still and as peaceful as she'd been in his dream. He loved her. The love was not passionate or lustful, and unlike how he felt toward Amanda, he knew it was not caused by the sway of a Greco-Roman god. It was natural. But he did not know what it meant.

He wanted to be afraid, but that was the toll that must be paid.

"It said I was ready."

***

Robert stayed behind to watch over Desiree, and to contact Sheriff Pat, while Amanda and Charles headed towards the shack.

Amanda was speeding, whipping around each bend in the winding country roads. The windshield wipers batted back the rain, but even in the headlights the yellow lines on the road were barely visible.

As she took a sharp turn, Charles's shoulder slammed into the passenger door. His seatbelt locked.

"Amanda, slow down."

"I can't." Her hands gripped the wheel.

The girl's face was set like stone, her dark eyes fixed on the road.

"I know you're scared, but this ain't helping," he said, his southern accent thick. He cleared his throat.

"But Desiree—"

"I know. But this isn't about Desiree right now, is it? It's about you."

Amanda's eyes turned on him. "Excuse me! You don't know what you're talking about."

"Yes, I do. You finally felt something for the first time since your parents died, and it hurt, and everything right now is too much to deal with. It's raining, and you're driving too fast, and if we crash…we won't get to the Oracle. We won't get back to Desiree. If we crash, it won't be your parents' fault. It will be yours, and that's what all of this is about." Charles paused to take a breath. "You blamed your parents because it was easier than blaming yourself, and after what Robert said you don't know who to blame. So, here's a little thought for you. It was no one's fault. The fact about life is that it makes no sense. It ain't fair, and it hurts like hell, but sometimes shit just happens. So, before this shit runs off the road and into a goddamn tree, slow the fuck down."

She took her foot off the gas, and the Nissan slowed. Gravel popped underneath the tires as she pulled off to the side of the road and turned off the engine.

"Sorry." She lowered her gaze.

The rain pounded down on them.

Charles sighed, and collapsed back into the seat. "I'm sorry." He had lost his temper. Those words had not sounded like *him*, but he, too, was afraid and confused. The expectations he once had for himself were gone. The person he'd once been had started to vanish, like a ghost in the rain.

"That…" Charles shook his head. "It's none of my business. I—"

"No," she interrupted. "You're right. I used to have this plan, you know? Trying to have my whole life together, so that

I was together, so that everything went...*right*. And I found this man. He was great. He *fit* in my plan. We moved into a perfect apartment together during our Junior year. We had it all working right, you know? But...he had big plans, and I didn't always fit. He was possessive and jealous. I couldn't go to study groups if there were other boys. I couldn't go to parties without him." She tipped back her head to stop the tears. "He...um...he had to control everything. Everything. What I wore, where I went, and if I was late coming back... I was scared, and I wanted to leave, but with the lease and my friends being his friends, I couldn't. It sounds stupid."

"No. No, it doesn't. It's okay..."

"I tried to make it all go away. Told myself I was crazy, because he was perfect. I told myself I didn't need to be hanging around other boys, and that those clothes I wore made me look like a slut, just like he said they did. I convinced myself he was right. I tried so hard, but I... I caved." Her tears turned into sobs. "I never told anyone." Her face vanished into her hands. "And now they're gone. They're gone."

Charles was prepared to sit in silence. He was prepared to comfort her, to help her grieve, but instead Amanda wiped away the tears and took a deep breath. She started the car and pulled back onto the road.

Amanda cleared her throat and asked, "Why isn't

Desiree waking up?"

"Uh..." Charles looked out at the road, trying to adjust to the change of topics. "The Loa, when he came into my dreams the other night, he was looking for Desiree. We weren't there last night, maybe he—"

"Why did he show up in *your* dream when he was looking for Desiree?"

"I...I don't know."

"Is the Loa keeping her trapped in a dream somehow or something?"

"Maybe."

Amanda turned onto the dead end road Desiree had taken them to only a few days before.

She parked the car and they headed into the forest. Neither of them said a word, since the thundering rain made it impossible to hear each other. Amanda kept looking back at Charles as she led the way. The sopping ground oozed beneath their feet. The tree canopy was tossed this way and that in the undertow of the storm.

In front of Charles, Amanda froze at the tree line, where the field opened to the view of that tiny crooked shack, twisted and warped from vines and time. The expanse of the sky rolled in grey waves above the field of bent grass.

Charles touched Amanda's shoulder, and she glanced

down at his hand. With a solemn nod she stepped into the field, and he followed. Beyond the shelter of the trees, the wind stampeded across the clearing. Charles's wet shirt flapped around his midriff, and Amanda's hair was whipped into knots.

Thunder chased them both as they reached the shack. Amanda turned the door handle. The walls of the shack quaked, and Charles reached around her to help wrench open the door.

Jon Hart stood in the center of the shack.

Drenched to the bone and panting, Amanda and Charles looked at one another.

"Amanda," Jon said, smiling. "I see you're doing better. How's your uncle, Robert?"

"He's...he's fine. He told me about... How did you...?"

"The Oracle tells me many things."

Charles stepped forward. "Then you should know your daughter's in trouble."

The roaring storm shook the wooden slats of the shack. Charles looked in fear at the rattling boards and the dancing light. He felt his dreams catching up to him.

"I do," Jon said, staring into Charles's eyes.

"Then do something," Amanda whimpered.

Charles turned towards her and saw that she was shaking.

Her voice rose over the wind. "You're a priest. You have

magic or something. You're her *father*."

"That is not for me to decide." The priest's blind gaze never deviated from Charles.

"But they are after you," Amanda insisted, "and the Oracle, the gods. You obviously know about that."

"An Oracle cannot change or create a future, since futures are in flux," he answered. "Oracles foresee possible roads we might take to reach certain outcomes. It is up to us to create our fate."

"Then what the hell is the point?" Amanda asked loudly.

"Amanda." Charles attempted to calm her, but she was still shaking.

He looked at the priest. "Last time you said I wasn't asking the right question."

Jon nodded.

"Charles," Amanda said, moving closer to him, "we aren't here for you. We are here to save Desiree."

"This is about Desiree...somehow. My dreams, what if they're clues, what if we can figure them out? We could save Desiree."

Amanda's screwed up face showed her obvious disagreement.

Charles stared at the dirt floor of the shack, trying to remember details. His first dream was about the flood and the panic. His second one was a twisted version of his childhood memory. He was stuck up in a tree, only in his dream it was an apple tree. He either needed to eat the poison fruit or face the fear below him. He remembered his dreams of castles and kings and of wells and rivers. He recalled his most recent dream, of Desiree trapped in a death-like slumber. His mind began to wonder what Desiree might be dreaming of at this very moment.

"Okay," he said softly, his voice barely audible in the storm. "The road signs all said Tell City. The apple, that's knowledge like from the tree in Eden, and it's also poison fruit. There is this stone well everyone is trying to find. Truth, maybe... uh...fear. Fear is King, and you can't let fear in or you'll crumble. The kingdom will fall. *The Panther!*"

"What?" Amanda's voice came from behind him.

"The panther," he said again, as if it should make sense to her. "The cause of my phobia. Why is it following me? What does it want?"

"Charles," Amanda said, looking at him like he was a lunatic, "there hasn't been a panther following you."

He sighed impatiently and looked up at Amanda. "In my dreams."

"Oh." She forced a smile.

Charles frowned. "But what does all that even mean? It doesn't make any sense. Or maybe...maybe I'm just too stupid to figure it out. Why did *I* have to have these dreams? Life was *good*. I was *happy*, or I thought I was. Wasn't there anyone else, someone better with riddles and symbolism, who could have fucked up their entire lives to come to this crazy town? Am I *really* that important?" He laughed. "I can't fight gods. I can't break curses. I can't even change a tire. What am *I* supposed to do?"

Charles began to panic. His skin felt icy and he was afraid he might hyperventilate.

"I don't believe the Oracle can answer all of those questions," the priest said, chuckling. "Let's narrow down your hysteria into one question, hmm?"

Charles clenched his fists. He knew how much was riding on this one simple question. How could this man, Desiree's father, the priest of the Oracle, be so calm and lighthearted with so much at stake? His own daughter was cursed. His precious Oracle was being threatened.

Charles felt a heavy pressure inside his chest. If he failed, Clermeil would steal the Oracle and use it to open the gates between the worlds. Humanity would be under siege by pagan gods who had been evicted from the human world because of their ruthlessness. The world would be at the mercy of their every whim, all because Charles couldn't ask the right question.

And the priest was just standing there smiling.

"Charles," Amanda said, putting her hand on his shoulder, "they're just visions, right? Some sort of mental symbolism your brain comes up with to make sense of the world around you...which is in chaos right now. But just because you are the one having them doesn't mean it's all up to you."

Amanda's fingers fell away, and Charles's rage subsided. He turned to her and their gazes locked. Her eyes were no longer like her uncle's – they were like her father's in that photograph. They were kind.

"This *panther*," she continued, "you say it's a recurring dream. It keeps showing up. What else is there in the dreams with the panther?"

Charles's eyes lit up, and he grinned.

Amanda stared at his face. "What? Have you found the right question?"

Charles turned to the priest. "Jon, where's the well?"

The priest nodded and stepped forward, walking as if he was part of a dream.

His blind eyes led him straight to Charles, and he raised his aging hand to rest over Charles's eyes.

"You are ready, my son."

Marie Hart had been preparing herself for this moment for eleven months – ever since the Oracle had given her that dream. The dream that told her she would be giving birth to a little girl.

After months of agonizing over the lies, the fears, and the doubts, she knew she could not hide herself or her new family from the Loa for much longer. Desiree was two months old now and Jon could take care of her. He would keep her safe and hidden amongst the houses and churches of that quiet town. Her baby would never know magic. Jon's mother would help take care of Desiree for as long as he needed her to, and he would be fine in the end. Heartbroken, but alive.

Marie knew that she must sacrifice her soul to the well.

She glided barefoot across the center of town on a full moon night, her long white skirts flowing around her legs and trailing behind her like mist in a breeze. Moments later, Marie appeared to be nothing but mist. Her shroud glistening in the light of the full moon, she drifted down the street and down to the river. Where the water lapped onto the bank, the mist faded. Her fingers, legs, chest, and eyes reappeared until she was wholly visible.

She held her shoulders back and her chin high as she stepped into the current of the Ohio. It was different than the Mississippi in so many ways. The Mississippi was a stampede of rushing, mixing elements. The Ohio, though, had a power that was absolute. Knee-deep in water, she leaned down and placed her palms onto the rippling surface of the river.

At her touch, the water beneath her hands took on an electric blue illumination. Like lightning travelling across the clouds, the glowing blue water splintered and shot downstream. Seconds later it had vanished and all was still.

Marie straightened up, and standing in the water before her was Clermeil. He was as still as the rest of the night.

Moments passed.

"I was beginning to think you'd run away with that dear-Jon to a damn desert, Marie." When she didn't respond, he continued. "Some planet, some strange reality where water might not exist, because you were nowhere to be found for damn near an entire year."

"You couldn't find me because I did not want to be found, Cler." Marie met his eyes with a steady gaze.

He laughed a little nervously, and hid a hand in the pocket of his jeans. "You're not that powerful, Marie."

"Are you sure?" She glided in deeper, closer to him, trailing her fingertips along the surface of the water. "You only know of the powers you gave me."

His temper rose, and so did the water. Marie was waist-deep in the Ohio now.

"And with those powers you were to get me closer to the Oracle. You and I, together, but what? You fell in love with that simple-minded little man? After everything we've done, accomplished together? After we got so close? Why?"

Her gaze was unwavering. "It's not something you can just pick up and carry away with you, Cler."

He was silent for a long moment.

"Well, what in hell is it then? Have you seen it?"

"It spoke to me through the lips of its priest."

"And?"

"And it's over." Marie shook her head. "It's all over. You. Me. You're Oracle hunt. It's done, baby. I can't let you do it."

"Then I will put this entire town death-deep in water."

"Go ahead. Drown them."

In his passion and rage, he entangled his fingers in Marie's long midnight hair and plunged her down into the rushing water. She did not fight him as her body scraped against the rocks of the river bed. But soon her legs began to kick and thrash, her skirt twisting around *her body. Clermeil held her under the Ohio until she moved no more.*

When he finally released her, her limp corpse lifted to the surface, her black hair and white skirts pluming around her like an ethereal funeral shroud. As the water receded back to its normal level, and the tides calmed, she drifted downstream.

There Clermeil stood, panting and shaking, watching as her body disappeared into the darkness. She had not fought. She had known she would die. She had known his true plan, and had meant to leave him without her, fading back into the realms of the gods all over again.

***

Charles awoke to the sound of thunder. He rolled his head along the back of the chair to look out the window. No shock came at the sight of rain cascading down the glass. The alarm clock on Desiree's nightstand gleamed bright red numbers: 5:25 A.M. He cracked his neck as he got up from the armchair, and then he sat down on the floor next to Desiree's bed.

"I had a dream about your mama," he said. Desiree did not stir. Her breath was quiet. "I think you ought to know." Charles yawned and rubbed the sleep from his eyes. "She was working with Clermeil, but she…she changed her mind because of you. She did it to keep you safe. Did they ever find her body?"

Lightning illuminated Desiree's face. Charles nodded as if the lightning had been her answer. He stood, and glanced at her once more before leaving the room.

The apartment's living room was dark. A bundle of blankets was visible on the couch where Amanda lay sleeping.

Holding his breath and scanning the room, he saw the path across to the kitchen was clear of Desiree's three furry beasts. Slowly and cautiously, he made his way over to the linoleum of the kitchen.

He busied himself with the coffee maker. While it gurgled and spat, he rummaged through the fridge. Only after pushing aside bottles of cheap vodka and potion vials did he find a carton of eggs. He found flour in the pantry to make gravy. In the freezer, he found a half-empty bag of hash browns that looked freezer-burnt. Mind numb with exhaustion, he began to cook with what he had.

He tried to cook the food just like his mama would have made it – though she would have made it from scratch. Finding prepackaged and freezer-burnt hash browns in anyone's ice box would have sent her on a Paula Deen tirade, causing her to say *Oh, bless your heart* every minute or two. Promptly, she would have treated them to the most amazing breakfast southern cookin' could provide.

He flipped the eggs and then stirred the gravy.

Mew.

Charles's body froze. He found himself struggling to breathe. With a tense gulp, his gaze fell to his feet, where a tiny black cat looked up at him with piercing green eyes. It reached up with its splayed paws and hooked its claws into his pant leg. Again it mewed, its mouth opening wider to reveal needle-like teeth.

Charles's knees gave way and he went crashing to the floor. By the time he realized what had happened, the cat had skidded out of the room.

His chest felt tight as he scrambled and pushed himself into a corner. Coming back to his senses slightly, he could hear his own rasping breath as he struggled to fill his lungs with air.

Amanda appeared from around the corner and quickly sank to her knees at his side.

"Are you okay?"

Charles could say nothing.

Reaching up and over to the stove, Amanda extinguished the burners. "Was it the Loa? Did you have one of your visions or something?"

He shook his head and whispered, "*Cat.*"

Amanda's fearful expression vanished. "Cat?"

Charles nodded.

With a sigh, she grabbed his arm. "Okay. Up you get."

His knees still weak, Charles had to balance himself on Amanda and the cabinets to stand.

"You want some water?"

"Eggs."

"What?"

"They're burning."

"Oh."

He rested against the counter while Amanda took the eggs off the hot pan. "Well, they aren't burnt, just...well-done. They're fine."

Charles's breath steadied as he watched her stir the gravy. She prepared a plate with a paper towel to put the hash browns on.

"Thanks for cooking," she said. "We could use some real food. You know, my mom put the eggs on top of the hash browns and the gravy on top of that."

Charles smiled. "There's another way?"

"Uh-huh. Put the eggs on one half of the plate and the hash browns on the other. Some people don't even like gravy."

"Those people have no soul."

Amanda laughed heartily, and covered her mouth to quiet herself. It would not have awakened Desiree, but Robert had also stayed the night, and he had ears like a watchdog.

Charles grinned, almost proudly, at Amanda's laughter. The changes in her personality were vibrant and radiating.

"Um...where's your uncle?" Charles asked, as Amanda handed him a plate.

"Keeping watch downstairs."

"*Really?*"

With a raised eyebrow, she said, "Yes, *really*, Mr. I-am-going-to-watch-Desiree-sleep...oh, so creepily."

"I had to."

"Yeah." She gave him an understanding smile. "But if you ask me, you both are crazy over-protective. You both need sleep, and Desiree isn't going anywhere."

"You never know." He piled his plate high with food. "She could sleepwalk."

"Cinderella didn't sleepwalk," Amanda replied, and then grimaced at her failed attempt at a joke.

Charles smirked. "I think you mean Snow White or Sleeping Beauty."

"You're a Disney Princess expert?"

He shrugged, feeling no shame.

She laughed, and then shoved him along, handing him another plate. "Take this down to Robert. He needs to eat."

"Yes, ma'am." Holding his plate and Robert's, he made

his way out of the apartment, praying to whatever god was on his side that the cats were hiding under the couch.

***

Robert was sitting, looking old and haggard, in one of Desiree's distressed waiting room chairs, gazing out into the dark sky beyond the window.

Charles handed him a plate of food and then sat in the chair next to him.

In an attempt to alleviate the oppressing silence, Charles asked, "So, if a Loa walked through the front door right now, what would you do?"

"Kick his ass," Robert said, skewering some hash browns with his fork, "and then run like hell."

Charles laughed, and began to eat.

"Pat will be here soon with a doctor. Don't know how the hell that's gonna help, but he insisted."

"Maybe he'll have some ideas on how to keep her fed and hydrated."

"Ha! A food tube and an I.V.?"

"If it helps to keep her alive…"

"Desiree won't die, if she's anything like her daddy. He had his eyes scalded from their sockets, and wanted to go home to his daughter instead of to the E.R."

Charles struggled to swallow. "That's intense."

"Kid, you got no idea."

Remembering something lost from a dream, Charles said, "That's how he became the priest. He can communicate with the Oracle…because he, what, saw the other side?"

"You know as much as I do."

Charles was unsure about that, and set down his fork.

"Do you remember his wife, Marie?"

Robert gave Charles a meaningful look. "Oh, yeah. She was a looker. Had this air about her, like she was an empress or something. She walked around this town making all us boys drool, like she had the world on a string. Who'd she fall for? Some quiet square…Jon Hart." Robert set his half-empty plate on the chair next to him. "He was a writer back then. I heard rumors they'd stay up all night at the bar – only time you saw him in public. He was interviewing her for a book or something. She was his muse. A year after she rolled into town, her and Jon got hitched and were expecting. Right after Desiree was born, Marie committed suicide…drowned herself. They found her remains tangled in some tree roots in Windy Creek. No one suspected murder, not with the way Jon was. Postpartum depression, they said."

Charles just nodded.

"A little late for my curiosity, but why are you asking?"

"Just another dream I had. Marie…she had magic like…I don't know. Like something in a story. I didn't think things like that were possible."

"The way I understand it," Robert said, "is that magic, God, miracles, never work in the way we expect. Sometimes it's loud and in your face. Makes you think you're crazy. Other times it's so subtle if you don't look hard, you gonna miss it."

"No in between?"

"Not that I've seen."

Something dark passed by the window. Robert and Charles perked up like dogs. Someone was trying to get in. The door rattled and shook and banged.

Both Charles and Robert jumped to their feet.

"Who is it?" Robert barked.

There was a long silence, and then from the other side of the door a voice said, "Who the fuck are you?"

"Never mind who I am," Robert replied. "If you want outta the rain you're going to tell me who the hell you are."

"Fuck," the voice outside muttered. "The name's Rick. I'm a friend of Desiree. Pat tol' me everything."

Robert looked at Charles.

"Come on, man." Rick sounded desperate.

Charles gave Robert a nod.

With a grimace, the old man unbolted the door. As soon as it was open, Rick O'Connor sprinted inside and up the stairs, leaving puddles in his wake.

They followed him, mindful not to slip in the water. When they arrived at the door to the apartment, Amanda was waiting for them.

She looked startled. "Is that Rick?"

"Yeah," Charles said, as all three of them crept towards Desiree's bedroom.

The door was cracked, and Robert reached out a hand to push it open.

Rick sat on the floor next to Desiree's bed, holding her hand in his. His soaked plaid shirt hung heavily off his shoulders.

"Hey, girl," he said to Desiree, almost whispering. "Ain't you looking fine? Pat tol' me what was goin' on with you. Man can't mind his own business if his life depended on it, ain't that right?" He laughed as if Desiree had quipped back. "Girl, when you get out of this, when you figure this out…you owe me a drink, you understand?" He stood and wiped his nose on the sleeve of his wet shirt. Rick turned to see three pairs of eyes staring at him from the doorway.

His gaze fell on the Illinois sheriff. "Now…who the hell are you?"

"Robert Wood."

"Daniel Wood's brother? No shit? We all thought you was dead."

"Alive and kickin'."

"Sorry to hear it." Rick strode from the room, pushing himself through the space between Amanda and Charles. He walked straight to the kitchen and helped himself to the coffee Charles had made. He knew which cupboard the cups were in. He knew where she kept her creamer and sugar, though he passed over the creamer, and put three heaping spoons of sugar into his mug. Again, he squeezed past the three of them, and into the living room.

Robert broke the silence. "Pat and some doctor will be here soon."

"Why?" Rick pushed aside the blankets on the couch and got comfortable.

Amanda stuck a fist on her hip. "Because she's asleep, and not waking up. Because she hasn't eaten or drank anything or even moved in twenty-four hours. We shouldn't be having a house call. We should be taking her to a hospital."

"Tell us how you really feel, sweetie." Rick smirked, and sipped his coffee.

Amanda gave him a particularly long glare.

"Amanda," Charles said, "she is under a sleeping...

curse…or something. No one at a hospital would believe us."

Amanda threw her hands up in the air. "What the fuck is wrong with you people?"

Charles flinched.

"She needs proper medical attention. Whether they believe us or not they can at least see that."

"There's a phone," Rick said, gesturing to Robert's cell phone on the coffee table. "Call 911. Get an ambulance over here. Tell the EMTs that some Voodoo two-bit gangster-god put her under a damn sleeping curse. Maybe they can wave their magic stethoscope over her to break the spell. Go ahead. Call 'em." His smirk grew more taunting. "We're waiting…"

"You're an asshole, Rick." Amanda turned on her heel and stormed out the door.

"Great." Charles headed out after her.

Robert shook his head. "If she's anything like her mother, you might want to let her cool down a minute before chasing her."

"But she's right, isn't she?" Charles ran his fingers through his hair. "I mean…this isn't normal! This isn't sane."

Rick's laugh sounded bitter.

Robert said, "Welcome to Tell City, Mr. Garrett."

***

Charles had expected the doctor Pat brought to be a thin, balding elderly man with a leather bag in hand. Instead, the doctor was blonde and pretty, and she had a camo tactical backpack that Charles could have sworn was a repurposed carpetbag à la Mary Poppins. The camo bag had everything a doctor would ever need inside it, with countless zippers and pockets and Velcro straps.

The pretty blonde doctor put her stethoscope back in her bottomless backpack.

"Well," she stood from her crouching position, "as far as I can see, Desiree's fine except for being asleep. Her vitals are fine. She's not dehydrated. She's not even shitting and pissing herself."

"Eww," Amanda interrupted. She had been leaning against the window watching the rain fade into a mist.

The pretty doctor continued. "It's a good thing. Weird, but good. No mess to clean up. Considering everything Pat has told me, I wouldn't be concerned until something drastic happens."

Rick looked over at Pat, who had been sitting in the armchair by Desiree's bed. "Did you tell the whole damn town?" he snarled.

"She needed to know," Pat replied calmly.

"What do you mean, until *something drastic happens*?" Amanda moved closer to the doctor. "She's asleep and she won't wake up. What the hell is your screwed-up definition of *drastic*?"

"Severe dehydration. Seizures. Heart tremors. Asphyxiation. I know you're worried. I'll stay here to keep an eye on her. It seems to me like she's just…meditating."

Rick glared at the sheriff. "People don't need to know nothing but their own business, Pat."

"So what?" Pat stood. "I shouldn't have told you what happened to Desiree? I shouldn't have explained the situation to the doctor, so she understands what's causing it?"

"It doesn't matter what we *think* is causing it," Amanda roared. "Voodoo god or whatever, she needs a *real* doctor."

"I *am* a real doctor. I served three years in Iraq. I've had men run back into the battle with broken bones and infected bullet wounds. I know when something needs immediate attention and when it can wait."

"This isn't a war," Amanda snapped.

"Kind of is," the doctor quipped back.

"Amanda," Rick said, smiling viciously, "if we take Desiree to a hospital, Pat here will have to tell them everything about the Oracle and the gods and what not, and we already have enough problems without him running his goddamn mouth. The flood, the mayor, the *meth* explosion."

"That reminds me, Rick." Pat strode up to him, and they stood nose to nose. "Where are those boys of yours? They're needed for questioning."

Rick bared his teeth. "Brandon and Steve got nothing to do with that!"

Robert raised a hand. "Hey, shut the fuck up!"

When everyone fell silent, Robert, who was standing by the window, pointed down to the alleyway. Charles and Amanda walked over to join him. Standing in the alley below looking up at them was a curvy woman with pinned-up fiery hair. Her bright red dress and matching pumps looked straight out of the 1950s.

Charles recognized her as the waitress who had served him and Clermeil at the Corner Diner.

Pat and Rick moved close enough to look out the window, and when they did, the curvy woman strode down the alley and out to the street.

"Who the fuck was that?" Rick asked.

"Someone sent to distract us," Charles said. "Because they're getting close or running out of time or both."

"She's one of the gods, then?" Pat asked.

"But which one?" Rick added.

Amanda's eyes narrowed. "She was sent to distract us,

huh? They would only do that if they thought we even have a shot at thwarting them, which we don't."

"Jeez," said Rick, "if only we had an Oracle or something."

"Tried that." Charles was still looking out the window at the rain sprinkling down. "Nothing but riddles."

Charles's peripheral vision began to blur. He turned away from the window. People were still talking, but their voices were fading in and out

Robert leaned against the wall. "That is all it ever does, and good never comes from it. Hell, let them have it."

Charles's chest began to tighten. He was having trouble breathing as fog permeated the room.

"How can you say that?" Amanda's voice cracked. She sounded so far away. "My parents would never have met, and I would never have been born."

It was happening to him again, like at the water tower. He was in a tunnel. Charles was falling into a vision.

Robert's lips moved, but Charles heard nothing.

"Jon Hart wouldn't be blind," Pat's voice echoed, "but then he wouldn't be priest either."

Desiree wouldn't be there to pull him out of his vision this time. He saw her, resting so soundly on her bed – and then the wall behind it faded away and *she was lying in that tiny crooked shack.*

Charles tried to move, but his body would not respond. He tried to call out to the rest of the room that had yet to fade away. Robert was still leaning against the wall, and Amanda stood nearby. Rick and Pat were still glaring at one another. No one in the room could help him. To them it looked like he was just standing there listening to their argument. Their lips moved heatedly at one another, fighting over the nature of the Oracle.

Charles tried to fight off the encroaching vision as it made its way around the room. The bedroom faded away little by little, until finally the apartment was completely gone and he was standing in the shack.

Desiree's body began to rise and drift as if she were underwater. Her long hair plumed around her. She floated up and up until she bumped against the roof of the tiny crooked shack, like a ragdoll lost at sea.

In the corner of the shack stood Jon Hart, his hands folded atop his walking stick.

The priest smiled.

When he spoke, he spoke with the voice that only Oracles have, but there was no real voice, for it was a void. "The wheel is in spin, and you must die in order to be born again."

Desiree's body bobbed against the ceiling, the sound echoing through water that was not there.

"Into the heart, into the water, into the well, and into the slaughter."

It was the riddle, Charles remembered. It was the answer to the question he was given in the shack.

Jon Hart's hand was over Charles's eyes once more as before. "Lost in the forest in your mind, the shifting shapes will lead you to the well outside of time." *Jon removed his hand from Charles's face.*

Charles glanced up, hearing the sound of Desiree's body hitting the roof. Thuuump. Buuump.

Charles could hardly bare it. He started to look away, but from the corner of his eye he saw bubbles escape her lips. He noticed her finger twitch. Then her toes moved.

"Desiree?" *Charles asked.*

Desiree's eyes opened and she began kicking and thrashing against the roof of the shack.

"Desiree!"

She screamed without making a sound, bubbles erupting from her lungs.

Jon Hart grabbed Charles's wrist. "The battle, though not over, will be nearly won when the gods are deceived by the light of the setting sun."

This part was new. Charles did not remember the priest saying these words to him.

Desiree did not know Charles was below her. He tried to pull away from the priest's grip, but he could not free himself from what he knew was truly the Oracle.

"The Wanderer and the Lost Son will unite upon the other shore. Shared blood and cause will close the gates forever more. Listen to me!"

Charles stopped fighting to reach Desiree. He turned and looked into the eyes of the Oracle. "I'm sorry."

The weight of its words had brought a tear to Charles's eye, but he wasn't sure why.

"But the fall of one kingdom will mean the fall of them all. I cannot undo what has been done, and I cannot cease what is to come, for you and I are to become one. Just listen to what I'm telling you. Listen to the dreams. Listen…"

Desiree's thrashing had stopped. Charles looked up. She was gone. When he looked back at where Jon had been standing, he saw no one. He was alone in an empty, silent shack. He realized his hand was gripping something round and smooth and a little cold…an apple. A bite was missing from the last time he'd eaten of that poisoned fruit.

"I am listening," Charles said to the empty space around him. "I just don't think I understand."

"Yes, you do," said a voice from the void. "I am sorry I am using you."

"What do you mean?"

The vision began to fade. The voices of his friends re-entered his realm, and the dream shack's walls crumbled like clay to reveal Desiree's bedroom. No one had noticed he had left, but he had not truly gone anywhere, and it seemed as though only seconds had passed. The people in the apartment were still bickering about Jon Hart.

"Yeah, but then he would have had a happy normal life with his daughter," Robert disputed.

A shiver ran across Charles's flesh, as the gravity of the vision fell upon him. His mind had abandoned everything in front of him. He had left, and in the midst of the argument, no one had seemed to notice – except for maybe the doctor. She stared at him from across the room, as if she was uncertain what to make of him.

Charles tried to shake the vision off, and joined the squabble. "No, because Desiree wouldn't have been born either. That was the only reason Marie came to Tell City. She was helping Clermeil the first time he was here, or maybe it wasn't the first time. Maybe he has tried several times. I mean...this town is prone to floods, isn't it?"

They all fell silent and looked at him in irritation.

"Look, it's..." Charles rubbed his forehead, exasperated. His mind was still hazy and numb as the vision began to fade away like a dream. The harder he tried to hold on to parts of it, the easier other parts began to slip away. "It's all cause and effect, right? We're all here because in one way or another, the Oracle told us to come."

Amanda caught Charles's gaze. Her arms were wrapped around her chest. "Why *us*, right?" Her face was rigid. He could not tell if she was angry with him for his moment of self pity at the Oracle the night before, or if she truly meant it.

"Well, duh," said the pretty doctor, looking away from Charles, "it's all cause and effect. A series of unfortunate events led you all here to this room, with this problem. You're the only ones that know about the gods, right? Looks like it's up to you to stop it. A ragtag group of underdogs. Isn't that the usual story?"

"Up to us?" asked Pat, indignant.

The doctor sighed. "To slay the lion, save the witch, and bolt the wardrobe."

"Right…" Amanda frowned, her gaze dropping to the floor.

Charles shook his head. Even with her emotions freed from their cage, she was still an enigma to him.

"How did you all end up here anyway?" The doctor looked amused.

All four pairs of eyes landed on Charles. He looked around in bewilderment. "Me?" They kept staring at him, reproachful.

"No." He protested.

"But, I came here because of you," Robert jabbed a finger at him. "I would have *never* come back."

Amanda nodded. "And I went to Desiree because I *thought* I felt something after you asked me for directions. And because you brought Uncle Robert here, my prophecy from the Oracle came true. It all goes back to you," she glared at him in accusation.

Rick's eyes squinted at Charles in suspicion. "And how did you meet Brandon and Steve, again? Hitchhiking?"

Pat frowned. "Wait, this guy knows Steve and Brandon?"

"He doesn't know where they're at either, Pat," Rick snapped. "Drop it already!"

Pat stepped closer to Rick, his voice formiddable. "You *know* I can't."

Amanda turned to Rick, her tone stormy. "You *lost* the boys?"

"No, I just haven't... seen them for a few days, all right?" He said through gritted teeth. "Well, maybe not since I ran into y'all at the shack."

Pat turned on Charles, incredulous. "When were *you* at the Oracle?"

"A couple of times." Charles shrank.

"A *couple?*" Pat had reached his boiling point.

"Hey," the doctor interjected. "All of you need to go take a breather."

"We're fine." Amanda scowled at the doctor.

"No. You're not. You're all starting to pit against one another. Everybody take a walk. Look, the rain's stopped."

Clouds still covered the sky, but the rain had stopped. The doctor had promised to look after Desiree while the others cooled their tempers. The two sheriffs had hopped down to the station to check on *things*. Rick had gone only God knew where, and Amanda and Charles headed to the square towards Sunset Park.

The park was boarded off by the floodgates, which were supported by sandbags as well. Charles wondered how high the water had gotten. He thought about the panic the Loa was causing, and how long it would be until everyone had to evacuate.

"We weren't about to rip one another apart," Amanda said, pouting. "Who is she anyway? She doesn't even know us. Where'd Pat find her?"

"I think she was right," Charles admitted, and Amanda's gaze snapped at him with vehemence. "Well, that person – or god – down in the alley wasn't there without a reason. Clermeil wants us out of his way. Maybe she was the one causing all the tension."

"Are we really a threat *to gods*?" Amanda asked, laughing. "Two college drop-outs, two outdated cops, and a *Rick*. Oh, yeah. They should run the other way." She paused. "We can't stop a flood. Are they afraid we'll come after them in paddle boats?"

Charles suppressed a chuckle, and then said, "I had another vision."

"When?"

"Back there in the room. I couldn't stop it."

Amanda wrapped her arms around her torso. "What was it?"

"It was about the riddle the Oracle gave me…'the wheel is in spin, and you must die in order to be born again.' It was like a memory, but Desiree was drowning, I think, or trapped, and I remember Jon telling me he was sorry."

"For what?"

"I don't know. But maybe that's why we're a threat."

They were approaching the floodwall. The murals of the flood sent shivers down his spine, but it might have been because of what was behind the wall…the Ohio. His dream of Marie's sacrifice and the remnants of his vision only increased his unease.

"No." Amanda shook her head, her hair tangling in the wind. "We are *not* the stereotypical group of messed up counter-personalities that are destined to save the world. Talk about self-inflated egos. We're just people. You and Desiree, though, I don't know about you. I don't know what you are."

Charles laughed. "I think you're underestimating the stereotypical group of counter-personalities. I mean…us people… why can't we save the world? It's our world. Who else is going to do it? Obviously not the gods. We can't sit around waiting for some miracle to save us. Your uncle told me that."

"Right, well, how do you plan on saving us with dreams? Dreams aren't real. You can't do anything with them."

"They're clues, though, aren't they? The mental reimagining your brain does to understand what's going on around you. If we listen to them, maybe they can tell us how."

"Okay, let's assume Clermeil believes we can stop him somehow. How else can he distract us besides making us aggravated at one another and immobilizing us with the flood?"

"Charles!" A voice from behind them rang like a bell – a southern belle.

Charles froze.

Amanda looked over her shoulder. "Do you know her?"

Charles choked. "Jenna?"

He turned around to see the girl he'd left behind. She wore her ripped-off blue jeans and that pink plaid shirt he always liked so much. Her hair was a stream of golden waves. She was beautiful, and Charles was terrified.

"God bless, I never thought I'd find you! You look so... oh, bless your heart." She jumped onto him, her arms around his neck, her legs wrapped around his waist. She was giggling and crying at the same time.

Charles stood motionless.

She hopped down. "What are you doing here? I mean, I figured you'd be here. That's why I'm here, but...why did you have to leave like that? I could have come with you. Made it a road trip. I..." Tears brimmed in her eyes.

"Jenna..."

She began to wail on him, kicking him, punching him. "You. Had. Us. Worried. Sick." He caught her arms, and she kept thrashing. "Are you trying to give your mama a stroke? What about college? What about Breakfast at Tiffany's? And thanks for leaving me with the rent!"

"Er..."

"Charles?" Amanda asked, frowning. "Who is this?"

Jenna froze, and looked up at Amanda with blank

confusion on her face.

Charles let go of Jenna's wrists. "Now, Jenna, hold on. Let me—"

She stepped up to Amanda. "I'm Jenna. His *girlfriend*. Who are you?"

A smirk crossed Amanda's face. "I'm Amanda. His *friend*."

Jenna turned back to Charles. "Is *that* why you really came here? She's…she's…"

"I'm what?" Amanda's hand rested on her hip, and by now Charles knew what that meant. "Go ahead. What were you going to say?"

"No, Jenna," he interjected, ducking his head to look into her eyes. "You know why I came here. I told you about my dreams and you thought I was crazy."

"Of course I did, you were talking about dream castles and magic apples, honey. I figured it would pass and you'd forget about it. I never thought in a million years you'd be fixing to abandon us and vanish for it."

Charles looked away.

"Baby, forget all this craziness and your nightmares and come home. I got my momma's truck. We can stay in a hotel for the night and be back in Houston by Sunday."

"In time for church?"

She squinted at him. "For supper."

"Oh." He smiled.

"My momma can make you that barbeque chicken you like so much. Just...come home, baby."

"You drove all the way here to try to find me?"

"I missed you. We've all been so worried about you, Charlie."

He had never felt so selfish, so stupid, and so inconsiderate in his entire life as he did at that moment watching tears fill up her blue eyes.

"*Charlie?*" Amanda giggled.

Charles gave her a nasty look, and went back to gazing deeply into Jenna's eyes.

"Jenna, I can't. Why don't you stay here with me? Just for a few weeks?" When he saw her brows furrow, he continued his appeal. "I'll call momma and daddy to let them know I'm all right, and you found me, and that we'd be coming home in July and—"

"Why don't you want to come home with me?"

"I'm not done here yet. Baby, my dreams, they weren't crazy...they were real. And there is magic here, and I have a friend, and she's in trouble, and—"

"Charlie, if we don't leave now, then we will become victims of the storm."

"Jenna, I can't leave…"

"Hold on," Amanda said, tilting her head, "what did you just say? About the storm?"

"Charlie, this place is under a severe flood warning, and it's only getting worse. Let's leave now while the rain's stopped."

"That's not what you said." Amanda looked her up and down. "You said 'victims of the storm.'"

Charles looked between them both, but the direction of Amanda's gaze conquered his attention. It was like she wanted him to read her mind, and he could. He looked up and around for anyone out-of-place. And sitting at a black metal table outside a shop across the street was a boy in a black suit. He was straightening his heart-shaped cufflinks.

"Charles, I don't want to die." Jenna smiled up at him, tears streaming down her cheeks.

"I won't let anything happen to you, but we have to leave. Now."

"To go to Houston?"

"No, to Desiree's. It's safe there…sort of." He grabbed her arm, but she refused to leave.

"Charlie, please come home with me."

"We don't have time for this, Jenna."

"If you don't come home with me I'll hurt myself."

"What?"

"Come home with me. Take me back to Texas. I want to go home, and I can't live without you."

This was not Jenna. This was the love god. Jenna would never hurt herself, but Charles had seen what the young god had done to the mayor. Jenna had been poisoned by his arrows.

"Jenna, please."

"Girl, love can make you do some crazy things," Amanda cautioned, "but that's not the answer. I know how you feel, okay? Let's go sit somewhere and work things out."

Charles looked back over at the love god. The boy held out his hand with his middle and forefinger pointing at his head, and his thumb cocking an imaginary hammer.

Jenna lifted her pink flannel shirt and pulled a Colt Mustang from her belt. Charles recognized the gun as the one her mother carried. Jenna had never liked guns, though. She refused to carry one, despite her mother's pleas about women's self-protection.

There was a round in the chamber, and she flipped the safety off and put the barrel to her temple.

"No!" Charles lunged forward to stop her. She pulled the trigger, and there was a crack and a splat. Bloody matter dripped down Charles's face. He heard Amanda scream as Jenna's body crumpled.

***

It was poker night. Smoke filled the air as Wile E. and all her brothers squeezed around a small wooden table in Jack's kitchen. He lived in a dark two-bedroom house off of State Road 145 in the Shawnee National Forest in Illinois. Laughter echoed off the walls as cards flittered across the table.

"All right, all right," Bugs the Rabbit interrupted, and the room hushed. "What about the time Coyote took back the blanket she gave to Rock?"

The room erupted with laughter again.

"Now hold on," Wile E. said, grinning. "How about the time you lost your tail ice fishing?"

Tiny the Spider made a face at Bugs. "She's got you there, brother."

"If we really want to compare blunders," Smokey the Bear said over the jeering laughter, "we should be telling Old-Man's stories."

"No contest there. Old-Man's got us all beat." Buzzy the Crow eyed the growing pot of chips in the middle and laid down his playing cards. "I fold."

"Looks like it's just you and me, Jack." Wile E. looked up from her hand at her brother sitting across from her. The old tricker's staff rested against the back of his chair. Beads and shells and feathers dangled off the top of the twisted stick, and they swayed from the vibration of Jack leaning back in the seat and lacing his fingers. His eyes were wide and dark and fixed on her.

"Well?" the old trickster asked. He was waiting for Wile E. to sweeten the pot.

Wile E. grinned. "If I win, you accept my offer to accompany me to Tell City."

Her brothers all rolled their eyes in exasperation, except Jack.

Smokey put his massive hand on her shoulder. "Just let it go, brother. Gitchi Manitou, Wakan Tanka, Great Spirit gave the burden to *you* – though why it was given to you is beyond me – quit trying to drag us into your mess."

Wile E. smiled. "Hey, Jack doesn't have to take the bet. That's his decision." She looked back over at Wisakedjak. "What do you say, World-Flooder? Want to watch the world flood again? No more water, but gods next time. Maybe you can help rebuild the earth again or....maybe there was a reason I met Garrett on the road up *here* to see my brothers."

"Maybe," said Jack quietly. He leaned forward and put his elbows on the table.

Bugs sighed. "Come on, Jack, don't fall for Coyote's

tricks. Just fold and let's move on, already."

Jack's eyes narrowed. "But if you lose, Coyote...if I win..." Wile E. perked up, and her head tilted to one side. Jack continued, "You have to shape-shift into a man."

The room erupted with laughter again.

"And," Jack added, "stay that way for an entire year."

Smokey beat his fists on the table, and Tiny wiped a tear from his eye.

Wile E. only grimaced.

Bugs giggled. "Coyote, just fold and let's move on."

Buzzy started to pick all the cards up off the table.

"I accept." Wile E. folded her arms and fell back in her chair.

Her brothers all froze.

"What?" asked Smokey, with a look of disbelief.

Wile E. gritted her teeth. "I said...I accept your bet. You're on."

"All right, boys," Buzzy said. "Show'em."

Wile E. laid down three queens. Jack laid down a full house.

Jack smiled. "You lose."

Wile E. let out the breath she was holding. "Shit." Then and there in her ripped off jeans and Lynyrd Skynyrd tank top, she shape-shifted into a man. And with her same sharp-toothed grin she added, "Get used to it, boys. I changed my shape, but I'm not changing my style." Wile E. lit up a cigarette. "Give me a chance to win it back. Who's up for rummy?"

***

Charles could not remember the last time he had seen a road sign. The last thing he remembered was Jenna's eyes. They looked like glass. Hard and cold and lifeless marbles rolling backwards as she fell, and then he was walking. It was dark. The rain had not yet begun to fall, but it would. It would rain and rain and make anyone who stuck around Tell City *victims of the storm*. The victims of the storm would run around looking for the Oracle. It would be in plain sight, and the fear would come and paralyze them all, and their eyes would transform into marbles just like Jenna's.

Charles was walking down a road with farms and trees on both sides. The night was silent except for the sound of a rushing river. Headlights gleamed from a truck coming up the road behind him. He stepped off into the woods. The ground sank beneath his footfalls. As he stumbled through the dark, limbs caught on his clothes and his feet became tangled beneath roots and vines. The sky was shifting overhead, the clouds drifting like waves across the ocean. The pale moon was almost full and her light shone through the gaps in the dark heavens, painting the forest with flickering shadows.

The mud became thicker as he approached the river. It had spread all the way into the forest. With every step, his boots sank deeper into the mud. It took a grueling effort to trudge forward.

By the edge of the lapping water, Charles collapsed upon a moldering log. The soft, decaying bark was saturated with rain. The cold wetness seeped into his jeans as he rocked back and forth.

He remembered the love god aiming his fingers at his temple. He saw Jenna pull the trigger. Amanda's scream pierced his mind.

All because of a dream, he thought. It was just a stupid dream that led him here to this flooding town. It was an adventure, a mystery to be solved. He did not mean for anyone to get hurt. Their feelings, maybe. They'd be worried, maybe, but not dead.

He could see Jenna's eyes turn in their sockets as the hollow point carved across her brain. She crumpled at his feet. Charles's own scream rent the night air, parting the clouds as the full moon shone down upon the river.

Charles's voice died away. He did not realize he had stopped screaming until he heard someone say, "Hey, jack."

Steve and Brandon appeared before him in muck boots with the legs of their jeans tucked in. They wore camo jackets and hats. Brandon shone the bright light of a lantern into Charles's eyes.

"What are y'all doing out here?" Charles found his face was wet, and he dried it with his sleeve as he stood.

"Huntin'," answered Brandon, adjusting a strap flung over his shoulder. The matte black barrel of a hunting rifle peaked out from behind his shoulder.

"What're you doing?" asked Steve. There was a bundle of rope draped around his shoulder.

Charles's mind faded and the world became foggy, as if he were about to have another vision, and he heard himself say, "I don't know."

"Well, how 'bout we take you home?"

Brandon and Steve approached him.

Charles felt numb. He tried to force away the fog as he turned his back on the river, meaning to walk back the way he had come. Brandon seized his arms, and Charles felt a painful wrenching in his gut that caused him to buckle over. His vision faded from the intense pain, which became even worse when he took a blow to one side of his face, then the other. His tongue and cheeks were bleeding, and he tried to strike out to defend himself, but was thrown into a stump. His swelling eyes only saw the blinding light of the moon.

"You're dead, boy. You really pissed off the wrong magic man."

Charles felt a kick to his ribs, and heard a crack. He tried to stand, but Brandon's four-D-cell lantern crashed into the back of his head.

"*Woohoo!* You ain't gonna come back from this one, son."

His vision faded in and out, and their laughing and jeering filled his ringing ears.

"Why are you coming into town on your high horse to fuck up everything?"

Someone grabbed his shirt and hoisted him up. "And to think we gave you a lift, jack."

Something made of sharp, cold metal rested against his neck.

"You don't mess with our friends, son. That's how you get gutted, you hear?"

Charles's vision came back blurry and full of stars. Brandon stood in the background with rope and the lantern in his hands. Steve held Charles up by gripping his shirt with one hand. His other hand held a serrated bowie knife to his throat.

Charles spit blood out of his mouth. It dripped off his chin and down his shirt. Steven and Brandon laughed in the light of the lantern.

"You work for Clermeil?"

"We don't *work* for him," Steve said. "You see, we're on his side. It's a good place to be…got some jane, new rims, a little revenge."

"One way ticket to the good life," Brandon added.

"We just help out however we can, you know. Diaper-Boy and that red-head bitch might have distracted you, but Clermeil sent us to finish the job."

Charles looked into Steve's eyes. He slammed his forehead into Steve's face. Steve fell back, holding his nose.

Steve's knife had nicked Charles's chin as he had lunged forward. Wracked with pain and feeling dizzy, he took off running as hot blood streamed down his neck. His stomach clenched in agony, but he didn't slow down. Running feet were not far behind, and the voices were hooting and hollering and jeering.

"Now this is our game, son!"

"Man, I love a good hunt."

Charles slid behind a stump, out of breath and out of strength. He tried to get control of the pain, but it persisted. His raspy breathing echoed in his ears, but that was all he heard. The laughing and shouting had stopped. His eyes scanned the trees.

A little red light scurried about on the ground, atop the leaves. It stopped on his upper leg, and he heard the echoing crack of a rifle. Charles crumpled over with a scream, writhing on the ground. He heard the sound of twigs and branches snapping, and two bright lights shone down on him – a lantern and the radiant full moon.

He faded in and out of consciousness as he was dragged through the woods. *Charles could hear the haunting dirge of the ferryman calling to him.*

"Clermeil figured out who you are, freak," Brandon said.

"And he wants to cleanse your soul in his muddy waters," Steve added.

"Give you your last rites. Carry your soul downstream to the land of the...what was it, Steve?"

"Land of the setting sun, I think he called it."

"Yeah, buddy!"

The sun and the moon rose and set.

His arms had been bound behind him.

Animals cried and howled and roared to one another.

His legs were bound together.

"He tol' me the afterlife is hell," said Steve.

Charles felt their hands on his arms as they dragged him into the river. Brandon and Steve's boots sloshed through the water and the muck.

There Clermeil stood in the shallows of the Ohio, looking up into the light of the full moon.

"Hello, Dastan."

Brandon and Steve held Charles upright as best they could. Charles did not understand why the Loa of flooding waters had called him by his middle name, but pain conquered his visions, and he slipped in and out of consciousness.

"My buddy, Charon, he's got a seat saved just for you, chained down to the bottom of Acheron. I figure your soul should be payment enough, Wanderer."

Charles could feel the current growing stronger. It was hungry.

"Jus' let the water take you." The bells of victory rang in the Loa's voice.

His captors' boots became unsteady on slippery rocks and logs. Water splashed into his mouth, up his nose, and then he was plunged into the current.

He could not breathe. Each struggle for a breath seared his lungs as the water ripped at him, the pain in his ribs felt like he was being stabbed. He struggled against the ropes in vain, feeling helpless. His shattered femur made his movements agonizing.

Jus' let the water take you.

The next breath he took gurgled and expelled water from his throat and lungs. The hands holding him down had lifted him up, and magically, by the grace of the god, he could breath, labored though it may be.

"I'll tell you what, boy," Clermeil began, "I'll make you a deal." He paused as Charles coughed and wheezed.

Charles could hear Brandon and Steve panting as they held on to him shakily. He wondered if they were trembling because of fear, or fatigue, or both.

"You for Desiree," Clermeil whispered, with a devilish grin. He knelt down in the water only inches from Charles's face. "Deal?"

Clermeil already had Charles at the brink of death. Choking and quivering from the pain, he knew there was no escape. The only reason Clermeil would strike this deal was if Desiree was at the brink of death as well. Her fate was in Clermeil's hands. Somehow, the Loa believed Charles could survive this…that Charles had some sort of power to stop him. If he died now without making any attempt to survive, Desiree would be spared.

Charles nodded.

The hands of death lowered him to the water.

"Clermeil?"

Brandon and Steve paused, looking at him.

Charles coughed. "Why is the Loa of flooding waters afraid of *me*?"

Clermeil leaned closer to Charles's ear, as if his next

words were a secret that Charles was only being told because he was dying. "I have tried time and time again to get this Oracle. This may be my last chance. I've received *prophecies,* too," he spat. The Loa stood tall in the rushing river. "*The water's king will ferry an army to the other shore to open the gates forevermore. The Lost Son will return to where he's never been. The water's king will find him then. Born of spirit and of flesh, The Wanderer will put the gods to rest...forevermore.* But now I put you to rest. Let the water take you."

And Charles was plunged into the current once again. He did not fight. He knew he would die, so he did not struggle or scream. He thought of Marie, and he dreamt.

***

Clermeil stood tall in the river as he watched Charles's body float downstream just like Marie's had. He gave himself over to save someone else. It was just like them, humans, to do such a thing. It was predictable. Marie did it for Desiree. Desiree did it for Charles, and now Charles thought he was doing it for Desiree, when really he was doing it to pay Charon for the gods' passing.

Clermeil thought it was beautiful the way humans would throw away everything that they are for something they want. They would sacrifice their lives, their freedoms, their children, their passions, their sins for something they believed in. Clermeil wanted to be that something again. To be sacrificed to, to be prayed to, and danced for, and honored.

The Oracle was so close he could almost hear it sing. Once the land was flooded, and all the humans that would die to save it were evacuated or removed or dead, he would take the vessel to the well and trap the Oracle inside. He was worried that they had not found the well yet, despite the number gods that had accompanied him from the other side. But there was still time. Midsummer, when the veils were at their thinnest and when Charon would set sail back to the other shore, was still days away. They would find it by then. They were only through torturing half of the Oracle council. One of them would know. Clermeil was sure there was at least one amongst them that would feel it wasn't worth dying for.

"We killed him." A shaking voice came from behind him.

Clermeil turned to see Brandon and Steve. He had almost forgotten they were there. "Yes, yes, you have." Clermeil began walking towards them across the slippery rocks. "And for your loyalty and your devotion, I will give you all that I have promised. You'll see."

Clermeil could see the two young men were in shock and wide-eyed with fear. They had talked about killing people, which usually resulted in someone getting seriously beaten under the school bleachers and that was all. They never meant it. It was never real. Even as they watched the trailer burn with both of their fathers inside, they never saw it happen. It was someone else, some goddess of fire that had burned the trailer. Not them.

Steve stared at his friend. "Brandon..."

"Yeah." Brandon looked into the face of Clermeil.

"I'm sorry." Tears brimmed Steve's eyes.

"Can't be sorry now." Sweat ran down Brandon's cheek and into his beard. "You pussying out?"

"Nope." Steve gulped. "No, I am not."

"Boys," Clermeil said, clasping his hands together. "Now, I know what you've accomplished was difficult, but it was worth it. Have I not already rewarded you for your sacrifices? You can now live anew, reborn, free from the oppression of your meager birthright. When I lower the veils, and the worlds meld, when all of us can return home," Clermeil turned his eyes to the heavens, "you will be repaid. All that's left for you to do now is leave here before the roads close. Go live your new lives, boys."

"My son."

The Oracle's voice sang like a siren luring him out to sea and into the void.

He was submerged. The water moved around him, carrying him…taking him home.

From the bottom of the well, he could see himself at the top looking down at his own reflection. Charles reached up and the Charles above reached down to him. His fingers broke the surface of the water. The air felt cool. But the Charles above flinched away.

"No," Charles said, but the words disappeared into the waters of the well. The version of him above stepped out of sight.

"Come back!" Charles cried. Again the words were lost into ripples, but he was not alone for long. The other version of him had come back, and he had brought Desiree. That Charles gestured for

Desiree to look down into the well, and she did, her hands gripping the stone. Her eyes were full of fear and panic when she saw Charles at the bottom. She screamed down at him, but Charles could not hear her. She reached for him, and he for her, but this time his fingers could not breach the surface. Something was holding him down, holding him under the water. Charles looked at the bottom of the well. Nothing chained him down, but on the stone by his feet an apple swayed in the gentle current.

He picked up the apple and knew he must eat of it. But hadn't he already eaten part of it in the shack? Yes, and now he could see there was still a bite missing. He lifted it up, and his entire hand was able to breach the water.

With tears in her eyes, Desiree put her hand around his. She said something, but he could not make it out. Her warm fingers slipped away, taking the apple with them. She handed the fruit to the Charles standing next to her. He shook his head and gestured as if to say the apple was for her. Her eyes squinted, and the Charles above flinched. Gripping the apple in her hand, she thrust it towards the Charles next to her. Her face was stern. She scolded him.

Unwillingly, he accepted the apple. He looked at her once more with a pleading expression, but she shook her head. He took a bite.

***

And then Charles was standing in the shack. His clothes were still saturated. Water dripped off him.

The boards were shaking from the panther's raspy purr. The cat lurked just outside the door.

"My son," *a woman's weak voice said.*

"Desiree?" Charles dropped the apple. It wobbled across the floor. Two bites were missing.

He ran to her side. She slept so soundly in that tiny crooked shack.

"I am the Oracle," *she said without moving her lips.* "I speak for her now…my daughter."

His brows pulled together. "Marie?"

"I gave my soul to the well. For Jon, for Desiree, for you. You gave your soul for hers."

"I tried. She wouldn't let me."

The Oracle laughed.

"She can fight her own battles. Now you must fight yours. The panther is waiting."

The ticking of a clock could be heard now.

The door to the shack burst open, and the panther prowled in. Its shoulder blades rose and fell. Its glowing golden eyes locked onto Charles.

Charles began to hyperventilate, and then began choking. Muddy water began to flow from his mouth. His lungs burned and he

could not scream. His body began to seize, and he fell backwards into
Marie, who was no longer a disembodied voice. She was present in his
dream.

"Shhh."

Marie caught him and laid him down. She stretched out next
to Charles and brushed back his hair.

"Shhh, Dastan. It's only just begun, and yet it's almost
over."

The panther was next to him now. Marie stretched out a hand
to it, and placed her fingers atop its head.

"Take him now."

The giant black cat sunk its teeth into Charles's thigh, and
began dragging him across the dirt floor of the shack.

Water still poured from Charles's mouth and nose as he fought
to breathe. The panther pulled him through the door of the shack into
darkness.

***

Charles awoke coughing, struggling to breathe, pain
stabbing at his sides. His left eye was swollen into a slit. His
clothes and skin were damp with mud and blood and water. He
tried to move, but a pain more agonizing than anything he'd
ever felt paralyzed his right leg. He screamed.

And then he heard a low rumble. It was not thunder. The sound came from behind him.

The panther crept out from behind the tree Charles realized he was propped against. The river was out of sight. He was deep in the woods with a bullet in his leg, a few broken ribs, a possible concussion, and a black panther.

Charles tried to scramble away, but the pain stopped him again, as did the panther's roar.

Its eyes were inches from his. Charles could see the thick hair on its rounded ears, the whiskers on its jowls. Its long tail swayed lazily back and forth as it sat there staring at him.

The beast's paws seemed to be the size of Charles's head. Its claws were daggers peeping out of the creatures toes.

Charles gulped. "Hi."

The animal lowered its head and began rubbing against Charles's shoulder, knocking him back into the tree. It purred.

Charles laughed hysterically, hot tears falling from his swollen eyes. He quickly smeared them away into the mud on his cheeks, and his hand froze in front of his face. He raised the other hand and stared at it, then his feet. He was unbound, and not drowning, and not dreaming.

"You pulled me from the shack. You pulled me from the water?"

The panther tilted its head.

"But…Desiree…I gave myself to the water!" Charles tried to move, and a scream like a woman in utter terror forced him back down.

The scream had come from the panther.

When it was apparent that Charles was afraid enough to stay still, the panther lay down in the wet leaves next to him.

Charles could not stop staring at the panther. He had heard that scream once before. He had been in the pine woods on Grandpa Charlie's property in Louisiana. He had been running from something, he could barely remember what it was…a shadow, perhaps? It might have been his imagination, but he had climbed a tall evergreen to escape it. But it, too, began to climb the tree. Then he'd heard a scream, like a woman's, high-pitched and shrill. The hair on the back of his neck had stood on end, but the shadow had vanished. All that had remained was a black panther below. It had saved him then, Charles knew now, as it had just saved him from the river, but back then he had been so young and afraid.

He had gone back to Grandpa Charlie's house to tell him what happened. His grandfather and grandmother had been eating at the kitchen table.

"Monsters aren't real, dear," his grandmother had said as she sipped on a mimosa. "You only imagined it."

"But those panthers are real, Charles, no matter what

they say," his grandfather had said. "I've heard those screams. Sounds like a woman screaming, doesn't it?"

Charles had nodded.

"If you see it again come and fetch me, you hear? We'll shoot that monster down, and haul it in. See what those so-called experts have to say about that."

The memory comforted Charles. He leaned forward, his breathing still raspy, and stretched out his fingers. The panther growled at his sudden movement, but as his fingers touched the cat's coarse black fur, it began to purr again.

***

Charles fell asleep and dreamed.

He was at the base of the evergreen tree on his grandfather's old property once again. The old man had never caught the panther, Charles remembered, and when he died his grandmother had moved to Houston to be closer to the family. She never stopped talking about how much she missed her previous home, and with good reason. It was beautiful.

The floor of the forest was covered with the soft fallen needles of the towering pine trees, and when the sun shone down on those golden needles everything appeared to glow.

Everything was glowing in this dream, too. The needles, the trees, the panther, even Charles's own skin had halos of light around them. He sat there at the base of that tree he remembered, and stroked the panther's fur. There was no pain in his lungs or legs or ribs. The panther's tail swayed across the golden needles, and it purred.

***

"Charles?" Someone was shaking him awake. "Charles?"

Charles was in a haze of agony, and there was a little old lady in front of him with a twenty-gauge shotgun.

"What are you doing out here? What happened? Oh, your poor leg!"

"I died," he heard himself respond.

"No, you didn't."

"Yes, I did."

"I'm only supposed to do this in December, but…"

Each broken bone in his body snapped back into place. He let out a wild scream. For a second he thought it belonged to the panther instead.

"Merry Christmas." The old lady smiled without compassion.

As soon as the pain vanished, all of his senses returned to normal. His vision became clear and his lungs stopped hurting. He could move his leg.

He looked around. The panther was gone.

The little old lady standing over him wore a frayed dress and muddy hessian boots. He stared at her shotgun.

"Who are you?" he asked in wonderment.

"They call me Mrs. Claus nowadays."

"You're joking, right?"

"Serious as an elf."

She held out her hand. He took it, and she helped him up. She was stronger than she looked.

"Why are you...?"

"You were in my barn, remember? We wanted to know what your role is in this whole mess."

She laid a finger aside her nose, and his clothes were suddenly dry – not clean, but dry.

"We?" He suspiciously examined his clothes.

"My husband...Santa and I."

"Obviously," he quipped. "Er...friend or foe?"

The old woman raised her brows. "You're joking?"

"Serious as an elf," Charles deadpanned.

"Friend," she said, irritated. "Well, why are you here? I thought everything with Jenna and school was going well. Why are you *here?*"

"I had a dream...and now Jenna's dead." At the mention

of her name, his thoughts turned blacker than midnight again. In despair, he distantly heard the old woman respond, but her voice sounded far away.

"Oh, dear. I'm so sorry, Charles…Come on, sugar plum, let's get you somewhere sa—" She paused. "Somewhere else."

She laid a finger on the side of her nose, and they stood atop a rooftop overlooking the little town of Tell City.

"Oops." She smiled at his blank face. "I don't do this very often any-more."

Again she touched her nose, and they were in front of the psychic shop. The neon OPEN PSYCHIC sign was off. She looked surprised. "This is where you're staying?"

Charles robotically knocked on the door.

"Who is it?" Robert's voice bellowed.

Charles said nothing, still numb to the world.

Mrs. Claus answered for him. "Charles D. Garrett and… friend."

The door opened, and Robert Wood tried to mask his evident worry with a stern look at the little old woman and her shotgun. "Whose friend?"

"Well…everyone's." Her smile was as pure as fresh fallen snow.

"You're not my friend."

"Oh, nonsense. You just don't remember me, that's all."

Robert seemed unimpressed.

"Can we come in?" Charles asked, his voice barely audible.

"Of course, kid."

Charles stepped through the door, with Mrs. Claus behind him.

"We've been worried as hell about you. Almost called out a dispatch, but Amanda said that you might need some time alone."

"Charles?" Amanda's voice called, and without waiting for a reply she hurried down the stairs from the apartment above. She wrapped her arms around his neck and held him close.

Charles felt empty, but managed to raise his arms to hug her back.

"Who's that?" Amanda was staring at Mrs. Claus over his shoulder.

"Mrs. Claus, I think."

"You can call me Skadi, Amanda, dear, and you, too, Robby."

Robert raised an eyebrow. "I've had it with this crazy place." He shook his head. "How you holding up, kid?"

Charles did not answer him. He began to walk up the stairs to the apartment.

The lovely doctor sat on the couch. She had her hands wrapped around a coffee cup. Rick and Pat were standing in the kitchen whispering loudly.

"Well, Rick, I've got to do something. I have another dead body in the damn morgue!"

They fell silent, and looked around the corner at Charles as he closed the door.

"Hey." The doctor stood from her spot on the couch.

"I don't want to talk." Charles walked past her straight into Desiree's bedroom.

The light of the living room illuminated Desiree's face. She was still asleep. Either Clermeil went back on his deal or he knew Charles was still alive. He closed the door, and the light vanished. There were only grey shapes in the dark.

He collapsed in the armchair by Desiree's bed.

Minutes blended into hours. He listened to the rain, and the harsh beep of the emergency weather service warning on the television in the living room. The computerized voice was listing off the counties under severe thunderstorm and flashflood warnings in jerky unnatural words.

He felt helpless. He wanted to save Desiree. He wanted Jenna to still be alive. He wanted to stop the Loa. But he had no idea how, or where to even start. But…there must have been some clue he'd missed, some sign he'd overlooked, and the harder he tried to find it, the more frustrated and tormented his mind became.

He could not sleep or drink these feelings off, or forget them in the drone of the television. That is what he did back in Houston when life became unpleasant. He ignored it. Charles would pretend a fight with Jenna or a failed exam did not exist, and the situation faded away like a bad dream. Life moved on.

These nightmares, though, would not slip away. He turned them over and over in his mind, trying to interpret the symbolism, something he'd found himself struggling to do in his required art history and literature classes in college. Jenna had helped him with those classes, though.

He had been selfish, abandoning her like that. If he had simply left a note behind, or taken the time to call her, she would still be alive. Jenna was dead because him, because of some psychic dream.

Maybe if he slept he would have another dream, and when he woke up it would all make sense.

The door creaked open. A sliver of light illuminated Desiree's face.

Charles reluctantly turned his head and saw Rick standing in the doorway.

"I can take the next watch," Rick said.

"I plan on sleeping here. I'm fine."

Rick walked in, and sat on the edge of Desiree's bed.

"You know," he began, a coy smile on his face. "You're a lot like Desiree. Dreams and stuff."

"A lot of good those have done me." The flatness of his own voice was strange to him.

Rick pursed his lips. "Can you do anything else?"

Charles was confused. Did he mean like the things Desiree's mother could do?

"Not that I know of," Charles answered. "Can Desiree do other...things?"

"Didn't you see her voodoo-witch shop downstairs?"

"Yeah, but I've never seen..." Charles paused, and Rick's face crooked up into a smirk.

He continued. "Desiree did something once. She put up a protection spell or something, and I could *feel* it. The same day, when the mayor was killed...I don't know. I've had visions. They come over me like a fog and I can't control them." He remembered bits of his vision of the shack and the strange sounds he'd heard, images he'd seen as he was brought to the river. A shivered crept up his spine. "It's like I'm dreaming, but I'm awake. Does that count?"

"Hell, yeah, that counts." Rick gave him a peculiar look.

"Well, no. I can't do anything like what Desiree can do. Spells, magic, trances. I can't control any of it."

"Maybe you should try."

Charles laughed, thinking it was a joke, but Rick had a serious expression on his face.

"Did Desiree ever tell you how she learned it all?" Rick asked.

"I don't think so."

"She wanted to know who her mother was. See, Jon didn't talk about Marie much, and if he did it was in crazy Oracle talk. So, it's kind of tradition to go to the Oracle for the first time when you turn sixteen. Not everyone does it that way, though, but Desiree did. And when Desiree went, she made that her official request, to know who Marie was." Rick paused. "The Oracle said something about mothers and daughters and secrets and all that, and it gave Desiree her mother's powers. She started doing some weird shit, man. She was hearing things, seeing things. She woke up one morning in Sunset Park. Not a clue how she got there. Then, she started having these dreams of swamps and cotton fields and drums. So she ran away in the middle of December. Came knocking on my window that night to see if I'd go with her to New Orleans. Maybe I should have. She figured if she went there she would find out how to control all that psychic clairvoyant shit."

Rick took a breath, lost in his memories.

"And?" Charles urged.

"Everyone in town was talking about it, but Jon said that she'd come back. I don't know if it is the best thing or the worst thing in the world to have your own dad bein' an Oracle priest. Anyway, I got a letter from her in June telling me she was pregnant."

"Desiree has a child?"

"Nope," he said, shaking his head. "That letter just said, '*Gave him up for adoption. Figured it all out. Be home soon.*' She got back about a month or so after that. Hardly said a word about it, but everybody knew she was a witch after that. Just her aura, I suppose, and she could do that evil eye thing." With a sinister look on his face, he jabbed two fingers in the air towards Charles. "She always knew who was calling her phone. This was back before Caller I.D. and cell phones and shit. She knew when someone needed a sleeping tonic or creepy accurate advice. At first she went to them, but then they all started going to her. Paid her for it, too. Soon she had a thriving business. Well, for her lifestyle anyway. Point being…see what all you can do."

Rick stood and made his way towards the door.

"Okay," Charles said. "Why aren't you and Desiree together?" He smirked. "I don't have to be psychic to see you two got a thing."

Rick chuckled. "'Cause," he said, shrugging, "we do

have a good thing. If it ain't broke, don't fix it."

***

Charles was not sure when he had fallen asleep. When he awoke, he could hear people talking in the living room.

"You're a…what now?" That was Rick's voice.

"A Valkyrie," said the doctor. "So, Skadi, how's Odin?"

"Enjoying his retirement," Mrs. Claus answered. "Thank you very much."

"I'm sure he really appreciates giving out toys to snot-nosed ungrateful little brats."

"Christmas miracles can happen when one lays off the mead, but how would you know, you hovering little vulture?"

"How dare you! You steal the Great All Father from his throne and call *that* a miracle?"

"I stole nothing."

Charles rubbed his eyes, and pushed himself out of the armchair. He flung the door open and it hit the wall with a thud.

The room fell silent. They were all standing around glaring at each other, their stress levels maxed out, teetering on the verge of a brawl.

"Everyone, this is Mrs. Claus." He gestured towards

the old woman, and then looking at the doctor, he asked, "And you are?"

Mrs. Claus answered for her. "A vulture. She feeds off the souls of the dead."

"No," the blonde doctor snapped. "I take worthy warriors to the Grand Hall of Valhalla...or I used to."

"So, she is waiting around for you all to die. That is why she's here. Not to help any of you…or Desiree."

"You simple-minded giant." The doctor glared.

"Shut up," Charles said. "Friend or foe?"

"Friend." The pretty doctor sounded insulted.

Mrs. Claus tutted.

"All right then. We're all friends. So why are we fighting?"

"That hag reduced the great Odin, gave him a glass eye, and domesticated him into a fat, jolly old elf!"

"Our problem," said Amanda, who sat looking bored on the couch, "is not with Santa Claus or a Norse god. It's with a psychotic voodoo Loa who is trying to steal a magic Oracle and take over the world...just saying. So can the mythological creatures please put aside their archaic grievances for a short while to help us mere mortals?"

"Well said," mumbled Robert.

"We're going to help you," replied the Valkyrie.

"That's why we're here, isn't it?" Mrs. Claus asked the vulture.

"Yes," she snarled.

"It's not just the Loa," said Charles. "It's a whole horde of pissed off pagan gods trying to get back into this world." He looked at the Valkyrie and Mrs. Claus. "Why?"

Mrs. Claus sighed, and eased down into an armchair. "Mind if I smoke?"

Every human in the room eyed her in horror, as if their childhoods had just been crushed and tainted.

She shrugged and pulled out a pack of cigarettes from the pocket of her cotton dress. The tip lit up by itself, and she took a long drag. She blew the smoke out and began to speak.

"Our worlds and yours were separated many aeons ago by beings far more powerful than gods. Used to be, one could slip back and forth like that," she snapped her fingers. "Now, it's a lot more difficult. There are customs and paperwork and miles of red tape to cross before one is allowed to pass back and forth. It makes it hard for us pagan gods to intervene. Yeah, sure, there are rituals and prayers and meditations humans can use to contact us, but it's easier said than done. Very few have that kind of sturdy dedication like back in the old days, men and gods alike. It used to be a way of life." She ashed her cigarette into a coffee cup on the table. "So, back then when the veils dropped, many chose to either stay here or there…this world or that. Many took on other roles here like Santa Claus, or familiars, or rock stars, or doctors, trying to keep to their nature." She winked at the Valkyrie. "There are lots of us spirit folk meandering in plain sight. Others, though, got trapped on one side or the other and want to leave. But like I said, miles of red tape and visas, so they try to make shortcuts and cheat the system like our Loa friend."

"Not our friend," Amanda said with a glare.

"No, I suppose not." Mrs. Claus dropped her cigarette into the cold, stale coffee.

"How many of them are there, these other gods?" asked the Valkyrie, her tone approaching civil for the first time.

"Plenty enough," Mrs. Claus answered. "Many of them stopped by our place on their way in to say *hello* to the old All Father and me, and to see if we wanted to join their efforts. Let's just say they were less than pleased when he told them how awfully busy he would be over the next six months."

The Valkyrie huffed.

"Wait." Amanda's eyes narrowed. "You said 'on their way in' meaning that some of the gods that were here all along joined him too? They want to return?"

"Some of us don't enjoy laying low, playing human, as some call it. They want their old power back to control the seasons…and destiny, war, and love. They want to be worshiped. When the veils dropped, nothing was the same after that. We weren't the same."

"So what the hell do we do about it?" Pat got up from the couch and began to pace the floor.

Mrs. Claus and the Valkyrie were silent.

"We must *put the gods to rest*," Charles replied, remembering Clermeil's words, remembering what the Oracle had said. He wanted to go back to sleep, to dream in hope of finding some answers. Or maybe he wanted to wake up in Houston with Jenna next to him. He had not missed her this entire time and now that she was gone, he could not stop missing her. It was a pain far worse than his ribs being crushed by steel-toed boots, a pain worse than brass shattering his femur. It was an agony living inside his entire being…a wish to undo it all, to rewind time and not be that stupid kid looking for adventure. An aching dread inside his soul reminded him that no matter how much he wished it, Jenna would be gone forever.

Her parents did not know. Her brother did not know. And he had to tell them. He had to be the one to tell them he watched her commit suicide, but he could not tell them why. He had to admit it was his fault she died because she went looking for him, because he ran away looking for answers. But now he did not care about the truth. He wanted Jenna *alive.*

A mist began to creep over his vision. The world began to blur.

Charles was freezing. In the room around him there were metal sinks and metal tables and metal instruments. The walls were steel with many little metal doors stacked one upon the other. The tile beneath his feet was as cold as ice.

Someone was humming a dirge he had heard when the mayor fell, and when he himself had nearly drown. Someone was taking their lives as a sacrifice, as payment. One of the little doors in the wall opened and a cold mist seeped out from the darkness within.

A metal table slid out from the opening.

And as if he had been there the whole time, a mortician pulled the shroud off the face of the girl on the metal slab. Her golden hair lay flatly around her mangled head. Her lifeless blue eyes looked up at the ceiling, seeing nothing.

Charles was afraid. He was so afraid of loss.

There was a toll to pay. One sacrifice away. The apple had to be eaten. True love's arrows would nearly destroy him. The king must be beaten or the kingdom would fall, and down would come Charlie, cradle and all.

The mortician covered the dead girl's face, and pushed her back into the black void behind the door. The remaining wisps of mist vanished.

"Charles?"

He did not know how he'd ended up on his knees. He was shaking and cold.

"Give him some air." The doctor hovered over him. For a moment he saw that she had giant wings upon her back, but then the image vanished. "Can you hear me, Charlie?"

"Yes. I'm sorry."

"Don't be."

"They killed Jenna. She's dead."

"I know."

"Is she in Van Halen or whatever?"

The Valkyrie smiled. "Valhalla? I couldn't tell you. I haven't been to the Great Hall in a long time."

Charles looked around the room. Amanda and Mrs. Claus sat nearby looking on with great concern.

He covered his eyes with both hands, wishing he could forget the vision he'd just seen.

"Where's Pat and Rick and Robert?"

"You were out for a minute before you hit the floor, weren't you?" the doctor asked. "You don't remember?"

He shook his head.

"They went to the station, dear." Mrs. Claus blinked. "To...do something about Jenna."

"Oh."

"You told them to do what they needed to do, gum-drop."

"He's been through a lot, so can't we just let him sleep?" Amanda asked.

"Sweety, we still need to know what happened to him before I found him." Mrs. Claus smiled. "How about some peppermint hot chocolate, Charles? Oh, that's right, you don't like it. How about some tea?"

The Valkyrie scoffed. "How about a drink?"

She helped him up with ease. She was much stronger than the average doctor, and he liked the medicine she called *mead*. It was sweet, like honey, but he was drunk before his third glass, and he told them everything, starting with the panther from his childhood and then about his dreams and about meeting Wile E. He rambled for hours.

And when he arrived at the part about Jenna, Amanda helped to fill in the gaps Charles did not remember. However, Amanda had not seen anyone sitting at the tables across the street, let alone a boy in a black suit.

Charles then began to tell them about the woods and Steve and Brandon. He noticed Amanda rummaging through her purse to find her phone. He figured she was texting Robert. He told them about the shack and Marie and the panther.

"Marie called you *Dastan*?" Mrs. Claus eyed him.

"Yeah." Charles went to drink more of the sweet nectar from his glass, and found it empty.

The Valkyrie smirked, and took his glass away. "I think you've had your fill."

"Well, *Dastan*," Mrs. Claus said, "is that your middle name?"

"Yeah, weird, right? So then the panther bit me. Drug me away by my leg outta the shack into nothing and then...I woke up."

"Charles Dastan Garrett. Nice ring to it." Amanda smiled.

"Right, so, then I woke up, an' the panther growled at me every time I moved, an' I wasn't tied up anymore, then it screamed, an' I had another dream—"

"Dastan?" Mrs. Claus interrupted him.

"What?"

"Oh, never mind, continue." Mrs. Claus smiled to herself.

Charles rambled on, "I remembered the panther was actually good, because it helped me when I was little, and everything was all gold'n'shiney in the pine forest—"

"Wait." The doctor interrupted, having caught the secret smile. With her obvious dislike of Mrs. Claus returning, she asked, "*Skadi*, what were you going to say?"

"Now's not a good time." Mrs. Claus brushed her off.

"Why not?" the Valkyrie sneered.

The old lady gritted her teeth. "Because. I. Said. So."

"You're going to end up on the naughty list." Charles laughed drunkenly. The Valkyrie did not look amused. "Sorry."

"I have an idea," the doctor offered, contentiously, "why don't you tell me now, and when it's a better time for *you*, you can tell the whole gang."

Amanda rolled her eyes at their squabbling, and then looked at Charles. "I'm going to go check on Desiree."

"Meeee too." He stood, and the world began to spin. He slowly followed Amanda into Desiree's bedroom and collapsed into his usual armchair. Thunder rolled across the sky for the first time in hours. The room was dark and still.

"Charles, I'm worried."

"You had another emotion!" He began to giggle. "Oh, shit, I'm sorry. That was…"

"About you, dumbass."

"Oh. Me?"

"Yes, you. You're the threat! They tried to get you out of the way. Then they tried to kill you, and now that you're not dead…" She sighed. "Why? Why do they want you? He said you were the one destined to send them back. And there is how many of them? And look at what they've done to us already.

They've killed people. They have Brandon and Steve under their thrall."

"*Thrall*?" He giggled again. "Sorry."

"They thought they killed you and look," she grabbed his chin and forced him to look at Desiree sound asleep on her bed. "You traded yourself for Desiree, and they didn't give her back, which means they know you survived, or they were going to kill you both anyway."

He nodded.

"Why?" She looked him up and down. "What are you?"

"Dunno. Let's do a spell!" His southern drawl was at full strength.

Her nose crinkled and she threw her hands out. "What?"

"You and I should go down to Desiree's reading room, and get Desiree back. Chant something out of *Charmed* or *Buffy* and hope it works."

"Well, that sounds dumb."

"No, it doesn't. Okay, maybe it's dumb, but do you have a better idea? I can't keep sitting around being scared and waiting and hoping I have some goddamn prophetic dream, because you know what, all they do is give us riddles…riddles only Desiree can solve. They did good taking our queen off the chessboard. Well, whether they think I'm dead or not, we're going to show'em we ain't pawns. We're going to show'em why their prophecy said they should be scared."

Amanda crossed her arms and pursed her lips. "How?"

"With…with a spell to…to get Desiree back."

"You're drunk, Charles."

"So?"

"Okay, so," Amanda looked around the room, "down the fire escape?"

"I have *always* wanted to do that."

Amanda creaked open the window. The springs squeak-
ed a little at first, but then the bottom half glided up with ease.
The fire escape was rusted and slick, and for a moment they
had second thoughts. Despite his drunkenness, Charles went
first…one foot after the other out the window onto the old metal
structure. It was more stable than he expected, and he held out a
hand to help Amanda through the window.

At the end of the ladder they had a short drop of only a
few feet, and there at the side of the building was the back door
to the psychic shop. The lock had been busted from when Robert
had kicked it in. Charles and Amanda crept into Desiree's lair.

It had a certain atmosphere about it due to the stereotypical accessories Desiree had added…the glass ball, the roots,
the mirrors. But there was also an actual aura to it that Charles

could feel on his skin. It was like silk running down the back of his neck and his arms.

"Do you think they heard us?"

"Probably not. Or maybe they did and they're pretending to let us get away with it anyway."

She shrugged. "So, uh...how do we do this?"

"Light some candles? Go into a trance?"

They nodded in agreement, and went about in search of candles, which were easy enough to find. Finding a lighter was another story. Amanda found some matches in a drawer under an altar, and began lighting the candles in the tall candlesticks next to her. Charles crept up behind her and examined the altar, which was covered with cutouts of obituaries, candies, pennies, dry leaves, and shells. And there was a picture. The photo was of a woman he'd met in his dreams.

"That's Marie," Charles whispered, reaching for the picture.

Amanda slapped his hand away before he could pick it up. "Don't touch it."

"Why?"

"I don't know. It just seems wrong, I guess." They looked at each other for a moment. "So that's her, huh?"

"Yeah. I feel this...I don't know...connection with her every time I dream of her. It's powerful."

"Didn't you say in your dream that her voice was the Oracle's voice or something?"

"She said, '*I am the Oracle. I speak for her now. My daughter.*'"

"Do you think *she*…?"

"She said, '*I gave my soul to the well,*' so yeah. She's at least a part of the Oracle. Maybe that was her sacrifice."

"Christ. What was mine?"

Charles looked at her.

"You know…my sacrifice? I don't think I did anything *sacrificial* enough to be able to *feel* again."

Charles took the box of matches from her and began to light a set of candles on the other side of the altar. "Well, opening up to the truth about your folks, accepting what happened, accepting that they didn't mean to abandon you…forgiving them for leaving. That's hard. I'd say that's a worthy sacrifice."

"Yours wasn't fair."

Charles felt his buzz from the alcohol wear off suddenly. An uncomfortable ache settled in his chest. He waved the match around to put out the flame. The ancestral altar was illuminated with light.

"I don't know if that was a sacrifice or a," Charles gritted his teeth, "*necessary casualty.*"

Amanda couldn't know what he meant by that, but

she reached out and touched his hand. His head fell onto her shoulder. He tried to hold back the tears.

"She came here to save me…to take me home." He caved, and the tears fell. "It's *my* fault."

"No. No, it's not. I know how you feel, and do you remember what you told me?" She lifted his chin. "Sometimes life doesn't make any sense. It's not fair and it hurts like hell, and you can't control it. You can't change it. It's not your fault."

"I don't believe that, though."

"You believed it when you said it to me. Were you lying when you told me that?"

Amanda wiped the tears off his cheek.

"No."

She squeezed his hand, and then sat cross-legged on the floor. "Wanna try to save Desiree?"

He sat down in front of her. "I don't know how to do this."

"You acted like you knew before you began sobering up." She grabbed his hands, and closed her eyes. "I guess we chant, right?"

"Er…I guess." He sniffed and blinked the last of his tears away, closing his eyes. He swallowed hard, and took a deep, shaky breath.

"Say something." Amanda nudged him with her knee.

"Um…Marie, come to me. Take me to where I need to be?"They both opened their eyes. "Like…take-me-to-Desiree's-spirit sort of thing," Charles clarified.

"Will that work?"

Charles shrugged, and they both closed their eyes again.

"Marie, come to me. Take me where I need to be."

"Marie, take him. Marie, take him. Marie, take him." Amanda added.

They repeated the words over and over until they mingled and became a chant.

Take him. Marie, come to me. Take him, Marie.

Take me where I need to be. Take him. Take me.

Take me where I need to be.

Marie. Marie. Marie. Marie…

A mist began to creep across Charles's mind.

"My, son…"

***

Charles stood on a street corner, squinting in the blinding sun. Across from him was a building lined with doors one right after the other. It looked as if the wall of doors was without end, until his eyes adjusted to the blazing sun, and Charles realized it was a motel – The Days Inn. He had stayed there when he first arrived in Tell City.

One of the doors had light bursting and beaming from around its frame. He walked towards it, moving effortlessly as though he were mist or smoke. He was dreaming, he realized. His body was with Amanda. He knew she would guard it well.

The parking lot was filled with beautiful, gleaming cars – all luxurious and expensive. The chariots of the gods.

As he approached the door, the blinding light vanished. It was Room 126.

Charles was not sure whether he should knock or just enter. He placed his hand on the door handle, and it slipped right through, as if he were a ghost. Hand outstretched, Charles stepped forward through the door and into the motel room.

Clermeil sat in a chair stirring the contents of a plastic cup with his pinky. Cupid was stretched out lazily on the bed. He puffed on a thin cigar, and exhaled smoke rings in the shape of hearts with arrows through them. The thick and curvy woman, who had been standing in the alley behind the psychic shop a few days before, was arguing her case to Clermeil. Charles now knew her to be Strife, or Discordia, the sender of the Golden Apple. Though she spoke very curtly with the Loa, Charles could not make out what she was saying. Her voice faded in and out beneath a buzz of white noise.

The bathroom door opened and a pale man with wire-rimmed glasses stepped out. Though there was blood on his lips and his neck, and his trousers were sticky with it, he was cleaning off his hands with a white motel towel. Charles could not hear him either as he politely intruded upon the current conversation. Clermeil waved a hand, and the gentleman, who Charles knew to be Xipe Totec, retreated back into the bathroom. He was performing a ritual sacrifice for the good harvest of their venture, and Charles knew that was not something he wanted to see.

Another goddess rested against the air conditioning unit, which was on full blast, by the window. Charles knew her to be Yuki-Onna, Snow Queen, and this heat was making her impatient.

There was another man who had his chair pulled into the front corner of the room away from the group. He appeared old, wrinkled, and dirty. His hair was white and wiry. His filmy eyes were a misty blue-grey and his clothes were tattered, stained and torn. He sat in his chair with legs spread, fingers laced, and his eyes distant. He said not one word, moved not one inch.

Then Charles heard a thud beneath the white noise. It sounded like an effect you would hear when you were at the bottom of a swimming pool. The sound vibrates all around you. It came again and again. Then he heard the sound of screams underwater, muffled and strangled. Charles had heard that noise before.

Against the wall was a dresser, and like other motel dressers it functioned as a TV stand, or in this case, an altar table. The altar was set up before the mirror, but the glass was shrouded with a bed sheet. The items adorning the altar were much like those kept on Desiree's, but these bones and shells and gri-gri bags were old and powerful. A thick red line of dust was placed in front of the mirror. Brick dust, Charles realized, only real brick dust, unlike what Desiree had thrown together.

Buuummp. Thuuump. Thuuump.

The noise came from the mirror. Charles reached out his shaking hand to pull the sheet away, to see what lay behind it where a reflection should be. He was only inches away from touching the sheet when he felt a scorching heat, as if he had just touched a hot stove. Charles flinched away, and examined the smoke rising off his blackened flesh with fear and awe. The brick dust was keeping him from the mirror; it was also keeping something in the mirror.

"She's at it again, Loa." Yuki-Onna let out a sigh.

He could hear them now. He wondered if they could hear him.

Clermeil pushed himself out of his chair and squeezed his way between the bed and Strife. "Pardon me, darlin'." He glowered at the mirror as he stormed over to it.

Charles was frozen in fear, like a child hiding under the sheets, praying and pleading not to be seen or heard by the monsters in the room. Clermeil stepped right through him. For a moment in time they shared the same space. Charles let out the breath he'd been holding, as Clermeil reached for the sheet.

"Clermeil?" said the old man in the corner, and Clermeil stopped. The Ferryman's voice was gravely and harsh, and it rang

with an almost terrifying authority that even Clermeil heeded to,
though begrudgingly.

"Yes, Charon?" he asked through bared teeth.

The Ferryman stood up slowly from his chair. "I thought you
said you killed the boy?"

"Dastan? Or, Charles," he corrected, "Yes, I did. Why?"
Clermeil turned to face the old man as the thumping on the other side
of the mirror began again.

Charon laughed and rocked back onto his heels. "If that be the
case, then why would 'e be standin' right o'er there next to ye?"

Cupid, interested now, started to sit up on the bed.

Yuki-Onna raised her hand. In a wave of fabric and snow and
ice, Charles felt himself being split in two. He felt his body jar and saw
Amanda reach for him. He felt his mist-like self tremble. Both sides
were being ripped and pulled, forced into one, until the snow settled,
and he was staring dead into the eyes of the Loa.

Charles backed away from Clermeil and Yuki-Onna as
they reached for him, and he fell backwards into the altar on
the dresser. Shells and bones and candles scattered everywhere,
and the line of brick dust was broken.

"No!" Clermeil pinned Charles to the altar. The Loa
reached around him and ripped away the sheet from the mirror.
Charles tilted his head back to see Desiree, floating in a sea of
muddy water, her hands pressed up to the glass.

"Desiree?" Charles tried to turn around, but Clermeil slammed his back down onto the dresser.

Desiree's eyes glinted with power and a hint of pride as she dissipated into light, vanishing from the mirror.

Clermeil's fingers seized Charles's T-shirt and ripped him up to eye level.

"Now you really are trading yourself for Desiree, aren't you?"

Charles grinned. "Maybe if your magic was more than just dirt..."

Everyone was standing now, even Cupid.

The bathroom door opened and the man with the wire-rimmed glasses stepped out. "I suppose that means I'm not quite finished in here then, am I?"

"Why, Totec, what an excellent idea."

"No," Charles heard himself say, as the Loa grabbed him by the arm like a petulant child and dragged him to the bathroom.

"The witch, Desiree, will be awake soon, and coming after him. Let's speed things along, shall we?" All the other gods, except Charon, vanished from the living room. Charon sat back down in his chair as thunder cracked across the sky. Clermeil pushed Charles through the open door of the bathroom.

Charles's boots slipped on something wet and he fell. The floors, the walls, the sink, and the tub were dripping with blood. Sheets of flayed human flesh hung off the towel racks. The trash can and toilet bowl were filled with entrails. Charles looked up at the two men. Even Clermeil grimaced at the state of the bathroom.

"Find out how he's still alive, will you?" Clermeil sneered, and the Aztec god nodded. "Oh, and Totec, don't kill him yet. I have plans for this one."

"As you say." The Aztec god picked up a strange ritual dagger from off the counter. The handle of the knife was solid gold and it was decorated with hieroglyphs. The blade was polished black obsidian. It reflected the room around it like a black mirror.

Clermeil left, closing the door.

"Get in the tub or I'll put you in there in pieces."

"You can't kill me." Charles stood, weighing his chances of getting to the door.

Xipe Totec chuckled, and glided up to Charles. He put the point of his knife on the soft flesh under Charles's eye. Charles gulped and tried to steady his breathing.

"Oh, hail! The things one can live through." He moved the knife down Charles's face, down his neck, to his chest. "Do you know how long a human can live once their heart has been

                    Kaylin R. Boyd

ripped out? An average of three minutes and forty-five-point-six seconds, and that's from shock, but the heart *will go on* for quite some time after you are gone. It's a beautiful thing, really, the human heart. And just think! The things I can do to you. I am a god, you know? I can take it out, and put it back in. And take it out. And shove it back in again. Do you know which god I am?"

Charles was backed up to the tub. He glanced down at the stained porcelain, dripping with red.

"Harvest and regeneration. I can, technically, reap you all I want, just as long as I put you back together before Mommy comes home from the market. Got it? Now, get in."

***

Desiree awoke screaming, and surrounded by people.

She tried to ease her ragged breathing and racing heart, while understanding her surroundings. All eyes were upon her.

"Back off!" she barked.

Everyone stood back.

Desiree sat up, ripping her fingers through her hair.

"Desiree, baby, you okay?" asked Rick, on his knees beside her bed.

"No," she answered. "Shit." She rubbed the bridge of

her nose, and tried to remember what she'd been dreaming about. It was something important.

Amanda whispered, "Desiree, you were asleep…"

"I know." She rubbed a kink out of her neck. "What I don't know is…who are these people?" She was looking at Robert and the Valkyrie and Mrs. Claus.

"Long story," Pat answered. "We're just glad you're awake. A lot's happened."

"Yeah. Where's Dastan?" She suddenly remembered everything. "I mean, Charles. Where's my—"

Amanda swallowed hard. "He vanished."

"When you two idgits did a goddamn voodoo ritual!" Robert growled.

"It wasn't my fault!" Amanda yelled. "And I said I was sorry, okay?"

"Wait," Desiree interrupted, "you guys did a ritual? For what?"

"You."

She smiled. "Good job, Amanda. It worked."

Amanda's eyes lit up.

"How long ago?" Desiree asked.

"Two hours."

"Shit!" Desiree flew off the bed and headed towards the living room. "We've got to go. We have to go now. I know where he is." She stopped in the doorway of the bedroom, and gave Mrs. Claus a quizzical look, "And...uh...tell me everything on the way?"

"Of course, dear. Where are we going?"

"The Days Inn. Room 126."

Mrs. Claus laid a finger aside her nose, and they all stood in the parking lot of the motel. Aside from an empty blue beat up pickup with a South Dakota license plate, the parking lot was deserted.

Desiree did not stop to understand how they got there. She grabbed the door handle and tried to rip open the door, kicking it and screaming at it until Rick pulled her away.

"Baby, come on. That ain't doin' no good."

"*They took him.*" Desiree freed herself from Rick's grasp and continued to throw herself against the door. This time both Pat and Robert had to pull her away.

"It's no good." A voice said from behind them. " We tried. The room's empty...Even the bathroom's gone...which is weird." Sitting in the bed of the once empty blue pickup were six tanned, dark-haired men.

"And you are...?" asked the Valkyrie.

"The name's Wile E. I'm a friend of that kid you're looking for. Kind of scruffy. Kind of lost. Goes by the name Charles. Horrible name." The man jumped out of the bed of the pickup. "These are my brothers. Bugs, Smokey, Tiny, Buzzy, and Jack."

"Hiya." Buzzy waved at them.

"Really?" asked Amanda. "No. Wait. Charles said Wile E. was a woman?"

"She lost a bet," Bugs said gleefully in his high-pitched voice, and Wile E. grimaced.

Mrs. Claus spoke up. "I know them. They're fine. They're here to help...most likely."

"And who are you again?" Desiree looked at the little old lady with the hessian boots.

Rick scratched the side of his nose. "Desi, that's...uh... Skadi...Mrs. Claus."

She stared at him, and he nodded.

Wile E. walked up to them. "So, where's the man-child? I'm kind of supposed to be looking after him, I guess."

"The Loa has him," Amanda said.

"Great." He rubbed the back of his neck. "Grandpa's not going to be happy with that one. So, we don't know where he ran off to now, huh?"

"No." Desiree shook her head, and wrapped her arms around herself.

"Well, we'll find him." Wile E. started to head back to the truck. "Why don't you lot head towards your priest before the roads sink. We'll catch up with you later."

The man walking away from them turned into a coyote. A crow flew off the roof of the truck. Jack lowered the tailgate and a rabbit and a bear climbed down out of the bed. A small spider slipped down to the ground on a thread of gossamer, and they all went different ways.

"I should help them," said the Valkyrie.

"No," said Robert. "I think we're going to need you for this."

***

"You know," said Totec, kneeling on the floor and bending over the edge of the tub, "I don't look like my people. They imagined us, their gods, as fair ones. So when the Spaniards came across the oceans on their ships of famine and pestilence and blonde hair, my people thought they were gods.

"Fools, though I love them. Fools, and not just the Aztecs. I was adopted into that family. So I took on this visage. A pretty, golden Spaniard. I'm a people pleaser. They ask for blood, I give them blood. They ask for blonde and fair, I give it to them. They ask for my presence to return in my former glory, how can I refuse?

"I'm not the only god like that. Clermeil, his people

viewed him as a white man, and so he became one. Us gods, we work for our worshipers. They give to us, as we must give to them."

He sat down on the edge of the tub and cleaned the blood off the handle of his ritual blade. "Greeks and Romans did it, too. They saw the blonde hair and smelled the floral fragrance of the northerners, and thought they were gods. So their pantheon became fair and pretty. And then that became the image of angels as well, which I thought unfair. Angels aren't like us. They don't serve their worshipers, no. They serve their *God*, and what does He do? Condemn all of *our* followers to his hell and his purgatory. No."

Totec knelt before the tub again, and Charles screamed, thrashing and kicking, as the god commenced his ritual work. Blood splattered the shower curtain. "We weren't going to let that happen, but out of fear they began to believe and abide Him. The Christians came to our people and brought their horsemen with them. They told my people they'd be saved if only they filled their soul with Jesus. Good marketing." He paused. "But that God, He can't come here like we can, can He? And it's hard enough for us with all the red tape. His angels can, but as warriors of God, not servers of humanity. They can't and won't adapt and give people what we give."

Charles's whimpers turned into a deafening cry. Totec

smiled, and brought a piece of Charles's flesh up to his mouth to eat it.

"And He killed His own son," he said, his mouth full. "That's a sin. But, oh, how I digress! The point is we aren't - nothing is - quite as it seems. We have masks, shrouds, costumes, and you seem like a young, succulent, human, mortal man...but you're not, are you? You certainly don't taste human. No, *you've* got something in you. Tell me what it is, what you really are, and I'll stop. Simple as that." Totec rested his elbows on the edge of the tub, his hands dripping with blood. Charles continued to whimper. "Still don't know, huh? Hmm…"

There came a knock on the bathroom door. "One moment," the Aztec god called. He reached up, and on the backsplash of the tub, he drew a symbol with Charles's blood. He pressed his palm against the symbol, and Charles let out a muffled scream as all of his organs and flesh grew back.

"You can come in now, Clermeil." The door opened, but instead of the motel room, it was a dark and rainy wood.

Clermeil grimaced as he glanced into the bathroom. "We've safely moved elsewhere, Totec. Give us a minute if you would?"

"As you say." Totec stood, and pushed his glasses up the bridge of his nose. He placed his ritual dagger in its spot on the sink and left.

Clermeil came into the bathroom and walked over to the tub. The Loa of flooding waters looked ill as he peered down at the bound and bent young man covered in blood. He stooped over and removed the gag made of intestines from Charles's mouth.

"I've had enough of this, Dastan, as I'm sure you have. This is hardly a fair fight, don't you think? Even I have my limits. This is…" Clermeil looked away. "How did you live? You gave yourself to the water. You were in my grasp when you went limp."

Charles slipped as he tried to sit up in the tub. Blood splattered and landed on Clermeil's face. As stoically as he could, he wiped it off.

Charles panted. "I was saved. I was saved by a black panther."

"A panther?"

"Yes."

"That is the most ridiculous thing I have ever heard." Clermeil began to walk away.

"It's true. I swear to God it's true."

Clermeil stopped and turned around. "I wouldn't go swearing to Him around here, Dastan." He laughed. "You're bound to get another lecture."

"Why do you keep calling me that? Why does everyone

keep calling me that?" Charles tried to stop shivering, but couldn't.

"Because that is your name."

Charles looked at him with squinted eyes. "It's my middle name."

"The gods know you as *Dastan*."

"What did you mean when you said you had plans for me? Why do you think I'm the one in your damned prophecy? Prophecies are kind of vague. It could be anyone! Why do you think it's me?"

"They gave me your name, Dastan." Clermeil leaned forward. "We don't have Oracles on our side of the fence. We have three useless, bitter hags that call themselves Fate. They warned me of you, but they never told me that I could use you." A smile slid across Clermeil's lips that could have wooed a serpent.

Charles's eyes narrowed.

"Can't pick up and carry away the Oracle. It's an essence, but that is why I found Marie. Something in her blood made her a perfect vessel for such an immense energy. But she's gone, and you and Desiree, why, you're her blood."

Charles shook his head, uncertain if he'd heard him correctly. "What?"

"Neither of your mommies told you? Child, Desiree

handed you over to social services the moment you were born. She never even held you."

Charles heard Rick's voice in his head. *You're a lot like Desiree. Gave him up for adoption. See what you can do.*

"You didn't notice? You are the spitting image of Jon when he was young. The dreams. The visions. Now the question remains, who's your daddy?" Clermeil smirked.

"*Please*, tell me it's not you."

"No," Clermeil snarled. "No, it is not me. Now me and Marie, we had something special. But Desiree...we still don't know who your father is, you see. I doubt Desiree even knows. She's a little harlot, your mama. Getting knocked up and throwing you aside. But the Oracle...it could tell us. It could tell us all about you and your daddy, if you take us to it."

"No."

"I know people who can take me if you won't. Now sit tight. Don't go anywhere." Clermeil stood. "I don't need to get Monsieur Totec to babysit, do I?"

Charles said nothing.

"Good."

Clermeil walked out of the bathroom, and as he closed the door it vanished, leaving a blank wall in its place.

***

They were soaking wet and covered in mud by the time they reached the spot where the tiny little shack stood.

"I wish we could have used magic to get us here," groaned Amanda as they crossed the meadow. "Magic should make things easier, not more complicated."

"When has magic ever made anything easier?" Robert scowled at the little shack.

Mrs. Claus trod through the mud and the field with perfect ease. "When you have to deliver Christmas spirit to every man, woman, and child who believes…all in one night."

"And, conveniently, you choose one of the longest nights of the year," quipped the Valkyrie.

"It's called 'opportune timing.'"

"No." The Valkyrie smirked. "It's called 'cheating.'"

Pat mumbled under his breath, and quickened his pace to escape the constant bickering. He reached the door to the shack, and raised his hand to knock, but the door creaked open.

"Sheriff." The blind priest smiled at him as he stood in the doorway. "It's been so long. Fifteen years, hasn't it? Come in. You'll catch your death out there." Pat entered, and Desiree followed. "Ah…Desiree, you slept well?"

"Not in the slightest." She squeezed his arm.

Her father had turned sixty-five that spring, and his age was beginning to show. His always cautious movements seemed even slower now. The grey in his hair was beginning to conquer the brown, especially in the stubble on his face. His personality, however, had not changed. Even as a little girl, Desiree remembered him being a gentle and wise soul, seemingly wiser and older than the grandmother who had raised her when she was not staying in the shack with her father.

"Mrs. Claus, what a pleasure." Jon clasped her hand as she entered. "Welcome, welcome. I've never had so many people here all at once. I don't know how we'll all fit. Oh! And who's this? The last Valkyrie?"

"Dad," Desiree began once everyone was inside, "please tell me you know what's going on."

"I do, and I'm sorry I can't offer anyone a seat, but feel free to claim a spot on the dirt floor as your own."

Awkwardly, everyone sat, and listened to the wind howl around the shack.

"We, uh, appreciate it, Mr. Hart—" Pat began.

"Please, you know you can call me Jon."

"Jon, we've got big problems here. We need your help."

Jon sighed, feigning exasperation, and sat down on the one metal folding chair in the room by his card table. "You all know by now, and have been told since you were young, aside from you two perhaps," he gestured towards Mrs. Claus and the Valkyrie, "that *that* is not how any of this works."

"All right, Dad, we know." Desiree forced her voice to be calm and level. "But there are gods, plural, coming after the Oracle, and we don't have the slightest clue what to do. And…they have him, Dad." Desiree's voice cracked. Amanda, sitting next to her, reached out and squeezed her hand. Desiree squeezed back.

"I know."

"We're adults now, Jon, all grown up," Rick urged. "We need to know how this shit works, man."

Amanda looked up at Jon. "Where is the Oracle? What is it? Is it an apple or a panther or a castle? Is it just a voice inside your head or...something else?"

"Yes. I do hear the Oracle as a voice, or a whisper, like wind chimes in my head. I can see the Oracle as swirls of static and pixels in my mind. I can feel her like waves of color coursing up my spine. She'll consume me…engulf me like a tidal wave. The Oracle is not a *thing* it is an *essence*, and it is beneath you."

All seven of them looked down at the dirt floor of the shack.

"What the hell are you talkin' 'bout?" Rick looked up at the priest.

"It's in the ground," answered the Valkyrie. "Like at the

Oracle of Delphi. It's an underground river."

"In this case," added Jon, "a well."

Mrs. Claus smiled at the Valkyrie. "Mímisbrunnr." The Valkyrie squinted at her, so she clarified. "The well of Mímir. Odin's eye."

"I get it," the Valkyrie snapped.

"Well, Clermeil can control water at his will," said Desiree. "He can make it rise out of the earth like a geyser."

"It is not a thing, Desiree." Jon said. "It's an essence. It's the spirit of the well."

"Okay," Robert said, "what do we do?"

Desiree's body lurched as if electricity had pulsed through her, and she gasped.

"They're here."

The boards of the shack began to rattle and quake as the winds gusted across the field. They could just make out the emergency weather siren droning beneath the sound of the wind. Everyone stood.

"Jon Hart," Clermeil's voice cried over the wind, "would you mind coming out of your...*office* so we could have a word?"

Jon stood up slowly, as if he were older than the stars, and walked towards the door.

"Dad! No."

The blind man opened the door.

"Our fate, Desiree," he said, smiling lovingly, proudly, "is set."

The wind ripped the door from his hand and slammed it against the side of the shack. Clermeil stood out front with a host of gods behind him. There was Strife, Yuki-Onna and Cupid. There was an enchantress with flowing hair, who had a grace so effortless she appeared to be moving underwater. There was a beast following behind them with a human countenance and a feline body, which had resting on its back a set of wings. Behind the beast were two young men, adorned in camo and muck boots.

Brandon and Steve had shown Clermeil the path to the Oracle, for one can only be taken to it by those who have gone before. The two of them quickly slipped out of the meadow and into the woods.

"You must be Clermeil." Jon smiled. "My wife sends her condolences."

"Condolences?"

"Yes. She's told me this will be your last vacation here. She knows how much you love this place. Our condolences."

"Jon...Jonny. I appreciate your vim and vigor, considering your age and your condition, but I'm not going anywhere yet. However, it might be easier if *you* did."

"Mmm. I see. But this shack is not the Oracle. This is the

Oracle's throne. This is where she speaks. Not where she sleeps."

"All right, fine," Clermeil said. "Where does she sleep?"

"I cannot say."

"Then I'll kill you, old man."

"I would be honored if my death came from the hands of a god."

"But once the keeper of the well is gone, well, we can all storm the castle." The Loa's smile crept cautiously back onto his lips.

"The storm will reign, and ferry the Oracle to another plane. The floodgates will open. Where the sun does set upon the west, there The Wanderer will put the gods to rest."

"I tire of riddles."

Water began to fill Jon's lungs. It began to pour out his mouth and nose. He crumpled to his knees.

"Dad!"

In a flurry of wings and grey clouds, the Valkyrie moved Jon into the shelter of the tiny shack. Mrs. Claus hurried over to him. The Valkyrie gave her room, and Mrs. Claus tried to stop the water.

"I can't stop it."

Jon reached his hand out to her. She held it as he went limp.

Charles was slipping and sliding in the bathtub, attempting to hook his bound feet over the edge. He was tired of being
helpless. Sick of being tied up.

With the back of his knees thrown over the tub, he
worked with all of his strength to pull the rest of his body over
the edge. He slipped, and fell backwards, landing hard. Charles
groaned in frustration. He turned around in the bloody tub and
used his arms, which were bound behind his back with entrails,
to hoist himself into a sitting position on the ledge. Managing to
keep his body balanced, he brought his legs over and stood. He
looked at the place the door should be, and then at the dagger on
the sink counter.

His brain told him to walk. He tried, but immediately
lost his balance, crashing to the ground, his shoulder receiving

most of the impact. He whimpered, flopping over onto his stomach. His chin on the floor, he looked up at the knife on the sink.

Charles flipped himself around, his feet getting caught up on the base of the toilet. Pushing himself across the bathroom floor, he wedged himself so his back was pressed to the cabinet doors beneath the sink. He began to move his feet backwards, and worked himself up into a standing position. His fingers stretched behind him and felt around until they touched the cool gold handle of Xipe Totec's ritual blade. He tried to maneuver the blade to where he could saw away at his bloody binds, but the knife fumbled from his hands and landed at his feet.

Frustration and agony and panic were rushing over him. He eased his body down and crawled to the knife, his fingertips struggling behind him to position the blade against the entrails that bound him. Charles moved the blade back and forth as best as he could. He could feel the stretchy muscles starting to tear.

He smiled. "Hell, yeah!"

He could feel the slimy intestines starting to give way when the door reappeared in the wall, and Totec stepped in.

Charles's heart began to race. A bead of sweat ran down his temple.

The Aztec god pushed his glasses up the bridge of his nose. "Awake from your nap and wanting to play?"

Charles continued to work at the binds subtly and frantically. He felt the entrails tearing and stretching.

Totec bent over, unaware, and rested his hands on his knees, looking down at Charles as if he were a toddler.

"You know you're not supposed to get up out of the tub until one of us tells you to, hm?"

He crouched lower to heave Charles back into the tub.

The binds broke.

Charles seized the hilt of the blade, screaming as he brought the knife forward and ran Totec through.

The Aztec god froze. Blood trickled out of his mouth. His breathing became shallow as he stared down at Charles in disbelief.

The god's blood poured over Charles's hand. It felt warm and thick.

Magic like electricity sparked across Totec's flesh. His limp body fell on top of Charles, the dead weight feeling immense.

Totec's body swiftly began to decompose. The bowels released, the skin withered, the eyes shrunk in a matter of seconds. Charles let out a cry, pushing the decaying corpse off of him, skin and bile coming off on his hands as he did so. He scrambled to cut the binds on his feet, and flung himself at the door, afraid it would disappear again. The bathroom door opened to reveal a flooding swamp.

***

Charles did not know which direction he should run, but he sprinted forward through the murky water, washing the blood and bile off his skin and clothes as he went.

The swamp became deeper, and the current stronger. He was lost in the woods, with fear in his heart and knots in his belly. With legs that trembled like limbs in the wind, and eyes that stung as though he were staring at the summer sun, Charles fell to his knees in the water.

Above him a crow flew, and when the scavenger saw the man he landed upon a nearby tree branch. "The end is nigh, human brother," he cried. "Run to higher ground."

"Which way?" Charles asked. He knew the bird was known as Buzzy.

The crow flew away. Charles waited a long while. He replayed the memory of killing his torturer. He recalled Clermeil sitting on the edge of the bloodbath, but the words the Loa spoke were lost.

When the crow returned he had in his beak the dark round glasses of the priest. From the branch on which he perched, he dropped the glasses into Charles's hand.

"The way is rough," the crow said. "Head west."

Charles stood and headed in a westerly direction to find higher ground. As he trudged along, the water became shallower. Then the land became mud.

His parents had told him he had looked like a younger version of his grandfather. They had not lied. They just had not known how true it was. But his skin was still darker than any of theirs, adoptive or otherwise. Or maybe Clermeil was lying, but he did not know why the god would use that as a distraction.

Where the earth became softer, he stumbled upon a bear. He was not afraid. He knew the bear was known as Smokey to other spirits like him.

"Where to now?" Charles asked.

The black bear stood up straight on his back legs, and cocked his head. "Fuck if I know," he said grumpily. "We've all been running our tails off looking for you."

"Oh."

"The way I took is clear. My paws have padded down the weeds and mud," said the bear. "Follow my prints back to the path. I'm sure it will lead you to safety."

So Charles followed the way of the bear.

Getting to the well before Clermeil did was what mattered the most. Saving whoever he could, that was what mattered, especially after he could do nothing for Jenna.

When he reached the path the bear spoke of, there was a rabbit hopping down it.

"Excuse me, Mr. Rabbit. Where are you going?"

The rabbit scoffed, and said, "Oh, dear! Oh, dear! I'm late." They looked at each other for a moment, and the rabbit sighed. "The flood has begun."

"But where are you going?"

"To have tea with a mad hatter," the rabbit deadpanned.

"Oh."

"Coyote has sent us to search for you." The rabbit sat upon its haunches, and looked around. "This path will lead you to the road. I will find Jack and have him meet you there."

Then the rabbit pulled from his back a black circle and he threw it upon the ground, where it became a hole. He jumped into it, and was gone.

Charles figured that was why the animal spirits called him Bugs.

He followed the path that led to the road. On the edge of the road was a trickster, who leaned upon his staff, his broad-brimmed hat covering all of his face but his dark crooked lips. Charles knew the trickster was known as Wisakedjak, or Jack for short.

"There is a well," Jack said. "Its waters run deep

through the veins of this land. The ground pulses with its force. Brother Spider is waiting there at the well, the heart of the land. I will take you there."

"Where is Coyote?"

"Chasing his tail looking for you. Come now."

So Charles followed the trickster to the heart of the land. His heart felt still, but he did not know why.

The land's heart was an old stone well in the woods. He had seen that well in his dreams.

A tree stood near the well. A tiny spider had built an intricate web in the low-hanging branches that stretched above it.

"Hello, Dastan," said the smiling spider known as Tiny.

"Hello." He approached the spider. "This is the Oracle?"

"Wakan Tanka," answered Brother Spider.

Charles groaned. "Not that shit again."

"It is a mystery."

"Where's Coyote?" He looked back and forth between Wisakedjak and Tiny.

"Wakan Tanka," the spider repeated with joy.

Charles lowered himself to the eye level of the spider, and gave him an inquisitive look.

"So…you don't know?"

"None of us will ever know."

"Are we still talking about Coyote?"

"The keeper of the well has fallen," Jack interrupted. "Now the keepers of the land must watch the well until a new gatekeeper is appointed."

Charles glanced down at the pair of sunglasses in his hand. He set them down upon the cold stone of the well.

"You are the keepers of the land?"

Jack nodded.

"What is your sacrifice?" The spider lifted its two front legs in celebration.

Charles thought for a moment, and said, "Wakan Tanka."

Jack and the spider looked at each other.

"I don't know what I'm sacrificing. It's a mystery, isn't it? We never know what it is we are sacrificing when we set out. We never know what the cost of our actions will be, what we must pay to get what we want…if we ever even know what it is we want."

"What is it you want?" asked Tiny with a smirk.

"I want a lot of things, and a lot of them I won't get. I want Jenna to be alive. I want to go home, but I don't *want* to want to go home. I want to have never left Texas to start with, but I want to stop Clermeil." Charles looked down at his feet.

"I want to talk to Desiree, and I want...I want to know who the hell I am. I feel like I never could find where I fit. I never felt right. When I had that dream though, things started to make sense, and now I might know why that is. Maybe that's what Wile E. meant when she said she knew who I was *going* to be."

"Wile E.'s a *he* now," said Tiny.

"Huh?"

"Never mind," interrupted Jack quickly. "It doesn't matter who you are, does it? What's important is what you do. What is it you must do?"

"Defeat Clermeil."

"How?"

Before they could answer his question, a coyote came out of the trees. Its fur was speckled with different shades of white, brown, and black. The coyote bared its teeth as it trotted up. When the scavenger shifted into a man, the bared teeth transformed into a toothy grin. Wile. E. laughed a laugh that sounded like an animal's cry, and gave Charles a hug.

"You gained weight, kid. Good. You used to look like a skeleton." He pulled away, his hands on Charles's shoulders. "So, what's the plan?"

Charles remembered a priest who was not a priest speaking to him in rhyme. "*The battle though not over, will be* *nearly won, when the gods are deceived by the light of the setting sun...For you and I are to become one...*We trick them."

"How?"

"Apparently, I'm a vessel. I can take the Oracle into me...somehow. Clermeil is convinced the Oracle can help him open the gates forever, and he tried to kill me because he was told I could close them forever. I can do that if I *am* the Oracle."

The tricksters all grinned.

***

Desiree stood over her father's body, her fists clenched and her jaw set. Tears trickled out of the corners of her eyes.

"Dad," she said, swallowing hard, "you were always such a damned fool." She fell to her knees by his feet. He always wore those beat up tennis shoes, even with his slacks.

"Why? Why are you always so damn stubborn? Leave it to you to die with a smirk on your face." She smiled a bit in spite of herself. "What am I going to do without you?" Desiree let out a deep shaky breath. "You know…it was hard being your daughter. I never thought I was good enough to be the *daughter of the priest,* and it didn't help that you weren't really around." She took off his dark round glasses. "You were always out here being the voice, the prophet, the sage...instead of being my dad." She lowered her head and began to sob. "But…you knew I could handle what the Oracle gave to me. You knew I would come back home. It wasn't the Oracle that foresaw that. It was you. You always had faith in me. You distanced yourself to give me faith…not in some Oracle, not in status, not in magic, but in myself. Sometimes I wish that I had asked the Oracle to let me know you instead…"

She took in a raspy breath, and listened to the wind. "But there's a war going on, Dad, and they have my *son*…and I don't know what to do. Please…help me."

Lightning struck a tree outside the shack, and the deafening crack and brilliant illumination turned the field into a battleground. Desiree's tears fell like rain. Water began to rise from the ground pooling around Jon's body, saturating his tweed jacket. Desiree watched without fear as the dirt floor of the little shack softened and opened, and the water of the land pulled Jon's body down into the earth. The land was reclaiming its priest. Thick wet mud swallowed him down whole, until all that remained was a puddle of water.

Caw!

Desiree opened the door. A crow bobbed and danced in the doorframe. Light flashed and shot across the field. A gun fired.

Desiree set the round glasses down in the puddle. The

bird approached her, unafraid. He hopped inside and inspected his reflection in the darkness of the glasses, and then picked them up with his beak. Desiree and the crow known as Buzzy looked at each other for a moment. She knew he was giving her his condolences, which always seemed to mean more when it came from an animal. Desiree nodded to him, and he flew out the door into the storm.

***

Outside the little shack, the war was waging. Mrs. Claus pumped her twenty-gauge and tried to shoot through the whipping snow and ice that was Yuki-Onna, but to no avail. Rick charged at Strife with a new four-wheeler that Mother Christmas had materialized for him. He rammed the goddess and her body flew over his head. He spun the ATV around to face her once again.

"You know, Strife, I've been fighting you my whole life. So this? This ain't nothin'." He charged her again.

The Valkyrie flew overhead and snatched Cupid's arrows from the air before dissolving her human form into shadow.

"Damn you!" He shot at her from the edge of the tree line, aiming an arrow towards her wispy silhouette. She smiled as she snatched it from the air, and reformed into her human-like visage, her long grey wings outstretched against the shifting clouds.

"You miserable coward," she called to him. "You call yourself a martyr of love, do you? You know nothing of what it means to die with honor, to die for those you love. Your cause is weak and selfish, and you call yourself a god! You're just a boy. Faint of heart. Fickle and bitter. If you were a god, Romeo, you'd know that is exactly what love is. Love is pain, and the ability to fight through that pain so you might someday know what it is to love something greater than yourself. Crawl back to your mother, lover-boy! So she can coddle you at her Freudian bosom, and maybe give you a diaper change."

Cupid's fists clenched. His outstretched wings rivaled hers in size. They gleamed with golden feathers. He soared above her, and his arrows rained down on the soldiers below. The Valkyrie dove to catch them, and seized all but one.

The arrow pierced its way deep into Pat's heart.

"No!" cried the Valkyrie.

Pat's hand reached up slowly and pulled the arrow from his chest. He looked up with glassy eyes to see a goddess. She was dressed in a robe that looked like the sea. Her hair ebbed and flowed like waves on a beach. He walked up to Calypso, picking wildflowers as he went. Her eyes were focused on the clouds, making them circle above the field as if they were in the eye of a hurricane.

"Excuse me, Miss?"

She scowled at him.

"I...uh...brought you these." He handed her the weathered down wildflowers.

"For me?" She blushed, taking the flowers. "Why… aren't you handsome? Want to come to my place?"

Pat removed his sheriff's hat. "And where might that be, beautiful?"

"A sea cave off the coast of Ogygia."

"How exotic, just like yourself." He smiled. "I'd love—"

A bullet cracked through her skull, and her body fell. Pat looked up to see Robert holstering his firearm.

"What the hell? Robert, that was the love of my life. You bastard!"

Pat charged him. Robert pulled his firearm once again, and slammed the butt of it against Pat's temple. The sheriff fell, unconscious.

"Sorry, Patty. But…er…you'll forgive me when you wake up."

Calypso was beginning to claw her way up off the ground, her skull and her flesh fusing back together. Robert aimed and fired three more rounds into her head.

"You ain't that pretty."

It wouldn't keep her down for long, but hopefully it would be long enough.

Amanda found herself in a life or death riddle match with a sphinx. They stood near a still-smoldering tree that had been struck by lightning. The winner had to answer two out of three, and so far they both had lost one. But Amanda was not playing fair.

"What has four legs in the morning, two legs in the afternoon, and three legs in the evening?" the sphinx asked.

"That's easy. The answer is man."

"All right, fine." The winged cat snarled and sat on its haunches. "Your turn."

"Okay. There are two coins that equal thirty cents, one is *not* a nickel. What are the two coins?"

"Wait...what is a nickel?"

"A coin." Amanda smirked.

"What kind of a coin?"

"You don't know? Do you give up?"

"No. No, I don't give up. Let me think on it." It closed its eyes, lost in thought. "But how can I solve it if I don't know what a nickel is?"

"I didn't know that a snail had a foot. I still lost that one. And before, you didn't know what a train was, so you lost that one."

"Fine." The sphinx glared at her.

"Do you give up? You said you can't solve it."

The sphinx's eyes brimmed with tears. "But I don't want to die."

"Neither do I." Amanda placed her hand on her hip.

"Call it a draw?" pleaded the sphinx.

"Fine." Amanda rolled her eyes. "But remember that I spared your life!"

"Absolutely. Of course." The sphinx bowed its way into the woods and was gone.

***

Inside the shack, Desiree drew an intricate symbol on the dirt floor with her father's walking stick. It was a circle with circles inside it, and stars, and ancient words in forgotten languages. When she was done, she stood outside the circle. She closed her eyes, and began to chant.

***

In the field, Cupid vanished from the air. His estranged arrow pierced the dirt. The flying ice and snow slicing across

Mrs. Claus's face like the north wind vanished. Strife and the other gods vanished one by one, and appeared inside Desiree's circle in the shack. They stepped on each others' toes and tried to exit the circle. They found an invisible wall holding them inside the close quarters.

"Hey, guys." Desiree smiled. She held her father's cane in her hands. "An eye for an eye. You trap me. I trap you." She scanned the faces of all the gods within the circle. Some were glaring at her, others were firing whatever magic they had against the force field of the trap, but one god seemed to be missing. The one god that would be coyly trying to talk his way out of the confines was missing from the circle.

Desiree gritted her teeth. "Where is Clermeil?"

Mrs. Claus, the Valkyrie, Amanda, Rick, and Robert shuffled in. Mrs. Claus and the Valkyrie had a few bleeding cuts, but were otherwise unharmed. The gods and spirits inside Desiree's circle were in the same condition.

"You...all of you were just here to distract us. Where is Clermeil?" Her body was trembling. Tears streamed down her cheeks.

"Now that your daddy is out of the way," Strife said, "the Oracle is unprotected. Clermeil, I'm sure, is taking your son to *where she sleeps* at this very moment."

"Clermeil doesn't know where that is," Amanda

replied. "No one does."

"You mean, you don't?" Strife asked Desiree.

"No, I don't," Desire snarled. "Did Clermeil think that because he has my...son, I'd spill? I didn't know during his water-boarding sessions, and I don't know now."

"Your son?" Robert interrupted.

She waved him away and continued.

"So his entire venture was pointless! He lied to you. He said finding the Oracle would be no problem. Torture the council, he said. Kill the priest, he said. He, my dad, was the *only* one who might have known. And Clermeil's bloodthirsty, hell-bent action plan is what screwed you. You'll never find it. It was all a waste of time."

Calypso's eyes squinted with frustration and determination. They turned an electric blue.

"Talking to you has been a waste of time," she said. "Entertaining your sad persuasion. You mortals are so weak-minded. I doubt finding the Oracle will be much of a task after you vermin are drowned."

The Valkyrie laughed, moving closer to her. "Rats can swim. Now tell us, you lonely whore, what did Clermeil promise you in exchange for your partnership? A sea-weary sex slave? I can assure you they don't make men like Odysseus any more, sugar."

Calypso smiled, as the door to the shack creaked open. Pat shuffled in like a zombie.

"Want to join the interrogation?" The Valkyrie smiled. His limbs were dragging, his head slumped. "What happened to you?"

He looked up to see the piercing blue eyes of Calypso. "My love," he whimpered and ran to her.

"No!" Robert called, but Pat ran into the circle and grabbed Calypso.

There was a burst of light as his shuffling feet disturbed the circle drawn in the dust. The summoning trap collapsed.

Everyone outside the circle flew back and landed hard on the ground. Dust flew up into the air and hung there like fog. Cupid was hunched over laughing behind the rest of the gods. He could not bring himself upright, no matter how he tried.

"How trivial." Calypso stroked Pat's hair then pushed him to the ground with the rest.

Yuki-Onna stepped up to Calypso. "Finally." She pressed her hands together in front of her chest, and bowed her head in one swift movement.

The Valkyrie stretched her wings out as far as they would go, as shards of ice like piercing glass raced towards the humans behind her. Mrs. Claus had just enough time to grab

Amanda and Robert, who reached out and grabbed Pat, and they vanished. The Valkyrie and Desiree's bodies lurched back and forth as shards of ice pierced their bodies. Blood trickled down the ice daggers.

"Like Christmas in July." Strife smiled, and straightened out her three-piece suit. She walked up to the Valkyrie, whose wings had collapsed. Blood trickled from her mouth and down her feathers.

"Oh, honey, you know, you're cute, but you're just one missed facial away from being a harpy. Now tell me, you lonely whore, who's going to carry your soul off to Valhalla?" She smiled. "No one. You're the last one on this side of the fence. So sad."

Strife put her palm to the Valkyrie's forehead. Her spilling blood began to turn grey and crumble. Her head sank forward as she died on her knees, her wings drooping, her body solidifying into a stone angel.

***

Clermeil passed through the crowd of gods and spirits who hung around the fires and elegant tents and hovels and cauldrons and chess games. He was headed to a door that had been set into the trunk of an old oak tree. It led to a motel bathroom that had been bestrewn with blood.

He opened the door. "All right, Dastan, it's time to..."

The tub was empty. On the floor, laying on a red-stained suit, was a baby. He cried and wailed, for the obsidian bladed dagger in his tummy was blessing him repeatedly with its ritual intent – death and rebirth.

Clermeil leaned upon the doorframe and began to laugh. His stomach wrenched in pain from his hysterical laughter. "My, my, Totec, bless your heart! You, born again by your own ritual blade. Magnifique! Poétique! And now you're just...useless." The re-birthed god wailed on the floor as the electricity of the blade coursed through him. Clermeil leaned down and wrapped the baby in the suit jacket. He grabbed hold of the blade's hilt and pulled it from the babe's stomach, setting it on the sink counter. The Loa rocked and consoled the infant until the blade was removed and the wound had healed.

"There now, you can't go leaving your toys lying around where the vessel can get to them, can you? Now we're behind schedule."

The Loa carried Baby Totec out to the fire where several gods and spirits sat. He handed him over to a humanoid creature with claws and a tail and a deer skull for a head.

"Here, Wendigo, hold on to this for me, would you?" The creature tilted its skull to the side and with a forked tongue licked its teeth. "I think you'll find y'all have a lot in common." Clermeil smiled. "For starters, you both have a taste for flesh."

He waved as he walked away, suddenly vanishing.

He appeared again outside the shack. The gods were stepping through the tiny crooked door.

"Did you do it?" Clermeil asked them, apprehension in his tone.

"The wicked witch is dead." Strife laughed.

"Damn!" He ripped his fingers through his hair.

"Why?" Cupid snarled. "What happened?"

"Our lovely friend Xipe Totec let our Oracle vessel escape, that's what happened, and now the other potential vessel is dead."

"Like mother, like daughter," said Calypso.

Clermeil's face was as rigid as stone.

"Go find Charles, or Dastan, or whatever. Find him now, and do not tell Charon what's happened."

The goddesses vanished, heeding his urgent command.

Cupid, however, lingered behind. "This isn't working out well for us, Clermeil."

The Loa laughed, deeply and menacingly. "Did you honestly expect everything to go as planned without a hitch?"

"That is how you made it seem…easy…just small mortals in our way. This has been nothing but annoying and frustrating."

"Bless your heart. What a naive child you still are, Cupid."

The young god's eyes narrowed.

Clermeil continued. "The plan is always easy. The plan is always perfect. It's the execution that takes work."

"Charon won't be pleased with this. Our time is running out. We only have a short window left on this plane until he ferries us back or leaves us behind. The solstice is nearing."

"Well, then, Cupid, I suggest you help us look for the only living vessel we have left in our grasp."

"In our grasp? If I recall, you just said he slipped through your fingers, just like his mother and grandmother did. Bless your heart. All your vessels keep outwitting you."

Cupid vanished.

***

Charles awoke from his meditation. *See what you can do*, Rick had told him, and he saw Clermeil carrying a baby god and fighting with the god of love. He sat up from the forest floor. Damp leaves stuck to his elbows and his back.

"Well," said Tiny, "did you do it?"

"Yeah, I did." Charles felt a brief surge of pride. "I

dreamt Clermeil was at the shack. And...Desiree's dead." His head lowered. The spit dried up in his mouth. His chest felt as if it was filled with daggers, piercing him at each breath.

"Hey, now." Wile E. gripped his shoulder, and sat next to him. "We need your pea-sized brain to stay focused here." His amber eyes were sympathetic.

"He sent the other gods to look for me, because I'm the last one. The last vessel now."

"Good," said Jack, who had been hovering over Charles. He now stood and was pacing. "I'll find Bugs. We'll shape shift and lead him straight to you. Smokey can save your mother."

Charles was uncomfortable with Desiree being called his mother.

"How?" Charles asked.

"There is a song and dance only the ghost people know," he answered. "She will not be the same as she was. There will be a toll to pay. She will, however, be reborn."

Charles was not sure if he liked the sound of that.

"Dastan," Tiny said, as he dropped from a branch on a string of gossamer, "fear makes a man's heart weak."

"*Fear cannot dwell there*," Charles muttered to himself. "*For if it does…* All right."

Coyote looked at the spider. "I don't know what you're

talking about. Fear's saved my furry ass multiple fucking times." He grinned.

Jack was blunt. "And your heart is weak, brother."

"I find it better to err on the side of caution." Wile E. sat cross-legged in the wet leaves.

"Bravery will serve you better."

"Not the way *Old*-man made me."

The spider crept closer. "Old-man is not your best argument, brother."

Wile E. snapped his teeth at the insect.

"Thank you, Jack." Charles interrupted the bickering and stood. With that, Wisakedjak walked into the trees and soon melted into the shadows.

Charles walked over to the well and peered into its depths. "Marie, if you're in there, because I think you are...I need your help to pull this off. You..."

Wile E. had joined Charles and stood uncomfortably close to him. He looked down into the well. "Who you talkin' to?"

"Marie."

"Oh, so, you've gone off the deep-end since we last met, huh?"

Charles thought for a moment. "No...Maybe...Yeah, I probably have."

"Crazy suits you. Keep up the good work, and the talking to, you know, nothing."

"It's not nothing. It's the Oracle. It's Marie."

"Okay. Sure. Whatever you say, man-child."

Charles smiled. "Can I continue?"

"Go for it. Didn't mean to interrupt." Wile E. smirked. "You know you missed me."

***

Mrs. Claus returned to the shack, finding a stone angel kneeling on the dirt floor. Her hands quaked as she reached out to it. Her fingertips touched the shoulder, and where her fingers lay the grey skin began to crumble. She drew back her hand as if she had touched smoldering ash.

"I'm sorry Valkyrie of Valhalla. May your sisters fly you home. May you find the Great Hall filled with friends, and I hope the mead is to your liking." Mrs. Claus pursed her lips and blew upon the grey Valkyrie. Like a dandelion, the Valkyrie blew apart and her ashes flew away.

Desiree Hart lay on the floor, pierced with icicles that were beginning to melt in the humid heat of June.

Mrs. Claus had to look away from the sight of two of those crystal bodkins sheathing themselves into her eye sockets.

The door creaked open, and a big leather-skinned man stood in the doorway.

"Hello, Skadi," said Smokey. "I did not know you would be here."

"Nor I you."

"Can you not heal her?" he asked.

She shook her head. "No. I cannot undo what's been done."

Smokey the Bear smiled. Then he crouched down, and with hands the size of bear paws he picked up the body of Desiree Hart.

"Would you like to dance with me, Skadi?"

"I hardly find that appropriate."

"It is a spirit dance. We will heal her body and return her soul to it."

Mrs. Claus' eyes turned to slits. "There are laws of nature, Bear," she said. "There are some things that cannot be done."

"My brother, chief of the ghost people, The Great White Owl, he owes me one...from poker night. I know his song and dance. He will come."

"She won't come back, or...she won't be the same."

"True. There are laws, Skadi, laws more mysterious than even gods can comprehend. There are wrongs to be righted here, a balance that needs to be kept. The gate has no keeper. The land must make a new one." He peered down at Desiree.

"Oh." Mrs. Claus glanced at Desiree's limp body.

"In other words, we have leverage." With big swaying strides, he left the cabin and walked into the rain and the flood.

***

Clermeil stood in the middle of the road and watched the water creep upon it. There were only so many places a man could be in this flood. The roads were closed, so the Loa knew Dastan could not have left town. The forest was a swamp. Traveling by foot would be too difficult. The Loa chuckled to himself. Maybe Dastan had built an ark like he'd suggested.

The sound of sloshing footsteps came from behind him. Steve and Brandon were running to him from the other side of the road.

The Loa greeted them with a politician's smile. "Boys, I thought I told you two to leave town. Why are you still here? I promised to find you when the time comes for me to repay you." Clermeil glared into the muddy water at his feet. "Unless you *too* have lost your faith in me."

"We did leave," said Steve.

"Started to," said Brandon.

"But…" They'd said the word in unison.

"But?" Clermeil urged.

They glanced at each other.

"We saw Charles," answered Brandon.

"No, man, his name's Dastan now."

"Right. Dastan. We saw Dastan, jack. He was just running down the road. Saw us and looked back at us like a deer in headlights." He laughed. "Probably thought we was huntin' him down like a dog again."

"Where?" Clermeil stepped up to them.

"Well, jack, we sorta followed him into the woods to a well."

"A well?"

"Yeah, man. It was all old an' shit. Had the bucket you lower in an' everything." Steve folded his arms in front of his chest. "I'd never seen it before. Kinda gave me the willies."

"Show me."

Steve and Brandon glanced at one another with raised eyebrows.

"All right." Brandon turned to walk away.

Steve grabbed his arm. "I don't know, man. I think it's a trap."

Clermeil chuckled. "Please, don't get ahead of yourself,

Stephen. Why don't you leave the thinking to me? You do what you do best. Track him. Take me to him."

***

Charles looked down into the well, and imagined he was looking down at himself. Was this what he was reaching for in his dream? Some better version of himself? He had always thought in the future he would be smart and have it together, but he had no idea what he was doing. He felt lost in the woods - in the dark without a flashlight or a Wi-Fi connection kind of lost - and he felt *free*.

He had had a plan: go to school, meet a girl, find a career, get married, have babies. Simple. But now he did not know the next step to the plan.

Adrenaline pumped through his veins. He did not know how to outwit Clermeil once the deed was done. Like a battle drum, his heart pounded in his ears. He did not know if he would live or die or be trapped on the other side.

Dastan grinned. Not knowing…he liked it. He liked it very much.

Desiree had not been this young in a long time. She had forgotten how smooth her hands were at the age of eighteen. She'd forgotten she'd had an obsession with plaid, and painted her nails black. The skirt she was wearing had been her favorite (Ricky always winked at her when she wore it). She remembered this bar in the French Quarter of New Orleans. And when the man sitting next to her asked if she remembered him, she nodded. How could she ever forget him? This was where they met.

"I don't remember your name though," she said, giggling despite herself.

"I don't blame you for forgetting. I only mentioned it once." He was handsome, exotic. He had a thick accent, though she couldn't place it. He had a bashful smile, and his perfect white teeth gleamed like pearls against his cocoa skin. "My name is Anenqui. It means

'Wanderer' in the Aztec language."

"I remember that now." She smiled, the memories and feelings all flooding back. "I'm sorry I left before you woke up."

"No worries." He eyed her. "How is our son?"

"You already know...don't you?"

He nodded.

"Then why ask?"

The Wanderer pressed his lips together, and set money down for their drinks. Desiree forgot that she had trouble holding her liquor back then, and was drinking something colorful and fruity.

"Because I'm in town and while I was here...I wanted to say hello." He began to walk away.

"Anenqui!" Desiree called after him. "I know now...you're not human, are you?"

"Oh, Desiree, I am human, among other things." His pupils grew large as he stared at her from the shadows. The dim light was caught by his eyes, which made them glow golden. "It was lovely to see you again, my love," he purred, and slinked out the barroom door.

***

Dastan's eyes were lost to the well. He saw visions and past dreams. He remembered a bullet casing tumbling to the ground for forever and ever. It had a human heart etched into the brass. He *witnessed Snow White waking up, gasping, blood streaming down from her eyes onto her white dress. Water rose and flooded beneath her bed as her fingers gripped the mattress. He heard a panther pacing back and forth outside the shack. He saw its breath turn to mist as it snorted and panted. While he waited he heard the ticking of a clock. The water's king was coming ever nearer. Fear could not dwell here. He could not be afraid, nor was he.*

"Hello, Dastan," said a gentlemanly southern voice.

"Cler." Dastan smirked and turned around. He saw Brandon and Steve hiding in the woods. They transformed into their true selves, an old trickster and a rabbit, and they made their way into the shadows of the trees.

Clermeil laughed. "I'm beginning to notice a personality disorder in you, son. I like this side of you better."

"Clermeil, talking takes up too much time, and you don't have a lot of that left."

"Come again?"

"Charon is losing patience with you and your boat's about to set sail west, with or without you or the Oracle. It's in the well, Clermeil. The essence of the Oracle is in the well." Dastan dropped to his knees, arms outstretched. The Loa took a cautionary step back. "I have seen it, and I cannot outwit my destiny."

"Well, you and your family have quite a habit of

outwitting me by *letting* me win. Fool me once..."

"How many options do you have, Cler? Really? Marie's dead. Desiree's dead. I'm all that's left. Whether you trust me or not, that don't really matter right now."

"You're a good salesman." Clermeil paused. "All right, Dastan. You know there's no going back home again after this?"

"What home? Desiree's gone…I have no home here. And Jenna is dead. Do you think I can ever show my face back in Houston again?" Tears welled up in his eyes. He closed them and took a deep breath, swallowing the lump in his throat. Looking back up at Clermeil with agonizing desperation in his soul, he screamed, "Stop talking! You took Desiree, Jenna, Jon, and Marie! Shut up and take me too! Just shut up and do it!"

"Fine." Clermeil gave a nod.

He raised his arms like a preacher to the choir. The water in the well began to rise, until it rolled over the stone edge of the well in a torrent, spilling upon the land. The soil, having been touched by the water, began to glow with swirls of sparkling light.

Dastan's body lurched, and he found his ankles bound and his arms tied behind his back.

"Really?" he called back to Clermeil, who glided up to him. The water was already past Clermeil's ankles, and Dastan struggled to prop himself up on his elbows.

"Yes, really. Like you said, I don't trust you." Clermeil stood with the palms of his hands facing out towards the well. He lowered his head and began to chant with the rhythm of a Congo drum. The lights in the water looked like sparklers on the Fourth of July. As Clermeil chanted, the lights began to encircle Dastan. He was not afraid. He smiled, welcoming them.

Ahead of him in the forest, he saw something short and brown moving about the tree line. A coyote spied on them through the brush.

Dastan smiled and winked at Coyote, who tilted his head.

Clermeil had ceased chanting, and all was still. The lights rose up and out of the water, and began to come together as one essence, one form. Dastan thought he heard them whisper. It sounded like a song, a mother's soft lullaby.

Then the light rushed him. The luminescence pried its way down his throat and into his soul.

Dastan saw everything. He saw Marie and Jon. He saw the stars of the sky and the waves of the ocean. He saw the shifting sands of the desert, the swaying trees of the jungle, and he saw the panther. He knew the truth now. All of it. Everything. And it was such an intricate thing, like a spider's web. It was beautiful in design, in shape, the way it glistened.

But how dangerous it was…this castle, this truth. Fear

cannot dwell here or else the truth will crumble like a thousand falling dynasties lost to time. The truth was so simple, one thread after another. One glistening strand of life, one twist to connect it to another thread, and then...perpetual weaving strands where there is neither beginning nor end. How mysterious, all the colors, all the feelings, all the thoughts. Never ending, never ceasing, not even in death, for that was another thread, another turn.

***

The gods carried Dastan in one of the Ferryman's gondolas. It drifted atop the flood, as they guided it like pallbearers down the streets of Tell City. The water was up to their chests. The pretty little shops and houses were all empty and boarded up. Sunset Park was now the bottom of the river bed.

Dastan's body tossed and turned in the hull of the little boat. His eyes fluttered open and rolled back into his skull. His muscles convulsed and rolled in waves underneath his skin.

Cupid appeared in the boat to watch the human's seizures. "What if he bites off his tongue?" Cupid asked with honest concern.

Strife, who was helping to guide the boat, chuckled. "Well, then we won't have to hear him complain."

"If," said Yuki-Onna, "he can ever bring himself to the surface. The Oracle's power will undoubtedly consume him."

"Undoubtedly," confirmed Clermeil. He led the procession of gods and spirits back to the cemetery outside the Catholic church, where Charon waited.

"Ah, Clermeil, you've succeeded then?" Charon stood atop the church, holding his rowing oar like a staff that towered above his head. "And here I thought you'd push your luck and miss the portal."

Clermeil glowered at him. "It's a pleasure to prove you wrong, Ferryman."

"Aye, I'm sure it 'tis." The old man cackled. "Let us now venture back to our shores, where you can celebrate your *noble* victory." The Ferryman's tone was facetious.

He pointed at the flood with his oar, and the water began to swirl and part like the Red Sea. The submerged cemetery's consecrated ground opened like a mouth. The other side of the entrance was dark and cold. Another gondola waited for them there.

They pushed the boat carrying Dastan into the waters of the Acheron. Then the gods and spirits climbed into the two boats. Charon tied one boat to the other, bow to stern, and climbed into the first. The Ferryman pushed off against the rock bottom of the Acheron with his oar.

Along the channels of the underworld the boats drifted. Charon began to hum a dreary tune. It reverberated off the cavern walls like a million souls singing their dirge.

Dastan's body was still twisting and turning against the hull of the second boat. Clermeil leaned forward to look at him.

"What's goin' on inside that head of yours, boy? Is the Oracle eating you up alive?" Clermeil smiled at the thought, and leaned back.

He looked up, and sitting across from him was the Wendigo, still cradling Baby Totec. They were giggling and playing a game where they took turns eating each other's skin. Clermeil shivered as he watched the infant slurp up a piece of the creature's rotting flesh.

***

Desiree awoke from a dream that was like a memory. She opened her eyes to a blinding white light. She reached her hand out to shield herself from it, but someone she could not see took her hand.

"Desiree?" It was an old woman's voice.

"What the…where am I?"

"You're in your apartment, dear."

"What? No, I'm…"

The blinding light began to dim, and pixilated blurry shapes began to form in the whiteness. The static shapes she saw were sprinkled with different colors. She only saw them if she focused, but it stung her eyes to do so.

"Who are you?"

"Mrs. Claus, dear."

"Where are you?"

"She's blind," said a man's deep voice. He laughed. "Seems to be a trend with the gatekeepers."

"What the hell are you talking about?" Desiree reached out into the static field.

"Desiree, sugar, you were dead, and through song and dance, Smokey and I brought you back to life," Mrs. Claus explained. "And, trust me, that song and dance was no Disney movie. I had to wear a bear skull on my head."

The man named Smokey spoke up. "And now you are to take your father's place as Keeper of the Well. Guardian of the Gate. Priestess of the Oracle."

"What? No, I can't. Where is everyone? Where's Charles?"

"Your son," said the man with the deep voice, "is in the passage between worlds with the gods."

"Yes, I'm afraid so, dear. The others are safe downstairs."

Desiree sat up. She realized she was on her bed.

"No, you shouldn't be up yet," said Mrs. Claus.

"I can manage a few *fucking* stairs."

Desiree stood and felt her way to the door.

A big hand cradled her elbow. "You are brave, and I respect you, but all wise men and women recognize when they need help."

Desiree snarled, "I'm letting you help, aren't I?"

Smokey eased her down the stairs. She wanted to go faster than her guide, but he kept her steady, kept her from falling down. Downstairs in her waiting room, the floor was soft and wet. She saw several blurry shapes. They each had different colors, like an aura, spreading through them and around them. It gave her a headache.

"Desiree," said Amanda, her voice trembling as she embraced her.

"Hey," Desiree said softly, her hands stroking Amanda's tangled hair. She counted the pixilated shapes that pulsed. There were ten. "Who's all here?"

Mrs. Claus cleared her throat for introductions. "Rabbit, Bear, Spider, Coyote, Crow, Jack, Robert, Rick, Amanda, and myself."

Several voices said hello to her.

"Where's Pat and the Valkyrie?"

"Pat is, uh, tied up at the moment," Robert said, sounding amused. "He got struck by Cupid's arrow and is all bent on being with some goddess-woman."

"And the Valkyrie died saving us," Amanda said, her voice choked with emotion.

"Oh…"

"Look," said an unfamiliar voice, "I'm Wile E., Charles's friend. Glad you're back and all, but we don't have a lot of time. We, uh, need you to contact an old flame of yours. Someone who can travel between worlds. Know who I'm talking about?"

"Charles's father?" Desiree asked carefully, recalling her dream.

"Yeah. That guy."

"But he already knows—"

"Listen," Wile E. urged, "the Big Chieftain is going to personally hunt me down and disown my ass if we don't fix this. I kind of screwed up, I guess. We should know by now that a trickster's plans usually don't work out too well."

"Coyote," said Jack, "that's the great mystery. It worked out the way it was meant to."

"Yeah, well, still…." Wile E. sighed. "He can travel between the worlds, right?"

Desiree shrugged at the strange blurry shape before her.

"He's a Shaman, right?"

Desiree started to make her way towards her reading

room. "Yes."

"Help her," ordered Smokey the Bear.

Jack gave her his walking stick. She nodded in appreciation.

"Amanda, get me copal incense. Rick, get me my pendulum, it's upstairs."

Amanda started scanning the shelves. Rick ran upstairs.

"Does anyone have a pack of cigarettes?" Desiree made a whimpering sound as she sat at her reading table.

"Oh! Yes, dear." Mrs. Claus put her pack of Marlboro Reds in Desiree's hand.

"Right…someone else light the candles over there." She pointed to her spirit altar, and Jack pulled out a Zippo and lit each one.

Amanda found the copal incense. It released a rich, lemony sweet scent when placed upon the coals on a cast-iron plate in the center of Desiree's reading table. Rick handed her the pendulum. It was an obsidian stone on a metal chain, which she turned over in her hands like prayer beads. She rocked back and forth for a while, everyone lingering, watching from the periphery.

Desiree began to hum as she lit up a cigarette from Mrs. Claus' pack. She inhaled then blew the smoke onto the incense in front of her. The two clouds of smoke twisted and danced with one another. Desiree continued to rock back and forth and began to chant under her breath.

Taking a deep breath, Amanda stepped forward and sat in the chair opposite Desiree. She began to hum the song Desiree had hummed, while Desiree continued to chant. The smoke billowed and twisted between them. Thunder began to rumble once again outside. The water in the streets made sharp waves, which crashed against the brick walls of the shop. Flickering shadows cast by the candle flames danced like ghosts upon the walls. Desiree blew her last breath of smoke upon the sizzling copal incense. The incense dimmed and extinguished. The candles blew out, and a black panther strode out of the shadows to Desiree's side. It transformed into a man, who reached out and took Desiree's hand.

"Long time no see." He sounded like he was smiling.

"No shit." Desiree set the cigarette butt on the cast-iron plate. "And never again."

"Hey, friend," said Buzzy the Crow. "Your son is in the underworld. He has the Oracle inside of him."

The wandering shaman stood.

Coyote stepped up to him. "You're the only one here that can travel between worlds. The only way we knew to stop him was to stop him at the gates. This way he can't turn around. This way we make him a fool in front of all the gods, and he will *never* be able to return, and no other god will try. That is, *if* you can stop him, get your son back, and return the Oracle to the well."

***

The Oracle coursed around him and through him as if he were an ocean cave, hollow and a part of the whole. Everything past, current, and future was one, one with him, and he knew the details, no matter how trivial, were the very essence of life. But Dastan knew he could not stay there in the castle forever. He tried to call out to the Oracle, to the mass of colors and images and threads that flowed all around, but his words became tangled in time and were lost.

Then Marie appeared, swimming out of a cumulous cloud before him. She hovered in front of him, the tangles of fabric she wore pluming around her. Her long ebony hair waved in the current. She beckoned him forward, bubbles escaping her lips as a sly smile graced her face. She began to swim straight up, and Dastan easily followed. He pushed off with his feet as if he were at the bottom of a swimming pool and swam after her. His clothes now flowed around him, too. Holding his breath was easy. He did not need to breathe.

They shot up through thunderclouds, then through the stars. Past movie reels of people's lives and books filled with all their lies and daydreams. They swam through the hall of mirrors which reflected back

*to them the interiors of bathrooms, dressing rooms, makeup compacts,
and antique malls. They swam through fire, past the door of Akashic
Records, and out through the cave of wonders, which Dastan found
quite plain after everything he'd seen.*

*Dastan followed Marie's flowing spirit up and up until they
passed through a tight cave with rocks. He had to push and propel
his way through the sharp and narrow crevice, but once the passage
opened, he found himself looking up through the river bed of the
Acheron. Marie, floating next to him, pointed at the two long boats that
drifted high above them.*

Charon's oar cut through the water and landed on the
riverbed with a thud. The mud and dust stirred and clouded the
water.

*Dastan wiggled and squirmed his way through the rocks. He
sunk his fingers into the soft riverbed and heaved himself through the
tiny opening. He swam up to the surface, but could not breach it. The
water was like a wall that was keeping him below.*

*Dastan turned back to Marie, who smiled and mouthed the
word* wait. *So he did. When she again pointed at the surface, he looked
up to see a large black panther spring off the banks and land on the first
boat.*

The gondola nearly overturned. The gods screamed as
one by one they were attacked and thrown into the water. Some
of them returned to the surface to fight the beast, while others

bobbed back to the top, blood rushing from the vicious bites in their necks and the gashes in their stomachs.

The Acheron ran red.

Clermeil stood up in the second boat. He towered over Charles's body, still convulsing in the hull. Anger rippled off of the Loa of flooding waters in waves, and his loathing reverberated through the water with a deep rumble.

The current suddenly reversed, *sending Dastan hurdling into a rock at the bottom of the river. The water began to rush past him. He pressed himself up against the rock so he did not get swept away, and then the wave came. Dirt and rocks caught in the current rushed against Dastan,* and a tidal wave tore through the caverns of the underworld.

The wall of water capsized and destroyed both boats, dumping everyone into the churning water. Charles's bound, seizing body sank and skidded across the rocky, sandy river bottom. *Dastan headed towards it. As he swam, he caught a glimpse of the panther swimming to the surface, followed by Strife.*

Above the water, he saw lightning flash as the wrath of the gods came down on the panther, his father. Dastan quickened his pace towards his body, while the current pulled back again, forming another wave. It would be coming soon.

Like a salmon against the current, Clermeil swam towards the vessel. *Dastan knew he would not reach his own body before Clermeil. He needed the Oracle. He was one with it…it was a part of him, as it always had been. Dastan cleared his mind, and time stopped.*

The river was still. Clermeil was frozen in the water. The light show above had paused. Dastan swam through the river with much more difficulty. With time stopped, it felt like he was swimming through marmalade.

Dastan went to untie his own wrists, but the moment his soul touched the flesh of his body, flesh and spirit became one.

His lungs felt like they would burst. His eyes opened to the sight of Clermeil seizing him like a hungry piranha, and ripping him to the surface through the pounding of the second wave.

Dastan gurgled and choked with the first breath of air. Water expelled from his mouth and nose, as he lay coughing on the banks of the underworld. Clermeil pulled Dastan up by his shirt.

"How in the *hell* are you alive?"

Dastan laughed. With a strained voice he quipped, "A panther saved me."

Clermeil grabbed Dastan by one arm and dragged him across the rocks. Dastan was so weak he could not stand, though he tried. The Loa threw him to the ground before the panther, who now appeared quite human wearing jeans and a black button-down. Dastan's chin split open upon landing, and he rolled onto his shoulder to look up at the panther.

His father still smiled, despite the blood between his teeth, and the two gods holding firmly to each of his outstretched arms.

"I knew you were up to something, boy." Clermeil put a boot to Dastan's chest and forced him back to the ground. "Now where is my Oracle?" His raging voice caused the water to rise.

"You still got it. It's inside me."

"Then how are you talkin'?"

"Because the Oracle is letting me."

Clermeil's eyes narrowed.

"What are you?" Strife said to the panther. Her hair was soaked and tangled, and that appeared to be the main source of her temper.

"I am Anenqui. I am a shaman, a walker of worlds."

"Wanderer," said the voice of a small child. All the gods turned to see Baby Totec holding the hand of the Wendigo. "Wanderer."

"*This*," Cupid pointed at Anenqui, whilst baring his teeth at Clermeil, "is The Wanderer? Not the boy?"

"How could I have known that?" Clermeil snapped.

"This," Charon said with a hint of glee in his voice, "is the prophecy. Clermeil, Loa of waters, savior to us all! This be the prophesy, and you made it."

"No!" Clermeil snarled, and turned to walk down river. "We still have the Oracle. Grab the boy and drown the kitten. We will not return empty-handed. Not when we're this close!"

The gods raised the panther to his feet, as Cupid gripped Dastan's arm. The young god took an arrow from the quiver on his back, and used the sharp arrowhead to cut the binds around Dastan's ankles.

"Walk," he ordered, and Dastan stood. The other gods were already far ahead of them, following Clermeil. Dastan watched them dragging Anenqui to the river.

"I said *walk*." Cupid put the tip of his arrow under Dastan's chin.

Dastan's mind cleared, and the man the gods were holding in the water became a panther once again. It tore away from them with thrashing claws and snapping jaws. They jumped back, though not unscathed. The giant cat was low to the ground, and it let out a roar that reverberated off the stone walls.

"Damn." Cupid ran towards the bloody scene, readying his bow and arrows. He leapt into the air and golden wings unfolded from his back, but the raging animal was already atop the gods.

Dastan cleared his mind once more and became the Oracle again. *He saw all of history, from the first painting in Lascaux to the last tour of The Rolling Stones, which happened to be after the invention of flying cars, because The Stones would never die, just like Bob Dylan.*

Dastan liked how Houdini had escaped his binds so many times, so he followed the master's moves, and was free. He stood, and looked towards Cupid.

The god was trying to take careful aim, lest he shoot the heart of one of the gods. The arrow itself would not kill them, but they would die from a broken heart.

Cupid danced about in the air, trying to take aim, while the panther swatted away the gods with his massive claws as easily as if they were flies.

It came to Dastan how David had struck down Goliath. He picked up the rope that had bound his wrists and tied it in knots to make a sling, in which a nearby rock fitted perfectly.

Dastan watched the bouncing pattern of the god in the air, which almost had a rhythm. *One, two, three. One, two, three.* He whirled the sling in the air around his head and when the god flew back to his first vantage point, he let go.

He heard a crack as the rock connected with Cupid's skull. The god's wings fluttered and tangled around his body as they lost wind, and he crashed hard on his back on the rocks. Blood trickled from his temple as he writhed in agony.

Dastan found it poetic. He approached the god.

Cupid tried to reach for the arrows in his quiver, but could not move without suffering spasms of pain.

Dastan squatted on the rocks next to the young god. Cupid began to laugh incessantly.

"What do you plan to do, hmm? Kill me? You can't."

Dastan's brows rose as he remembered Totec's obsidian dagger, *and he knew how the rebirthing magic of it worked. It was so simple to understand, once you had seen how the ties of death weave their way from life to life.* Electricity formed in his hand in a perfect ball, as he manifested that magic into his palm.

Cupid's eyes grew wide as Dastan moved his hand to Cupid's chest. Once the blue lightning made contact with Cupid, it electrified him, just as it had done Totec. It coursed through Dastan and into the god, whose wings shrunk and shriveled. Soon all that remained was a small child, lost in a man's deflated suit.

Dastan stood, and the panther prowled up to him. The bodies of two gods now lay on the ground in puddles of blood on the banks of the river, and a toddler wailed and cried upon the rocks.

The panther's fur was sticky with blood. It licked its jowls and they began to walk together along the river, Wanderer and son.

Around the bend, they saw the other gods surrounding

an enormous door set into the rock face. It was made of wood and metal and a large tree was carved upon it. The tree's branches were adorned with symbols that resembled decorations hanging off a Christmas tree. In front of the door, arms outstretched, stood Charon. The gods all kneeled like a worshiping congregation behind its priest. But one of them kept looking back towards the river bend, waiting for three gods that should have been kneeling as well.

Clermeil was watching for them to drag Dastan through the door. Instead, he saw Dastan and the panther walking towards them. With a cry of frustration, the Loa stood.

His rising disturbed the meditation of the others, and beckoned them all to stand. But the ritual had been completed and the huge wooden door began to open, pushing against the dirt and rocks that were in its way. Clouds of dust fell from the rattling rock ceiling. The ground began to shake.

The land beyond the door was flat and barren and cracked. The horizon was lined with gold and faded into a dark purple. It was starless, cloudless, moonless, sunless, but it glowed like the setting sun.

Clermeil gawked at his vessel in awe and panic.

"Well, well, what have we here?" asked Charon with a greasy smile. "A Lost Son and The Wanderer come to put us gods to rest?"

"Forevermore?" Clermeil pondered under his breath.

"Where is Cupid?" asked Strife.

Neither the panther nor Dastan answered.

"Clermeil," Yuki-Onna cried, "you've only made the prophecy come to fruition."

He snapped his muddy eyes toward her. "Not true." Clermeil pointed at Dastan. "Get him!"

No one moved.

"Have we ventured all this way to fail now? Are y'all that weak of constitution?"

"Aye," Charon said, stepping forward, "when I can see the course that Fate has set, you best believe I step out of her way. This voyage be damned the moment we set sail. Trial after trial, we found but troubled waters, and here at the end it seems we best not tempt the Fates any further, lest we have this door closed forever."

Strife turned to Charon. "But the doors will be open forever if we quit bitching, old man, and drag the brat and his cat through with us."

"If anyone wishes to stay, be my guest, but I won't be staying 'round for this disaster, lest we be trapped on this side rather than the other."

The gods and spirits glanced at one another, weighing the odds.

"Cowards," Clermeil said, sounding unsurprised. His twisting hand gestured towards Dastan, and Dastan felt the familiar sting of water filling his lungs.

But now he knew how his father, the panther, could change, how he could transform into an animal. It was actually rather simple to Dastan now that he understood how everything was connected. He shifted the way Anenqui did, becoming a fish. His lungs moved up his body, as his neck melted into his shoulders. Dastan's respiratory system changed into gills, and Clermeil could no longer drown him. Dastan flapped on the ground, feeling the tickling ebb and flow of his gills fanning through the air.

Clermeil marched up to the fish and laid his boot upon it, but then stopped. The Oracle was now inside the tiny fish as well, and he could not know what Dastan's death would do to his precious prize. The Loa bent to pick up the fish and take it with him, but it squirmed and twisted, becoming a viper. Its fanged head struck at his hand and his boot. Clermeil jumped back. Blood dripped off his hand from two perfect tears in his flesh.

The panther strode up to the viper who was curling on the rocks for another strike.

Dastan's tongue flicked. The air tasted like the cold wet rocks and dirt of the underworld, like the taste of decay. But the air that trickled in from beyond the gods, beyond the door, tasted like power. An enveloping, burning mystery overtook him, one that both beckoned him and told him to turn and run.

It was a dusty, lonely universe filled with books of unimaginable and forsaken knowledge. It was a place that never ceased, never died, but was ruled by Death. It was a dreamscape dominated by real nightmares, soothed only for seconds by masqueraded love. It was Magick, ancient, alluring, and poisonous, and he could *taste it*.

Dastan's head turned towards the panther, whose eyes glowed in the darkness. Dastan's body morphed again, slowly this time. Adding limbs was much harder to do than ridding yourself of them, but they grew out from the marrow of his spine. His heart grew ten sizes as his rib cage expanded and his right lung was pulled back up to rest across from his left. Dastan's new tail felt freer and looser now as it ticked back and forth.

Many of the gods had turned and were walking through the door. Clermeil still held onto his wounded hand. The blood that was pooling in his palm bagan to seep back into the puncture wounds, healing his injury.

"Blood is water, Dastan. Thicker than water, but still mostly water." He looked up to see two panthers beginning to stalk around the few remaining gods. He was uncertain which one was the boy and which was The Wanderer.

One leapt onto Strife, while the other climbed onto the rocks piled high aside the massive door. Yuki-Onna raised her hands, and shards of ice flew out of her palms towards the panther atop of Strife.

The panther screamed and thrashed his teeth as the ice shards pierced his skin, and then the wild cat sprung upon the ice queen. Her draping dress spun around her, and her essence turned into a cloud of blinding white snow. In the blinding white, Dastan could see nothing, until a monster with horns and decaying flesh upon bone came at him with needle-like fingers.

The fingers tore and ripped at him, the deer-skull head slurping down his flesh, until a southern voice called, "Don't kill! We do not know which one is the vessel!"

Clermeil was treading over the rocks to where the other panther had vanished.

With a crash and a shake, the giant door, still grinding open, reversed, and the gate began to close.

"Find the Wanderer!" cried Strife with urgency. She held onto her limp arm. Her chest was gashed with claw marks. Her shoulder was gnarled and ripped open.

Reeds and roots grew up from the bed of the Acheron at Calypso's command. Her eyes were glowing blue-green, as were the reeds that made their way upon the land.

Yuki-Onna solidified her essence back into the concentrated form of a Geisha.

Dastan lay upon his back, vainly trying to claw and bite away at the undead beast upon him. He managed to move his back paws onto the hip bones of the Wendigo, and he threw the monster off. Only part of his ear and shoulder were missing, but his underbelly had been eaten entirely away as if by buzzards. Even with the Oracle inside him, the pain was blocking him from clearing his mind to access it.

The reeds had crept up the bank to Dastan, and now they were beginning to grow around his paws. Distracted, he had noticed them too late. The glowing reeds encircled his paws and this throat. He tried to pull, tried to bite and claw, but they pulled him down to the ground. He struggled and failed to get up. Dastan looked up into the rocks and sniffed, trying to find Anenqui.

***

The Wanderer hid amongst the rocks. He sat, human, cross-legged on the ground, humming and chanting ever so quietly. He rocked back and forth to the rhythm, his song pulling the energies from the veils between the worlds to close the gate forevermore. The gap to the other shore slowly narrowed.

He, like other Wanderers, like his son, could slip subtly

between the veils, like ghosts through walls, but they were a rare few. Having a door open as powerful as this one cut the veils in two with the grace of a wrecking ball. So many worse things than gods could use this portal if it remained open; things that go bump in the dark corners of the ether; things that all the gods combined could not summon enough power to defeat. The door must be closed, locked forever, and so he chanted on.

Anenqui felt a searing heat begin to rise over him, course through him. He screamed as the water in his blood began to boil in his veins and bubble his skin. His scream was not like the cry of a panther or animal – it was the cry of a man. His song and chant and concentration broke under the seering pain, and the laborious swing of the door stoped, leaving the breach between the worlds splayed open and vulnrable.

***

Clermeil looked down upon The Wanderer from the rocks above. "Blood is thicker than water, takes longer for it to boil. A slow painful death might just be more than fitting. Too bad we can't stay to watch. Got a flight to catch." Clermeil smiled as he descended from the rocky overhang. "Let's go, girls. I should have known the gods would let me down. Goddesses always seem to have more fight in them." He winked at Yuki-

Onna, who glared back un-wooed.

Calypso's eyes turned an electric blue and the reeds holding Dastan down snapped at their roots. She gripped the one that wrapped around his neck and yanked it like a leash.

"Come on, kitty."

The door was almost closed, but it had stopped. Dastan heard the cries of his father grow weaker as he struggled against Calypso's leash. Though his abdomen flinched with pain, he summoned the dregs of his strength to shift one last time. His hips and spine repositioned. His shoulders locked back, and again he was a man. He sat on his knees and looked down at the wounds the Wendigo had inflicted upon him. The sight of his own flapping flesh and moving muscles and organs jarred him.

The Wendigo licked his lips at the sight of red human flesh, and Baby Totec was sitting on the ground clapping his hands and giggling.

"Come on." Calypso pulled again at his leash, more forcibly this time.

Dastan knew if he somehow forced the Oracle out, the Oracle would be safe, and Clermeil would kill him, returning to his world empty handed. Dastan was not afraid of death, but he knew it was not his time to die. He needed to see this through.

He could not shift into any creature, except perhaps a worm, that could survive his near-disembowelment, and the pain was too great to shift again anyway. Nor could he summon the knowledge and energy to heal himself.

If he gave himself back over to the Oracle, his body would simply lie there as the gods took him to their world beyond the door.

Dastan put his hands to the cool earth. His breathing became strained, and his fingers gripped and clawed into the sandy soil. He heard the chant of his father in his head. It was the song of the land, of the energies that coursed deep through its veins, and they were now in Dastan's.

The Oracle sang like a siren. The door began to close once more. The ceiling and walls and floors of the underworld shook and moaned. Heavy rocks were tumbling from where they had sat for centuries. The Acheron's waters trembled and rippled with the vibrations.

Clermeil raised his hand, his muddy eyes as dark as swamp water.

"No!" cried Strife. "You'll kill him just like you did Marie and Desiree, and then what will you do?"

"The door is closing…this land is through with us," Yuki-Onna said. "Goodbye, Clermeil." Transforming into a whipping wintery wind, she swirled through the narrowing crack at the door.

From around the bend in the river, a small naked cherub

with a quiver and an arrow flew through the air straight to the gap. He managed to give Dastan the finger before he fluttered, adorably, into the land of the setting sun.

Calypso looked between Dastan and the closing door. She thought of her island where she liked to hide, and knew if the door closed, she would never see it again. She glanced at Clermeil, rushing towards them. She dropped Dastan's leash and ran. Her bare feet padded past Baby Totec, who crawled across the floor, whimpering as he, too, made his way back to their world.

Clermeil grasped Dastan by his chin and forced him to stand. Then, gripping him underneath the arms, he dragged Dastan's struggling body to the door.

A voice came from Dastan's throat that was not his, but his grandmother's. *"What's it going to be, Cler? Would you rather be stuck here or there? Do you want to save us lowly humans or do you want to save yourself?"*

"You are coming with me, Marie," he said, panting as he carried Dastan. "I'm not letting you, or the Oracle, go this time. We can use the knowledge of the Oracle to keep the door open, travel back and forth at will and have our lands become one."

"You're lonely and you're desperate." She smiled and laughed through Dastan's lips.

Clermeil's anger exploded like a geyser. He threw

Dastan to the ground. They were but feet from the door, and it was nearly closed. "You and I, darlin', we were supposed to do this together, but you failed me. You left me stranded, alone. We are nothing without each other, gods and humans! You need us."

"No," said Dastan in his own voice. "We don't." *His mind cleared, and it was revealed to him how a god could die. Dastan thought of a vortex, darkness filled with nothing, a lack of existence.*

A misty veil appeared between him and Clermeil. It rippled like haze on the horizon, and it opened like curtains upon a stage. The dirt at Clermeil's feet was sucked into it like a vacuum. The Loa's clothes, still damp from the river, were being pulled in, and the Loa of flooding waters let out a cry that became lost to the void in front of him as he too was pulled into the darkness and was gone.

The void called to Dastan, this blackness that hung in the air in front of him, reminding him of a wormhole, or a black hole, but he knew it was neither of those things. It was nothingness. Yet it seemed so peaceful. No pain, no confusion, no thoughts, no regret. He so wanted to be there, to not feel anything.

A song, a chime, began to chant in his head. The Oracle sounded like a lullaby, soothing him, like the arms of a mother. He closed his eyes, the veil collapsed in on itself, and the gate to the other shore closed tight.

He opened his eyes to the dimness of the empty under-world. The light of the purple sky had vanished, and the tree carved into the wood of the door in front of him glimmered in the gloom. It seemed massive, larger than life, but it was the symbol of life, its branches radiating past the frame of the door. It was what the truth looked like, the castle, the webs of lives and stories. *I found this tree,* he had said, *and it was the castle.*

Dastan stood up slowly, carefully. Down from the rocks came The Wanderer, healed, and wearing a weary smile. He reached his son, and hugged him.

Dastan cried. The tears did not build up gradually; they fell like a sudden rain.

Without a word, Anenqui crouched in front of Dastan's abdomen, and a thick misty veil covered the wound. When the mist vanished, the pain was gone, his flesh had returned. There was not even a scar.

Dastan smiled. "You have to teach me that."

"Later." It was the first time Dastan had heard his true father's voice.

Anenqui turned towards the tree upon the door and the same thick veil of mist covered the portal. It lingered there for what felt like an eternity as they stood on the shores of the underworld. When the mist vanished, the door was gone. Only rock remained.

"We're Wanderers," Dastan said. It was meant to be a question, but it wasn't, because he knew it to be true.

"We are." Anenqui nodded. "We, my son, can walk the veils."

"How did I not know before?" he asked, then realized he already knew the answer – the Oracle was still inside him.

"Our secrets are buried within our hearts," his father said, his accent thick. "Revealing them is nothing less than the sacrifice of human art."

Dastan knew what that meant now.

"Now, Dastan, my son," he said, laying his palm against Dastan's face, "take us home."

A veil formed in Dastan's mind, and it pulled them both through to Tell City.

Dastan stood at the edge of the well. Surrounding him were Mrs. Claus, Anenqui, Desiree, Robert, Amanda, and Wile E. and his brothers. The sun shone brightly down through the tree limbs.

The river had receded to almost normal levels. A few cars and buildings had been destroyed, and there were articles in the Indianapolis newspapers about the tragedy that had fallen upon Tell City, about the mysterious deaths and disappearances that had occurred just before the flood.

The townsfolk and local farmers believed that the flood had made people crazy. Like animals before an earthquake, they had sensed the flood coming, and had killed themselves before the natural disaster could.

A few psychologists disagreed, and said a mixture of

chemicals were released in their brains due to a sort of primal panic caused by the sudden change of weather conditions, like animals before an earthquake.

"Go on," Wile E. said, grinning. "Slit your wrists already."

"Are you sure this will work?" asked Amanda anxiously.

"Yes," said Dastan, and he took the pocketknife from Robert. He ran the blade across his left palm. It stung and he grimaced. He had cut too deep. A pulsating pool of red filled his stinging palm, but then lights like sparklers began to drip with his glistening red blood back into the well. The light fell, sprinkling at first, and then grew until a stream of sparkling light fell from his cut, back into the veins of the land.

"Happy Independence Day!" Wile E. grinned, and Jack looked at him with narrowed eyes. "...What?" Jack said nothing.

When Dastan had purged himself of the Oracle, Desiree hurriedly and clumsily handed him a cloth bandage and a roll of gauze.

"I got it," he whispered softly, and a mist gathered around his hand. When it faded the cut was gone. "See?" He smiled.

"Was that supposed to be funny?" Desiree lowered the dark sunglasses on her face to reveal two clouded white eyes. She winked at him.

Dastan tried not to laugh. "Sorry."

She slipped her arm through his, and he carefully guided her steps through the woods back to the road.

"So are you going to stay here now? To catch up? To get to know each other? To be my personal walking stick?"

Dastan laughed, and took a deep breath. He felt lighter. Ignorance was bliss, and the days he had spent with the Oracle inside him, with the ability to turn his mind over and know everything, were dazed and blurred together. Often he had come to on top of a mountain, or out in the woods, or in the shape of a bird or a praying mantis.

"I need to go to Houston," he said, feeling lightheaded. "For Jenna. I need to go home and see my parents and…"

"Home is where one's story begins, and where one's story must end. For those that wander, they may never see home again, for it is not a place in time, but a place of mind." Desiree shook her head. "To attend her funeral," she said.

"Yes."

Dastan felt a pull. A veil in his mind was forming. He gripped Desiree's hand to steady himself, before he ended up standing in the middle of a Houston highway or in his old apartment.

"Well," she said, swallowing hard as though she were fighting back tears, "Robert is planning on staying here. He's moving in with Amanda. They have a lot of catching up to do, too, you know. And Mrs. Claus lives in Santa Claus half of the year, which is only a thirty minute drive. And, so...we'll be here when you come back." She stumbled on a fallen branch.

"Didn't mean to eavesdrop," Wile E. scampered up next to them, "but we can go with you to Houston. Moral support... or to make sure your family doesn't exorcise you if your head spins 'round."

"You did shapeshift into an owl the other day," Mrs. Claus quipped from behind them.

Without much thought, Dastan agreed.

"Pat said they sent off her body for burial yesterday," Robert said, lowering his gaze, "so we ought to be hitting the road tomorrow to catch the funeral."

"Her family will hate me," Dastan said. "And, my family..."

Rick looked sympathetic. "Charles...shit, sorry...Dastan. It wasn't your fault."

Dastan said nothing.

Anenqui slinked up to Dastan and Desiree. "Dastan, my son, Desiree, my love, I must leave you both now for I must keep moving. I am sorry."

Rick glared at The Wanderer before walking ahead of them into the woods.

"Don't be." Desiree reached up and touched his face.

He nuzzled her hand like a cat, and purred. "I will see you both again soon."

"Yeah, but I won't be seeing you, will I?" Desiree smiled.

"You will when you dream." His body began to fade around the edges. "Goodbye, my loves." He evaporated into the air and was gone.

Dastan wondered if that was how he looked when he drifted off to another place, becoming something else.

"*My loves,*" Rick mocked, having slowed his pace.

"Don't be jealous, Rick. He's the father of my son, and you...you get to be the one to keep me company in my nice new little shack, just me and you. Oh, and someone has to install the plumbing."

"Oh, how sweet." Rick frowned. "I'll gitcha an out-house."

"That would be bigger than the actual shack!"

"Well, I guess you can give your shit prophesies in the toilet where they belong."

Amanda giggled from a few feet away.

"Amanda." Desiree's jaw set. "Tell me exactly where he's at. I want to hit him."

Rick smiled, and gave Dastan a look asking to trade places. Dastan stepped away so Rick could take her arm.

"Come on, baby. You know I'm sexy."

"God, Rick."

"Hey, don't say their name in vain, ya hear? We don't want them coming back now." He kissed the top of her head.

Dastan and Amanda let the rest of the group walk ahead. Amanda waited until they were out of earshot before speaking. "Thank you," she said.

"For what?" Dastan was confused.

"Saving us from a world of narcissistic gods and overzealous psychopomps, and whatever else came out of that dimension. I just haven't heard anyone say *thank you* yet. I'm sure you're tired of everyone asking you how you're feeling. I know I got tired of that." She paused. "Don't turn off your emotions."

"I won't. I almost fell into blissful nothingness, but no, I promise I won't do that."

She nodded, looking satisfied, and they walked on in companionable silence.

***

The Wood house was filled with the aroma of coffee and stories of Native American tricksters and shenanigans at the North Pole. Robert showed Rick and Amanda old war wounds, and Desiree cursed every time she stumbled or bumped her knee on the coffee table. Mrs. Claus made gingersnaps, and Sheriff Pat dropped by to bring carryout from the corner cafe, and to harass Robert about job openings at the courthouse, which he less than kindly refused. Pat also told them what he knew about funeral arrangements for the mayor, Steve's and Brandon's fathers, and Jenna.

"There's going to be a candlelit vigil at the flood mural on Thursday for those that went missing during the flood."

Dastan did not even know what day it was, let alone when to expect Thursday, but he nodded. He knew where some of the missing people were, but did not say. They were in the sink and the toilet and the trash bin of the missing bathroom of the Days Inn. He wondered when the motel staff would notice that part of room 126 was missing, and if anyone would ever find it out in the woods. Then he imagined the smell...

Sheriff Pat tipped his hat before he left, and soon the house was quiet. Robert, Amanda, and Mrs. Claus were all snug in their beds, while Desiree and Rick had fallen asleep, cuddling on the couch. A pile of fur and blankets was on the living room floor. Jack had his hat pulled over his face, which rose and fell with the breathing of Smokey, currently a bear, against whom Jack was laying. Buzzy slept with his feathers fluffed in the center of the chandelier. Wile E. was snuggled up with Bugs underneath his chin, while Tiny had made a web in the corner of the room.

Dastan crept as quietly as a cat to the flannel shirt Wile E. had left on the armchair. He pulled a crushed pack of cigarettes and a lighter from the pocket, and he formed a veil in his mind that pulled him through to the steps outside. He sat down on a step and put the cigarette between his lips, lighting up. Dastan coughed on the first inhale, but did better on the second and the third.

The door creaked open and closed behind him.

"Tricking with tricksters? Stealing from thieves? Smoking? You've gone up in the world." Wile E. sat down next to him.

"Do you know who I am now?" Dastan asked.

"I'm no good with faces or names. Smells, though, that I can get on board with. You don't smell like garbage or sweat now, so that's a plus." The coyote took the pack of smokes and lighter from Dastan's hand.

"What do I smell like?"

"Sad," Coyote answered. "A little lost. A little confused. Wet."

"Wet?"

"Sure."

"Okay. Wet it is then. What did Charles smell like?"

"Like I said, garbage, sweat. A little lost, a little confused, and damned determined. Congratulations, you're a man. The adventurous naivety of youth, smells so sweet, tastes so bitter, like afternoon roadkill."

"So…what? A man isn't determined?"

"They just aren't *damned* determined. They've been there, done that, got the tattoo, and after that don't really care anymore. They live their life with one philosophy." He pointed his cigarette at Dastan. "The fuck-it philosophy. It's applicable to almost anything."

Dastan laughed. "Sounds about right."

"So, no-longer-man-child-but-actual-man…what tattoo are you going to get?"

Dastan scraped the cherry of his cigarette out on the concrete step. "I'll get the one I've always wanted. Fuck it."

"And what's that going to be?"

Dastan lifted up the sleeve of his T-shirt to show his upper arm. "Barbed wire."

Wile E. made a face. "…We'll work on it."

Dastan laughed, lowering his sleeve.

Wile E. gave him a long look. "What are you doing after the funeral?"

"Hell, I don't know." He ran his fingers through his hair. "Desiree wants me to stay here, but I…"

"Yeah." Wile E. flicked away his cigarette. "I hear ya."

They sat on the steps in silence until the sun began to brighten the horizon, and voices and footsteps permeated the house…the hustle and bustle of hastened morning routines. The door opened behind them.

Robert, carrying duffle bags, stepped around them both. "What? Couldn't sleep?"

"We're creatures of the night," Wile E. answered.

"Well, get to stepping. It's a long road to Houston."

Robert opened the trunk of his black SUV and tossed the bags in.

Wile E. stood and stretched. "Ready for the road again?"

Dastan stared at the rising sun. "Always."

THE END

ACKNOWLEDGEMENTS

Thank you first to my sister Raven, who lived with me and tolerated me during the years spent writing this book. You had to bear through my constant insistence that you listen to what I had written- usually pages at a time, but sometimes just a few paragraphs or only a few sentences. I know how irking it must have been. I hope I am able to return that support you gave to me as you embark on your own writing journey.

Next, of course, is Elise Rorick. I cannot begin to tell you how much your creative spirit has fueled me along on this journey. Thank you for all the editing road trips, the all-nighters, the bookmarks, the coffee, the art, the stories, the cover. I couldn't have met a better friend on Craigslist.

To Deborah Kahn, thank you for making the editing process so positive and so helpful. It was truly a delight to work with you.

My sincerest gratitude to my educators: Greg Richards,

Nicole Steel, Bill Kenley (who always wanted to see his name in one of his student's books), Solimar Otero, and James Rocha.

Thank you to Kali Begal for being in my life and letting me be in yours. We've grown so much together, and I can't wait to watch your girls grow up. Thank you for letting me read them bedtime stories. You and yours have a special place in my heart.

To my parents, Dan and Daina Boyd, thank you for everything: for all your support, for always believing in me, for raising me to be me. I cannot thank you enough. I love you both more than I can say...I'll be sure to call more often.

And to my sister Mrs. Devin Holden. I love you. I wouldn't be who I am without you. Thank you.

To my grandmother Janet Huddleston, who told me stories and read me books. You inspired my wanderlust, and you were always so kind and patient. I have your suitcase, and it will be well-used. I love you, and your memory will live on.

Thank you to all the people I've met along the way who inspired me in one way or another: Melissa Riggio, Yekaterina Komarovskaya, D.J. Wood, Gene Palmer, Christy Monroe, Dustin Templeton, Jon Ogle, Tommy Walls, Kelsey McCann, the guy walking up interstate 55 in the middle of the night in June 2012, Grandpa Coke, B.J. Johnson, and all my incorporeal friends.

ABOUT KAYLIN R. BOYD

Kaylin R. Boyd is a fantasy author. She was born in the Midwest, and raised on a strict diet of daydreams, myth, and magic. She has published an illustrated book of prose, *The Mountain*.

Tell City is her debut novel.

For more information, visit her online at www.kaylinrboyd.wix.com/stories, or on Instagram as @kaylin.r.boyd